FEAR IN THE BLOOD

FEAR IN THE BLOOD

C.M.W. HAWKINS

EDITED BY
MORGAN MUNRO

Undead Avian Publishing

AN UNDEAD AVIAN PUBLISHING PUBLICATION

First Edition

10 9 8 7 6 5 4 3 2 1

Cover illustration by Dani Smith.

Moonshiner fonts © Mattox Shuler.
Fallen Spartans fonts © Chris Vile and used under license.
Monthoers fonts © Agga Swist'blnk.

ISBN 13: 978-0-9952100-0-4

Printed through IngramSpark .

Please follow Undead Avian Publishing on Facebook or Twitter!

https://www.facebook.com/undeadavian/
https://twitter.com/undeadavian

*Wendy and Isaac,
without either of you
this wouldn't be possible.*

Love you both

I

The forest had fully settled into its nightly routine, with the clear sky letting the half-moon of the autumn night cast an ethereal glow across the area. A truck that had seen better days barreled along a dirt road running parallel to the edge of the woods, kicking up a small dust storm in its wake. The truck took a sharp turn leading into the woods and disappeared from sight.

A few moments passed before the nocturnal sounds of night returned and the animals hesitantly carried on with their interrupted lives. However, the new calm and silence was broken yet again by the blaring siren and lights of a police cruiser, causing the animals to this time scatter for safety.

"Goddammit, Wilk. If those fucking poachers get away again it's our hide."

"Hank, you're the one who promised the sheriff we'd 'bring them to justice' or some shit by the end of the week. Well, it's fuckin' Saturday, and I don't see where the hell they went."

Deputy Hank Murphy was an older man, just shy of his sixties, whose stark white hair and a salt-and-pepper beard weren't helping him in the youth department. Age lines crept from the corners of his eyes and mouth like cracks in a foundation. As Hank glared over at his partner, Wilk could feel the elder man's eyes burning into him with disdain. When Hank spoke he spit the words more than said them.

"We still got 'till Sunday."

"Either way, they're probably long gone by now."

Daniel Wilk was practically a baby compared to the older man. He was clean shaven, his black hair was neatly combed, and he didn't look a day over twenty-five. He glanced over at his partner, noting how white knuckled his hands were on the wheel, and couldn't help but smirk at the dogged-determination the other man had.

Hank had been a part of the small Sheriff's Department since Wilk was in high school, as Hank liked to constantly remind him. Instead of instilling a sense of reverence and respect, all it did was cause Wilk to view the man more as a dinosaur than any sort of experienced lawman. One thing Wilk *did* admire was Hank's ability to never give up on anything, even when the prospects were grim.

"No, they're still here. There's nowhere to...There!"

Before Wilk had a chance to react to the exclamation he was slammed into the door as the cruiser took a sharp turn down the only other road leading into the woods. Immediately the cruiser's headlights illuminated the truck they'd been searching for. The truck responded to being found by flashing its high-beams at them and started to accelerate right towards the deputies.

"They're gonna fuckin' ram us!"

Wilk was sure those were going to be his last words as he grabbed onto the dash in a futile attempt to brace himself for the impact. He shut his eyes tight, both by being blinded by the bright headlights of the oncoming truck, and in fear of facing his demise head-on. He was not happy his possible last moments were going to be spent with Hank.

"They don't have the stones!"

Jesus, Hank, neither do we! Wilk thought as he dared to glance at what was going to happen. The next few moments were somewhat surreal as he felt their cruiser accelerate and keep its head-on course right for the truck.

"They want to play chicken, then I'm obliged to accommodate."

The oncoming truck began veering off and on the road erratically, causing Wilk to believe they had flinched first and swerved to avoid the deputies. Hank uttered a gleeful shout as they roared past the truck. Was the truck really swerving so much before the impact? Wilk was sure he was going into shock from it all and maybe he was just seeing things. Either that or he'd finally snapped; he was fairly certain Hank had already. They had been trying to find these poachers all summer, and this was literally the closest they'd come to catching them.

As the truck passed, Hank didn't miss a beat; he grabbed the emergency brake, yanked on it hard and twisted the wheel. This resulted in the cruiser pulling a rather shoddy one hundred and eighty degree turn with the vehicle rocking roughly back and forth as it came to a stop. Hank disengaged the emergency brake as he gunned the accelerator again and took off after the truck.

"Yer heart racing yet, Wilk?!"

He's enjoying it! The crazy bastard is actually enjoying it! Wilk's thoughts ran through his head as he swallowed hard and concentrated on trying to calm his heart down before it beat right out of his chest.

"Are you fuckin' crazy?! What if they didn't swerve??"

"But they did."

"You're insane, Hank."

"Maybe," Hank replied, as he closed the gap between the truck and themselves rather quickly, "Gotta be a little touched to pull this off."

"Pull what o-"

Wilk didn't have a chance to finish the word as they rammed into the truck, locking the bumpers together. Hank slammed on the breaks, trying to cause the truck to stop with them. It certainly wasn't procedure, that was for sure.

For a moment it seemed it would work, which surprised Wilk. That is until the truck ripped the front bumper off the cruiser and went off like a rocket. The path of the truck was becoming more and more erratic and it seemed the driver was having serious difficulty controlling the vehicle as it rolled off the road into the surrounding forest. A few seconds later Wilk heard the all-too familiar crunch of metal against wood.

Other than having a missing bumper the cruiser still drove well and Hank pulled it to a nice stop, as if he were parking for church. Wilk was dumbfounded and more than a little impressed. The old dog still had a few tricks.

"Ok, call it in. Sheriff's gonna have a fit about the car, but I think, given the circumstances, he'll be a bit more forgiving."

"You're not going out there alone are you?" Wilk sounded a little more frightened than he intended which elicited a hard laugh from Hank.

"You leave your big boy britches at home? For all we know they didn't die in the crash and are headed to the next county on foot by now. Call it in, then get your ass out there. No telling what we're gonna find."

With that, Hank was gone, pulling out his service pistol and heading off in the direction of the crashed truck. Wilk could have sworn he saw a bounce in the older man's step as he ran off into the trees.

He started to fumble with the radio in the dash. Excitement didn't come to their little community very often. This was the biggest event Wilk could recall, even including the time before he was a deputy. He rather liked it that way. Hank, on the other hand, seemed to crave it. Wilk recalled overhearing someone say Hank used to be a city cop before moving to Stonesworth and that he came here with his wife to relax after she was diagnosed with a heart condition. After her death, being a cop was all he had.

He finally managed calm himself enough to flick the switch on the radio. Speaking as clearly as he could he shook his head as he thought about Hank. The man was anything but relaxing.

"Dispatch, this is car 54. We've cornered the poachers. Managed to run them off the road. Requesting backup and medical assistance to the scene as well. We're out on RR37, near the McCallum acreage. Be advised: suspects most likely armed and dangerous."

"Acknowledged, Car 54. Are either you or Hank injured?"

"No, we're both fine. Car's seen better days, however."

"Sheriff won't like that one bit."

Wilk was about to give a sarcastic reply when a shot rang out.

"Dispatch: shots fired. Repeat: shots fired. Proceeding after Hank, advise caution to all approaching parties."

He didn't even bother to place the receiver back in the dash as he jumped out of the car, pulling out his own service pistol and heading after Hank. A second shot rang out.

"Hank! Are you alright? Sound off!"

There was no reply as he moved through the trees, trying to discern where the truck and his partner had ended up. Considering how close together the trees were in this area, it was a wonder the truck hadn't hit one sooner. After a few tense moments he managed to find Hank's silhouette framed by the brake lights of the truck. Breathing a sigh of relief, he made his way over to the other man.

"Damnedest thing..." Hank was muttering under his breath, taking off his hat to run his hand through the messy strands of white hair.

"Hank, I heard the shots. You alright?"

The older man seemed dazed, as if he was trying to piece something together on the ground with his eyes. Wilk reached out and placed a hand on Hank's shoulder, shaking him gently.

"Hey partner...Are you hurt? What were you firing at? The poachers?"

Hearing the word poachers seemed to kick Hank out of his trance. "Thought I saw something. Uh...raccoon maybe."

Wilk remained unconvinced and prodded his partner further. "Where are the poachers? Have you secured the scene yet?"

Spitting on the ground and cursing under his breath Hank shook his head shrugging as he re-holstered his weapon.

"Nothing to secure."

"Why do you say that?"

"Look in the bed of the fuckin' truck. Nothing. And we know for a fact these guys have been getting out with a kill every time they hunt. We didn't see em dump it, either."

"Maybe before the turn off?"

"Maybe..." Hank didn't seem too keen on that idea as he moved towards the truck.

"Hank, there were two shots. Who fired first?"

Hank motioned for Wilk to come over to the driver's side of the truck and pointed in with his flashlight.

"They did. Happened before I got close enough. Saw the flash of the muzzle as the gun went off in the cab and then the passenger window blew out. Thought it was the gunshot at first, but the glass broke a few seconds after."

Wilk looked in and his mind tried to process what his eyes were seeing. At first he thought the driver had just slumped over the wheel and been knocked out. It took him a moment in the light to realize that the steering wheel had lodged itself up and into his throat, crushing his windpipe. He looked downright peaceful compared to the passenger.

The man looked ashen, which, in and of itself, was unusual. However, the jarring thing about him was the look on his face: frozen in pure abject terror. His jaw was locked open and his eyes were bulging. Wilk winced as he looked down at the man's hands and realized they were gripping the seat and door jamb hard enough to bend back the nails on a few fingers.

"Hank....what the fuck? Drug overdose?"

"It's a theory. Could also explain the gunshot not hitting whatever got out of that." he pointed his flashlight over the section of the extended cab where what looked like a cage hung open.

"It's like a trapper's cage for small game, but I've never seen one this big before. Looks like it could hold a black bear maybe."

"A black bear? Are you fuckin' high, Wilk? That thing is barely big enough to hold a cub."

"Fine, a goddamn cub then! Either way, this almost cinches it: these gotta be the poachers, Hank. Looks like they just bit off more than they could chew. Probably got free in the crash and clawed its way out."

"I highly doubt a grown-ass man is gonna be that fucking terrified of a bear cub or anything else small enough to be stuck in that cage." Hank flashed his light back onto the man's face as if to accentuate his point. His words were shaky and he seemed unsure of himself.

"Hank, did you see the animal?"

"...I saw something. Dunno what it was and sure as shit it's long gone now. Come on, we need to get the Medical Examiner out here ASAP and clean this shit up." Hank started to head back to the cruiser. "I need a goddamn drink."

Wilk continued to stare at the dead men, his eyes moving from the cage in the back to the look on the passenger's face, slowly going back and forth between the two. What the hell were they moving? Why was Hank so spooked?

"You coming, or do I need to send you an engraved invitation?" Hank called out back over his shoulder.

Well, at least he was starting to get back to his old self, Wilk thought as he followed after Hank. There was a movement just out of the corner of his eye in the brush, but there was no time to react before something that felt like a hot knife stabbed deeply into his stomach.

A wave of nausea and pain washed over him as he felt some sort of fluid spurt from whatever stabbed him. It retracted as quickly as it had struck, and he fell to his knees as his limbs became sluggish. He tried to call out but the words wouldn't come as he tilted forward and crashed face-first onto the ground of the forest. Pine, dirt, and a slight scent of decay filled his nostrils as he felt something mount his back.

Feeling claws begin to dig in, the terror in his mind was palpable. He tried to shake whatever it was off him but he could barely manage a slight shrug. His screams for help came out as little more than whimpers as his heart pounded faster and faster. The pressure on his back suddenly blossomed into white hot pain, and it felt like strips of his skin were being torn off and then...suction. Something was...sucking on him?! Tears started to flow as he coughed into the dirt, inhaling it more than air as he tried to escape.

A hot puddle of liquid was quickly forming underneath him, and at first he thought he was pissing himself. He was unable to comprehend the growing pool was not just urine but his own blood. He was in shock; a terror had him. A demon of the night was killing him. He hadn't even seen his attacker and that fact alone terrified him even more than the knowledge he was a dead man. It was then his bowels joined his bladder.

Whatever had him wasn't letting go. Wilk tried one last time to scream to Hank for help. The veins on his forehead and neck bulged as he strained, as his eyes rolled back into his head. It was a scream of silence and it left his lips as nothing more than a faint gasp as his body finally had enough.

"Wilk! What the fuck are you waiting for? Come on outta there!"

II

"Once more from the top, Hank."

Sheriff John Dragert looked at his deputy with something akin to pity, and Hank reviled him for it. A lukewarm coffee in a paper cup was the only thing on the table between them. He wasn't being officially investigated, but the way the sheriff reacted when he first told him what happened at the edge of the forest made Hank wonder why the tape recorder wasn't going.

"I already told you twice, John. Something those poachers caught killed them before I got to the truck. Then it...fuck." He took a breath. "It fucking killed Wilk, too."

"What was it, Hank?"

Here we go. Here comes the look of confusion and wondering if I've been drinking or some shit, Hank thought. *Just like the other two times I repeated myself.*

"I. Don't. Fucking. Know. Whatever it was, it wasn't any bigger than a large dog. Looked like some sort of reptile, but it stood on its hind legs, John..."

The sheriff just sat there, arms folded, watching Hank. The older man knew the tactic well, for he employed it regularly himself. Hank knew right now Dragert was going over the story in his head, looking for discrepancies and to see how much Hank was fidgeting in his seat as he repeated himself.

Anything to find a crack in the story to discredit it, because it was just too unbelievable. What possible animal could kill multiple grown men within minutes of one another without being seen until it was too late?

"Alright, Hank. I believe you."

"Bullshit!" Hank spat out, grabbing the cup and downing the bitter liquid. God, the coffee in the station sucked.

The sheriff gave a snort that sounded like a bull about to charge and rose out of his seat. The man was getting on in years but was not quite as old as Hank. Instead of a head of white like the older man, his hair had most of the dark brown color left. His bushy mustache and developing paunch gave him the appearance of a young walrus, and his bulbous nose didn't help to change that point of view. He was a good sport about it, usually, even going so far as to letting the kids in the community call him Sheriff Tusk. Right now though, he looked annoyed and downright aggravated.

"You ever know me to spit in your face and call it a handshake, Hank? I tell you I believe you, I goddamn believe you."

"John, even I dunno if I believe it!"

"It's insane, Hank. But I believe you saw something you've never seen before, and that it killed Wilk. How many shots you fire at it?"

Hank gave a dry, soulless chuckle. At least John had enough faith in him to know he'd at least try to stop it.

"Every last bullet; I was in shock though and I know it. Think I even hit Wilk's body, poor bastard."

"Julie will figure it out. For right now we need to get ahead of this thing. You and I both know we can't let this story of yours get outside this room. Even if that thing is some new creature, it'll still sound insane and hurt the reputation and credibility of this department. We need to keep this quiet and that means dancing around the truth a bit."

Hank felt a pang of disgust at that moment. First for not being able to kill whatever killed his partner, and then for having to cover it up. Sure, Wilk had been a gutless coward most of the time, hardly enjoying the job like Hank had, but in the year they'd been partners he'd grown to appreciate the man.

"Yeah, nothing says Small Town USA than a regular old cover-up."

"Oh fuck you, Hank. You really think telling everyone some lizard killed your partner is gonna make people side with you? Even you admitted it sounded far-fetched! Besides, if people *do* believe you, do we really want the woods filled with all manner of numb-nuts with guns looking for a payday or vengeance?"

It was hard to argue with the sheriff when he was like this. Dragert had already decided this was going to be the way it was before they even entered the room to talk, and there wasn't a force in the world that would change his mind. The fact that the sheriff was right only served to make Hank stew a bit more.

"No, of course that'd be stupid. I'm still telling you, John, whatever it was isn't from around here. It can't be. No way."

"For all we know they smuggled it in from China or some shit." The sheriff rubbed his chin, deep in thought for a moment.

"Look, we'll find out how Wilk and the other guy died, ok? That might give us some idea as to what this thing is so we..." He paused, looking Hank dead in the eye, "*and only we* can hunt it. For now, when the press comes to ask about Wilk, he was killed in the crash."

"That's a load of horseshit! If we crashed, how did Wilk die and I end up fine?"

"Alright, a fucking bear got him then! They were poachers after all. I really don't give a shit, Hank. Fucking make something up and run with it!"

He slammed his fist onto the table, causing the now empty coffee cup to topple over and roll awkwardly towards the edge stopping just short of falling over. For some reason, Hank couldn't help but be mesmerized by that cup for a few seconds. It seemed a good analogy for how he was feeling right now. Awkwardly rolling towards an edge that he was certain he would be pushed off.

The sheriff took a deep breath and let it out slowly, lifting his hand off the table and rubbing the bridge of his nose right between his eyes. He moved toward the door of the interrogation room and opened it for Hank.

"Come on. It's been a long fucking night and I still gotta tell Wilk's wife he ain't coming home."

Even for their all differences, Hank wouldn't wish that phone call on anyone. In the chaos of everything that occurred after he found Wilk dead he hadn't thought of the fact no one told his wife, Sherry, what happened. He looked down at his watch: 2:52am. He shook his head as he realized the coincidence. It was around 2:45am one night his mother got the same call.

"Go fill out the paperwork, and Hank..."

"Yeah, John?"

"Remember what I said."

"...Got it."

The fact that they were, for all intents and purposes, simply going to cover this up didn't sit well with Hank. While there was a point about how believable his story was, he got the feeling that the sheriff maybe knew something else. *Nah*, he thought, *that's just conspiracy talk*. Better to blame it on nerves and jitters from the night.

At least he'd managed to get Wilk into an honest-to-god car chase. It was something he'd promised the man when they first partnered up. Wilk hadn't believed that any car in their town could ever go above fifty.

He made his way over to his desk, turned on his computer, and waited for it to boot up as he tried to figure out what the hell he'd seen. It was both terrifyingly alien to him and yet somehow familiar. What he hadn't told the sheriff, was the size of the thing. He'd gotten a much better look than he let on, but he knew when to keep his mouth shut. No sense coming off as a total loon, so he didn't mention specifics. 'Some creature' was an easier pill to swallow than 'Godzilla's second cousin'.

Maybe it wasn't even a lizard, he thought. It was way too cold in their little town of Stonesworth. Autumn had set in strong, and winter was a hair's breadth away. Granted, the weather in the area was milder than most, but they got the occasional heavy snowfall and he knew enough about reptiles to know that cold was not their cup of tea.

He was also not so naive as to believe that he and the sheriff were actually going to hunt this thing. John was a damn fine lawman, one of the best he'd worked under, but a tracker? A hunter? Hank sure as shit wasn't one either. He started to wonder who he could bring in, discreetly, to help find this thing without alerting the town to the fact that something was out of place. Keeping something like that from the sheriff was another issue altogether.

He was still lost in thought when the phone on his desk rang, causing him to jolt out of his thought-induced daze with a start. He reached out and picked it up.

"Deputy Murphy," he spoke into the receiver.

"Hey Hank, it's Julie. Figured you'd be at your desk, all things considered."

His demeanor instantly softened. Julie was the Medical Examiner for county and not too hard on the eyes either. Although he'd not dated since his wife passed away, Hank still enjoyed viewing the beauties life had to offer. Not to mention she was damn fine at her job.

"What a fuckin' mess tonight. You figure anything out?"

"I found plenty, all of it making you seem less like a fruit loop."

She was one of the first on the scene, and the only other person besides the sheriff that knew his full story. He was still in shock when she came on the scene, and he just began unloading all of it on her at once. She'd managed to calm him down, and when the sheriff arrived the two men took a ride back to the station, leaving her to do her job.

"Like music to my ears darlin'."

He could almost hear her blush on the other end of the line, and despite himself he smiled genuinely for the first time since it all hit the fan just hours ago.

"Hank, I'm serious. This is like nothing I've ever seen before. I think you should get down here."

There was a pause, and Hank didn't even realize he was yawning until he was almost done.

"Actually, Hank, never mind After everything tonight you should get some rest. The weird shit will still be here tomorrow. Finish what you gotta, then go home and get some rest. Doctor's orders."

With that she hung up on him. That was how he knew she meant business. They usually bantered back and forth like that for several minutes as their way of saying goodbye, but when she was in no-nonsense mode she wouldn't even wait for a single goodbye. Hard to argue with a woman like that. Reminded him of an ex he once had, but in a more favorable way.

He looked at his computer screen glaring at him and rubbed his eyes.

"Fuck it."

He got up, turned his computer back off, and grabbed his coat. Paperwork could wait for the morning too. He was in no mood to deal with the tedium of filing a report as well as having to make up some bullshit story to cover the night's events.

***

"Yes, Sheriff...I understand the need for discretion. I'll make sure the death record is sealed...Your eyes only. Got it...Good night, sir."

After she hung up the phone, she took a long drag of the cigarette she wasn't supposed to be smoking. She'd never do anything so foolish as to smoke near the bodies; too much chance of contaminating evidence. Sneaking one inside her closed office was another matter entirely. The real issue was that she had promised Hank, and others, that she would quit this year. That phone call from the sheriff was worth breaking the promise, especially with everything else that had gone on that night.

Julie Black had only been the medical examiner in Stonesworth for about two years. She kept her dark brown hair short and easy to manage just in case she was needed out in the field at a moment's notice. She was also taller than most women she knew, which suited her just fine. It helped to intimidate a few of the more backwards-thinking men she encountered.

Exhaling another stream of smoke she looked out of the window on the door to her office at the covered bodies. The deputy's autopsy was unusually hard for her. While she hadn't known Deputy Wilk very well, she *had* known him, and the oddities in the autopsies she discovered were enough to cause her to sit in her office with a cigarette hanging out of her mouth.

Let's go over it again, she thought to herself. The driver was killed on impact and she figured she could determine cause of death in her sleep. So she did a cursory run of the standard check marks and then turned her focus to the passenger and Wilk. Those two were what really threw her for a loop.

Initially, there was no outward injury to suggest what had killed the second poacher, and Wilk's body was just covered in blood. A look of terror frozen on both their faces were the only thing both bodies shared. Getting a good look at those expressions caused a chill to go up her spine and she had turned on every light she could find. It was just so damned...creepy. Still, she was a professional, and she did her job. That was when she discovered she was well out of her pay grade on this one.

Extinguishing the butt of her smoke, she exhaled the last of her contraband vice and rubbed her temples. Maybe she needed to process it all from the beginning. She was exhausted, having just finished a late shift, when she got the call about the accident and attack. It was certainly possible she missed something or maybe she was giving something ordinary far more gravitas than was warranted.

Closing her eyes, she thought back to the arriving on the scene. Two EMTs were with her in the ambulance and she had been thankful for the extra muscle. Usually for a homicide she would have gone alone in the coroner's van, but the initial call only stated there was an accident and an officer was down. Deep down, she had hoped it wasn't Hank. Despite his prickly personality and usual grumpy demeanor, the old codger had grown on her.

When they arrived, the EMTs jumped out and went to Hank. They exchanged a few words, and their demeanor instantly changed. Instead of being ready to do what was necessary at a moment's notice and work quickly, their body language told her all she needed to know: there were no survivors to rush back to the hospital. As elated as she was to see Hank standing, her heart sank for his partner.

She remembered how Hank had seemed in a daze as she approached and then how he just let loose on her about some creature that had attacked Wilk. She managed to calm him down and figured the loss of his partner had really shaken him up badly. Until, that is, she went out and found the EMTs in a stupor over the body.

Her reassessment of the events of the night was interrupted by the loud, echoing clang of something metal being knocked to the ground. Sitting up, startled, her eyes darted out into the morgue, and she cursed out loud despite herself.

"Goddammit Hank! I told you to go home and rest, not come to the morgue and wreck my equipment!"

He looked like a kid in a candy store, caught with his grubby little hand stuck in a jar of gumballs. Holding up his palms in mock surrender, he tried to excuse his way out of her justifiable wrath.

"I know, I know, but what you said on the phone had me intrigued. So, I figured the paperwork can wait until tomorrow, and I should come down here and be, ya know, a cop."

"Sheriff Tusk finds out he's gonna blow a gasket."

"He'll blow one sooner if he finds out you're the one who started that nickname." Hank smirked at her before giving her a full on smile full of teeth and genuine amusement. Truth be told, they had both come up with it while sharing stories of Sheriff Dragert one night.

"Fine. You're here. May as well show you what I found so I can get you out of here just as quickly. Come on."

It was only when she rose up out of her office chair that she noticed Hank was glaring at the thin line of smoke rising from the ashtray on her desk. She had meant to hide it once she had enjoyed her lone cigarette, but he had startled her and so she just glared back.

"Like you haven't indulged in a vice under stress."

"Not one that could kill me, Julie. Well, unless I forget to drug the donkey..."

Refusing to dignify his comment with a response, she merely rolled her eyes at him and ushered him over to the middle of the room where Wilk was under a sheet.

"Normally I don't cover them once I finish the autopsy; not until they're ready for storage. I just couldn't stand to look at their faces after I was done. You sure you're up for this?"

All playful banter between them had ended, and she could tell he was switching gears into cop mode. She wondered for a moment if he'd always been able to disconnect so easily when the time called for it. A curt nod told her he was as ready as he ever would be, and she lowered the sheet covering Wilk's face.

Even fully prepared she heard him gasp sharply. Much like the passenger, Wilk's face was frozen in an expression of terror. The eyes were wide open, mouth slightly ajar, and the remnants of frothy spittle were dried at the corners of his mouth.

"Whatever killed him didn't just kill him, Hank. It drove him into a terrified frenzy. He was scared witless for each of his last moments. See here?"

She pointed to a section of his temple where the skin had a bruised discoloration. "He was under so much stress and strain that he literally blew a gasket. It looks like one of his veins ruptured just before his death. I've seen it happen before from trauma, usually to an arm or a leg pushed too far, but never something like this."

"What the hell could cause this much fear in a man, Julie? Wilk wasn't exactly the bravest man I knew, but he could hold his own."

"Well, it might have to do with whatever he was injected with."

"What?!"

She lowered the sheet down to his abdomen, the autopsy incisions already sutured up. Pulling on a pair of fresh gloves, she pointed down at a section of his abdomen that was covered with gauze and tape. Carefully pulling back the bandage she said, "Normally I wouldn't bandage a dead man, but watch."

Under the bandage was a small puncture wound. She pushed against the flesh near the wound and a viscous pink fluid seeped from the hole. Hank's eyes went wide.

"When I first made my incisions to begin the examination, I hadn't realized the significance of the puncture wound.

However, inside his abdominal cavity is more of that fluid. I'm not sure of the toxicity, or what its full effect was on Deputy Wilk, but I'd bet anything it was at least a component of his death."

Motioning over to the wall of cold storage she added, "I found a similar wound on the passenger, only not as much of the fluid. It was mostly superficial surrounded by some residue, so I can only assume that if there was any overflow it was absorbed by his skin and clothing."

Reaching over, she grabbed some wipes and cleaned the wound before tossing them into a bio hazard bag and disposing of it. Reapplying the bandage she finally removed the gloves.

"Until I know for sure what that stuff is, I'm not taking any chances. The substance could be highly poisonous or toxic. I was actually going to send some samples off to the university in the next county over. Their equipment is much more suited to determining what this stuff's chemical makeup could be. What do you think?"

Hank was silent for a few moments, looking down at his dead partner. Julie wondered if it was having an effect on him again, seeing his friend like that, but soon realized Hank was actually focused on something on the Deputy's side.

"You see this here, Julie?"

Moving next to him, she looked right where he was indicating. There was some discoloration on the side, barely visible, near the kidneys.

"Christ. How did I miss that?" Julie muttered under her breath. "Here: put on a pair of gloves and help me get him onto his side.

Once they had Wilk on his side it was Julie's turn to gasp sharply. The area of his back, near where his kidneys would be, were two nasty bruises. What was most disturbing was that the bruises looked like misshapen hands, with several puncture marks all throughout the 'hand prints'.

"Put him down."

They eased him down onto his back again, and Hank gave her a quizzical look.

"Don't you want to examine those marks?"

"Honestly, his gut is still full of that weird fluid. Putting him onto his stomach could cause it to leak out. If it really did have a hand in his death, like I think it did, last thing I want is it all over the place. Once we get a toxicology report back on it, and better containment, then we can examine those marks."

Maybe she was being overly thorough with this, but the fact was, she was terrified of what could cause as much damage to a single person as this. The weird fluid, the fear frozen on Wilk's face, and now these godawful markings all over his lower back.

Thinking back to the passenger, she made a beeline to table he was laid out on and dropped the sheet to his waistline. Raising the body slightly, she let out a sigh of disappointment when she didn't discover the same markings.

"The hell? Looks like it may not have had time or opportunity to do what it did to Wilk to this guy. There's nothing on his back."

"He was sitting with his back pressed up against the door originally. Maybe it couldn't latch on from that angle?"

"Maybe..." She let her voice drift off as she re-covered the man.

"Julie, send the samples off first thing. Don't even wait for John's approval; if it costs extra I'll foot the bill myself. I get the feeling the sheriff would rather this all just disappear without a proper investigation."

"You too, huh? He gave me a call just before you got here, telling me to keep the death records sealed until further notice. Thought it was odd but not in a 'cover-up' kind of way."

"Whatever his real intentions, if we're lucky whatever did this is long gone deep into those woods and no one else is in danger."

Julie bit her lower lip, a sign of apprehension Hank picked up on almost immediately.

"Don't worry. John may be a lot of things but, at the end of the day, he's still a good cop. His biggest fear right now is that if people heard and believed my story, they'd want to hunt this thing down. The last thing we need is a bunch of idiots traipsing through the woods at all hours, hindering a real investigation. Just get the stuff tested and I'll let you know if we find anything else out, ok?"

"Alright."

She placed the sheet back over the deputy's face, trying her best not to meet his gaze with her own, but found it nearly impossible to turn away from it. Julie couldn't help but shiver.

"I don't think I could handle more autopsies like these, Hank."

"If I'm right and actually did see some lizard, then maybe we'll get lucky and the cold will do our job for us. Lizards need heat to function, right?"

"Most. Depends on the reptile."

"Most? Christ, Julie, you know how to bring a guy down."

"Part of my charm, Hank. Now get out, go home, and get some sleep!"

She playfully pushed him towards the door as she headed back to her office.

"I'll let you know as soon as I hear back from the University."

"Fair enough. Night, Sunshine."

Again, with the winning smile of his. Despite the difference in age between them, a good twenty or thirty years, she couldn't help but be attracted to a man like Hank. Smiling to herself as he let himself out, she headed back to her desk. Looking at the ash tray, she sighed as she pushed it into the trash bin.

III

Hank woke the next morning to contemporary adult music, his least favorite, and the neon glare of eight am on his bedside radio clock. Muttering to himself he sat up in bed, popped in a few places he wished he didn't, and headed for the bathroom.

About forty minutes later he pulled into the station and sighed heavily. Sheriff Dragert was outside being yelled at by Wilk's now widowed wife. From the looks of things, he was getting the riot act read to him. Her face was red and flushed, probably from crying all night, and she held their young son in the crook of her arm. The kid was, thankfully, asleep from what Hank could tell. Probably had done his fair share of wailing already.

It wasn't that Hank disliked Wilk's wife, he just despised her attitude towards what Wilk did. She never agreed with it, nor made any attempt to understand why he did what he did. Merely went about guilt tripping the poor guy for doing his job. Saying things like he was 'abandoning his family' and 'what would they ever do if he died?' Hank winced; now they get to find out it seems.

He tried to slip past them to get inside, but she was on the warpath and he wasn't about to escape the torrent of verbal abuse she'd lined up.

"Hank Murphy. You disgusting son of a bitch!!"

"Sherry."

He knew she was grieving right now. Hell, he personally knew what it was like to lose a spouse, so he didn't blame her one bit for any of the words she spewed at him in that moment. Resigned to take his fair share of the hurt, he turned to face her fully.

"He trusted you and you let him die, you coward! You let him run off into those woods after those thugs and he died! Where were you?!"

Let him run off? Thugs? He glanced over at the sheriff. The expression on the man's face said 'just go with it' and he looked almost pleadingly at Hank. Guess this was what they were going to run with. Alright then. At least this bullshit story painted Wilk in a more positive light. Hank could live with that, for the time being.

"Daniel was a good man, but he knew the risks."

"RISKS?! What about his family?! At least he still HAD a wife you washout!"

That one stung a bit. He clenched his jaw and continued.

"Perhaps. He went after the suspects on foot after we cornered them. I'm not sure exactly what happened to cause his death, but he went down in the line of duty. That's all we can really say at this time. He was my partner and I will miss him dearly."

She just stood there, seething at Hank, tears beginning to well up in her eyes again. She turned away and said just one sentence that hit Hank in his core.

"It should have been you."

The words stunned him a bit as the gravity of it all settled in. Yeah, it should have been him. He was the one pushing sixty. He was the one with no family, and certainly no wife worrying for him at home. His own future was practically measured in minutes, while Wilk had decades left ahead of him. It wasn't fair at all and she knew it. He knew it. Hank decided to offer Sherry the only words of comfort he could at that moment.

"Yes, it should have been."

She turned back looking just as stunned as he had, and just started wailing again as the sheriff took her into his arms and let her sob against him. He gave Hank a look with his eyes urging him to make a quick exit. Pausing for a moment and watching the grieving widow, Hank then turned and entered the building with a heavy heart.

He finished the paperwork for the incident in about twenty minutes. Assuming Dragert hadn't said much to Sherry, he kept the report somewhat vague as well. They cornered the suspects after they crashed their vehicle in the woods. Deputy Wilk pursued on foot as Hank called for backup. Shots rang out, and by the time Hank arrived at the scene all three were dead. Open and shut.

So why couldn't he hit save? It still didn't sit right, having to lie about what happened. True, mass panic could send the town into a frenzy, with all manner of idiots looking to be famous for catching a new unknown creature, or trigger happy folks shooting one another. That was if the town even believed his story. At worst he'd just be branded the crazy cop. Despite the possible negative outcomes he still would rather have told the truth. At least he'd still have his integrity.

There had to be more to the reason that John wanted it covered up. As much as Hank wanted to go digging into why, however, he didn't even know where to start. He had just gotten up to go grab a fresh cup of coffee, to get his thoughts in order, when his phone rang.

"Deputy Murphy," he spoke, although he had a feeling he knew exactly who it was.

"Hank, I was just about to head over to the University, when I got an idea."

He groaned inwardly. Her ideas were usually a bit more trouble than they were worth, and he dreaded finding out exactly what she had in mind. "I'm not sure I want to know, Julie. Wait, you're *going* to the University? I thought you were going to send the samples via courier, not hand deliver them."

"I was going to, but once I spoke with the head of the Biology Department he was incredibly eager to begin analysis and wanted them ASAP. Since it's only about an hour drive I decided, what the hell."

Hank fumed a bit at that. "Julie. What part of 'keep this under-wraps' do you not understand? This could cost you your job, discussing an ongoing investigation like that!"

"Christ, Hank, who pissed in your cheerios this morning? Relax. As far as Jeremiah knows, we're doing this for a local farmer who lost a few head of cattle in an attack last night."

"Doesn't seem the kind of thing to rush, Julie. Sure he won't get suspicious?"

"Not one bit. When I told them about the fluid and the markings around the kidneys he practically begged to do the tests himself. He thinks he may be the discoverer of a new species."

"Ok then, Julie. Just be careful about this. Word gets out, we're all in hot water."

"Hank, I'm not a little kid. I can take care of myself. He said the preliminary results shouldn't take long and to bring him as many samples as we could. Which brings me to my idea: I was thinking you and I could head back to the crime scene and take a look during the day. See if there was anything we missed."

"We? I was gonna head out there myself to be honest. Lord knows we've never seen anything like this before and I doubt that the rookies did more than secure the scene last night." He paused a moment and considered something else. "It may be dangerous out there too. What are you gonna do if we find the thing still around? Autopsy it to death? Just hang back at the office. I'll bring whatever I find to you."

"You're an asshole, Hank. Meet me at the scene in thirty."

She hung up before he could argue, and he slammed the receiver down. "Goddammit," he muttered under his breath. He knew she meant well, but he couldn't afford to have her underfoot and in possible danger as he did a more thorough investigation. She may have been the medical examiner but that went as far as dead bodies. Looking for clues was a bit outside her purview.

He grabbed his coat and hat as he headed for the exit. On the way, he noticed the sheriff and Mrs. Wilk were inside his office now, her taking on a more somber and reasonable tone. Seeing her there, so utterly emotionally spent and broken, brought back a flood of memories of the passing of his late wife. Blinking a few times to clear his eyes, he cleared his throat and quickly made his way to his cruiser.

***

Even though the crime scene was on the outer edge of town, it was a pretty straight shot to get there from the highway. He managed to make the trip in about twenty-five minutes but wasn't surprised one bit to find Julie's car already there. She was sitting on her hood waiting for him.

Parking his car behind hers, he got out and moved towards her. He could swear he saw her toss something that looked a lot like a cigarette butt onto the road as he drove up, but before he could mention it she grabbed his arm and dragged him off into the woods.

"About time you got here. Come on!"

"Easy there, Nancy Drew...You seem far too excited about this. Wilk and two other men died here last night and we have no idea if the thing that did it is still around."

Her chipper attitude took on a slightly more serious tone as she let go of his arm.

"You're right. But that doesn't mean I can't enjoy the work to try and figure this all out, does it? Besides, we *need* to figure this out so we can give Mrs. Wilk some true closure."

"I suppose. Just try not to disturb anything."

It didn't take long to find the perimeter of police tape that had been put up haphazardly in the night. Hank frowned. He always hated shoddy police work.

Ducking under the tape, then holding it up a bit to make it easier for Julie to duck under, he headed right for the truck, trying to ignore the dark patch of earth where Wilk had died. It didn't surprise him that the ground had absorbed the blood, just that it still looked so dark. As if the stain of death had set upon the soil itself. Julie, however, made a beeline right for it.

"Watch where you step. Could be evidence anywhere."

"I'm not an amateur, Hank. I've been to a few crime scenes. Remember?"

Her tone was filled with annoyance, which got a smirk out of Hank. He knew she was good, but it was still fun to tease her. When he got to the truck, he looked in the bed. Last night he didn't see it, but there were deep scratch marks in the bed of the pickup, as well as metal cables that were unfastened.

"The cage was in the back? But why bring it inside?" He wondered aloud.

"What, Hank?" Julie looked up from the dark patch, examining the blades of grass with gloved fingers.

"Nothing. Just thinking out loud."

He turned his attention back to the truck. They were live poaching, which was not entirely unheard of. All it takes is some rich idiot who wants a wolf as a pet or some other stupid shit. But why bring the cage into the truck? He went to the cab and looked inside. The cage was wedged pretty good back there. It barely fit actually. So, whatever they caught, they felt it was far too valuable to leave in the back, and so they decided to bring it inside. Maybe it *was* something exotic. Were they afraid it would escape, maybe?

About to head over and see if Julie had found anything, he noticed something out of the corner of his eye as he turned. Opening the side door of the truck he peered into the cage and saw what caught his attention. It was a large patch of dark, scaly skin. He instantly recognized it as moulting, as he had snakes when he was a kid, and one of the most fascinating things about them was how they shed their skin when they grew.

Horror dawned on his face the next instant. His snakes *only* moulted and shed their skin when they grew. Whatever the hell this thing was, it was growing. He tossed on a pair of gloves and grabbed the skin, making his way over to Julie as he placed the skin into an evidence bag. "Anything good?"

"Sort of. This looks like blood, but not quite. Too dark and watery. Not all of it has been absorbed by the ground, so I was able to take enough for a proper sample. I also managed to find what looks like footprints. They just look...off? I dunno. Take a look."

She pointed with the end of her pen towards a patch of dirt near the stained soil. He got down on his haunches to inspect. There was a set of prints that looked like three long toes in the front and two smaller toes in the back, all five ending in what he guessed were claws. In-between the footprints was a line, as if something long and thin had been dragged behind it.

He thought about getting the supplies out of the truck to make a cast, but was there really a need? Not like it was a shoe print or tire tread they could track down. It was just some animal tracks.

"Hell of a tail on this thing too," he mused, getting up. He looked around the scene, slowly, from one end to the other. Something felt off about the whole thing, and he couldn't quite place it.

"This thing didn't kill because it was cornered and scared, Julie. I think it was pissed."

He moved over towards her and helped her off the ground.

"By the time Wilk and I got on scene, it had ample opportunity to escape. Both the poachers were dead and it took us a few moments to get over here. Yet it seemingly waited until one of us was alone and easy to attack and then it struck. We need to figure out what we're dealing with. Let's head to the University, I want to get this patch of skin tested. Hopefully it'll tell us what kinda reptile this thing might be."

Julie's eyes lit up as he held out the evidence bag for her to see. Snatching it from his hand she held it up to the daylight, squinting as if that would help her see it better.

"I can't believe you found this. Jer should definitely be able to tell us what did this now!"

She bounded off into the forest heading back towards the car. Her energy was infectious, Hank admitted, and he headed off right after her.

IV

Instead of heading back to the station, Hank phoned Dragert and told him he wasn't coming back for the rest of the day. He managed to get the sheriff to reluctantly agree that he needed the day off, all things considered. As they stopped at Hank's place to change, both decided it was wiser to take a single car, and for Julie to drive as she knew the way better.

An hour and some small talk later, the two of them were climbing the steps to the University's Radcliffe Building of Science and Research.

Being a Sunday only the most dedicated, or those woefully behind on projects, were there, along with a skeleton crew of staff. It had been literally decades since Hank even stepped onto a campus. The University had been established back in the 1960's and still held that old rustic charm he was accustomed to. It gave him a little comfort that not everything in the world was passing him by.

Julie walked right next to him with a small lunch cooler in hand. While it wasn't exactly the most professional means to keep the samples chilled, they both agreed it would be better to be discrete.

"Which way?"

"If I remember right, the lab is just down this way to the left. Apparently it's updated with all new and state of the art stuff. Some alumni with more money than sense donated most of it to get their name on the building. Lucky for us, huh?"

"It's certainly fortunate."

Stopping in front of a set of double doors, she peeked inside and turned to Hank.

"Ok, just wait here. I'm sure he's in his office so I'll just head there and grab him. I half expected him to be here waiting for us, the way he sounded on the phone. Try not to get hit on by any co-eds while I'm gone."

His response was an eye roll as she headed off. He placed his hands into his pockets, leaned against the wall next to the door, closed his eyes, and saw the creature.

He hadn't been fully honest with everyone. He got more than a glance at it: he saw the whole damn thing, clear as day, in the beam of his flashlight. Even hunched over Daniel, it was about three or four feet tall. It had gangly arms grabbing onto his back, and a tail that whipped back and forth, moving too fast for him to get a good look at the tip. Did lizards have stingers?

The hind legs looked powerful as it straddled the fallen man and he could see the muscle bulging against the leathery hide. The head was smooth, reminding him of a salamander, just a bit more scaly. That was another thing that stuck out for him, besides the eyes; the thing looked like it was part crocodile with dark and leathery skin. There were stiff, bony ridges along its joints and around the eye sockets as well.

Then there were the eyes. He'd never seen anything like them before. They were a stark contrast to the rest of the creature, having a bright blue, almost neon, hue. The iris was a slit, but not quite like a regular lizard. He couldn't be sure, but it looked like a sound wave almost. Thicker in some parts and thinner in others.

When he shined a light on it, a second set of eyelids shot up as it winced; it didn't like the light. Giving a strange honking cry, it leapt off Wilk, and ran into the forest. He'd fired after it but considering how fast it was there was no way to be sure he'd hit it.

Perhaps it was a bit of self-preservation that kept him from telling anyone the full details of what he saw. He was also highly unsure if any lizards anywhere in the world moved on two legs like this one. If he hadn't seen it so clearly he would've sworn it was a midget in a costume.

This case wasn't what he was used to. He was a facts man and got results based on that alone. He tended to take a few risks but that kept things interesting. This was some goddamn creature and he had no idea how to investigate something like this. At the end of the day there wouldn't be anyone to arrest, and no one to answer for the crime. Just some animal that would probably end up being captured and put in a zoo somewhere.

Huh. Kill two men and become a star. Maybe he could sell that idea to a TV network or something as a new reality show.

Hearing footsteps on the hallway floor, he turned his attention towards them as Julie and a much younger man came around the corner. He had dark skin and a short cut of black hair. Even with a well-groomed goatee he looked far too young to be the head of a department like this. *Nothing like getting old to think everyone is inexperienced,* he chastised himself.

Pushing himself from the wall with his shoulders, he moved towards the duo. They were busy exchanging excited chatter about the possibilities of the new species. *Like two peas in a pod,* he thought, feeling a small pang of jealousy towards the younger man. It was completely irrational and he quickly pushed it aside.

"...if this really is a new species of reptile it could completely turn on its ear everything we thought we knew about North American species! This could be the find of the century!"

"Exactly! That's why you were the first to come to mind when we needed some things tested."

Your access to state of the art equipment on a moment's notice had nothing to do with it at all, Hank sarcastically commented to himself. Extending his hand towards the approaching pair he interrupted.

"You must be Jeremiah. Name's Hank."

"Ah! Deputy Murphy," Jeremiah took Hank's hand and gave it a hearty squeeze and pump. Hank was impressed; a man with a good handshake always got his attention. "Doctor

Jeremiah Besson, but please, all my friends call my Jer. The pleasure is all mine, especially after bringing these samples. Julie told me you actually saw the creature?"

Letting go of Hank's hand, he moved past him through the double doors, letting them all inside, and turned on the lights. He then headed for a lab coat hanging in the corner. Julie placed her lunch cooler filled with samples on one of the stainless steel counters.

"Er...yeah I saw it. Only caught a glimpse, but it had these weird as hell eyes."

Jeremiah didn't turn around as he set about turning on various pieces of equipment and booting a computer on one side of the room.

"Can you describe them?"

All business. Hank was starting to see why Julie thought highly of this guy. "The pupils were slits, like a lizard usually has, only they weren't the right shape. Kinda like a sound wave or something. Thin in some parts and thick in others."

He wasn't sure Jeremiah heard him, as he didn't say anything for a few moments. Julie must have felt the same way as she piped up for the first time since they entered the room.

"Jer, you familiar with something like that?"

Silence was the only response they got as the other man busied himself around the lab. Grabbing a book from a shelf, he headed over toward Hank and Julie, flipping through pages, until his eyebrows shot up and a smile blossomed on his face. Placing the book down on the counter before them, he pushed it over and pointed to a picture on the page.

"Did it look anything like that?"

There on the page was a lizard Hank had never seen before. The eye shape and iris was identical, however the color was completely different. These eyes had a golden hue.

"Yes! Just like that! What the hell is it?!" He couldn't hide the rising excitement in his voice as he thought, maybe, they had just discovered what the creature was.

"That is just a gecko. But the eyes are the important thing right now. Eyes like this are usually only found on nocturnal species of gecko, which means the specimen you encountered last night probably had incredible night vision."

"Guess that explains why it ran off after I shone a light on it. It went off into the woods, and I fired a few rounds after it, but I missed."

Jeremiah looked aghast. "You shot at it?!"

Hank wanted to yell at the man, tell him 'of course I shot at it, it killed my partner!' but only he, Julie, and the sheriff knew what really happened. As far as Jeremiah was concerned, it was a cattle attack he happened upon.

"Reflex, I suppose. Wasn't even supposed to be out there that night but the...farmer heard some strange noises and I was sent out to investigate. Saw the thing, and popped off a few rounds. Cow was dead before I got there though."

"I suppose you were just doing your job. I can hardly blame a man for that, now can I?"

Jeremiah patted Hank twice on the shoulder and moved over to grab a pair of gloves.

"Was there anything else about it that seemed unusual or that you noticed when you flashed your light on it?"

Hank tensed slightly. He wondered if he should fully admit everything he saw at the risk of sounding more like a loon. He relented as, given the present company, it really couldn't hurt. The sheriff may have said he believed Hank simply to shut him up, but Julie saw the bodies; she believed he saw something dangerous. As for Jeremiah, he was pure science. Might even be able to tell what he saw from a description alone.

"Honestly, for a minute I thought it looked like a guy in a costume. It stood on two rather large hind legs, bony ridges around its eye sockets and joints, and smaller, almost frail looking arms. It hissed at me before jabbing its tail in my direction. Seemed pissed it couldn't reach me with its stinger and ran off."

At the mention of stinger Jeremiah dropped what he was doing and stared at Hank.

"I'm sorry...stinger?"

"You never said anything about a stinger, Hank."

He felt both pairs of eyes on him and his face started to burn a bit. This was it. This was when they both called him a fool and questioned everything he saw.

"No lizards, at least none known, have stingers of any kind. They deliver their venom through bites. This is most unusual. I can't wait to do further analysis!"

"Does that help you narrow down what it could be at all?"

Julie's question didn't have the disbelief that Hank had feared it would and seemed just as genuine as when he had told her it was a lizard to begin with. He appreciated that even more now. She was still in his camp.

"Not exactly. If anything it opens the door to far more possibilities. The creature may actually be a genetic hybrid."

He moved to the cooler and popped it open, beaming as he looked inside.

"Perfect! You've got everything prepared exactly how I specified. You even brought me a bonus!"

He held the evidence bag containing the skin up to the light, and seemed to marvel at it. Although Jeremiah's reverence for the whole ordeal made him uncomfortable, Hank begrudgingly admitted that the guy was making what could be considered the discovery of a lifetime. It was something a person in his field could work years towards and never accomplish.

"Alright, I'll place the samples in the mass spectrometer and we should know the results by tonight or tomorrow. Thankfully we've got a fully updated database of known compositions, which should make this fairly easy to identify."

Hank must have looked as dumbfounded as he felt in that moment, because he heard Julie make a noise that sounded like a snorting laugh and Jeremiah looked a little embarrassed.

"Uh, yes, sorry. I forgot you are not as well-versed in these items as Julie and I am. What I'm going to do is run the liquid samples through a machine that will analyze their compounds and give us some idea of what exactly they are made of."

"Right." Hank hated feeling out of his league, but he honestly had no idea what some of these machines were, let alone did. Hell, he felt he should be wearing a lab coat and goggles to just be standing there.

"As for the skin sample..." Jeremiah took it out of the plastic with a pair of tongs and put it into a specimen tray. Grabbing a nearby scalpel, he sliced off a small section and placed it into the middle of a petri dish.

"That may take a couple of days. Our DNA machines are fast, but there will still be a delay for them to compute the results. If this is a brand new creature, however, we may not get anything conclusive either."

That Hank understood. Most labs had a turn around time of a few weeks, so a couple of days was nothing. It would give him time to try and figure out where to go from here anyway.

He inwardly kicked himself as the thought of getting animal control out to the woods was only just now crossing his mind. He should have called them first thing, but was also glad he hadn't, because if that thing was capable of killing men with guns, like it already had, what chance would a couple of people with nets have?

"Just let Julie know whatever you find. She can relay the information to me." He tried gingerly to broach the subject of keeping things discreet.

"Jeremiah...uh..Jer. Did Julie impress on you the importance of keeping this to yourself for now?"

"Yes she did. You have my word that I will not go public and I shall have utmost discretion no matter what I discover. She told me you were afraid of farmers going off to protect their herds without knowing the full dangers. The last thing I want is more loss of life, no matter what discovery I make."

"Excellent. I know it's asking a lot, 'specially since you're using this equipment to help us out."

"Think nothing of it. Did she tell you my terms for its use?"

He flashed a toothy grin and looked right at Julie, who started to fidget a bit. Hank turned to regard her slowly, cocking an eyebrow as he did.

"Uh...terms, Julie?"

"He wants to name it after himself."

"Yes. And what else?" The same big grin. Hank was getting a little concerned when Julie started to blush.

"...And take me out to dinner." she muttered. It was now Hank's turn to snicker a bit.

Jeremiah continued to grin. "I'll call you later Julie. We can discuss the results over said dinner. Sound good?"

"Yeah, sure. Just call me and we'll set something up."

"Great! Now if you'll excuse me, I've work to do!"

With that, it was as if the two of them didn't exist as he set about his tasks of discovering what they were dealing with. All Hank could do was chuckle, and try not to feel a little jealous of Jeremiah, as he and Julie left the building.

V

"It's been two days and still no sign of 'em. Think they got themselves arrested?"

"Of course they got caught. They're fuckin' morons like you and your goddamn retard brother."

"Fuck you, Uncle Greg! Josh isn't a retard...he's just a bit slow is all."

"Andrew, if your brother were any slower he wouldn't move at all. Now hurry the fuck up. If Luke and Jeff got caught we need to empty our traps and get the hell out before we're next."

Greg cursed his bad luck. Andrew and Josh may have been stupid, but they were family and could be trusted. Luke and Jeff were just two idiots he met in a bar in town a few years back. At the time, they just needed some hands transporting the animals and hides. He had no idea back then just how sloppy those two were.

It was their fault the sheriff was even aware of what they were doing. There may have been a rumor or two in town, but they worked mostly at night and in remote locations specifically to avoid detection and suspicion. Those two loud mouths got cocky and tried to use what they did to get laid. Worked for them at the time but in the end they weren't the only ones to get fucked.

"Where the hell is Josh anyway?"

"I told him to head over to that cave we set traps up in a few days ago. See if we got lucky."

"Jesus fuckin' Christ boy, you sent him alone?? Yer both retards! What was the first goddamn thing I told you about this shit?!"

Andrew looked panicked suddenly as realization dawned on his face.

"Shit! Never check a live trap alone."

"Yeah. *Shit* is right. Let's go. Now."

It may have seemed stupid, but since these two were family, as well as morons, he had adopted a few extra safety precautions. He'd lost a careless partner years ago when they went to check a live trap alone. The trap had caught a bear cub, and momma wasn't none too happy about it. At least Greg assumed that's what had happened. By the time he got there all he found was his partner's maimed corpse and a cage that was torn to pieces. Ever since, he'd insisted on the buddy system.

"We may have to just say 'fuck it' and move to greener pastures, boy. If those two got caught, there ain't nothin' keeping them from turning on us."

Greg wasn't a criminal mastermind, but he'd been hunting and poaching the land for years. He was a firm believer that man had a God-given right to live off the land as he saw fit, even if that meant killing wolves and bears for their furs or selling off their cubs. Animals were there to serve, after all, and he was gonna make sure they served him but good. With the amount of poaching he'd done in the area over the years, Luke and Jeff were indeed small fish that could lead to the big catch. Greg didn't want to spend the rest of his life behind bars for doing what felt right just because those two pussies decided to save their own skins.

"Almost there, Uncle Greg. Josh will be alright, won't he?"

"Sure, Andrew. Let's just get there."

He shook his head at how utterly daft his nephew had been, sending Josh off alone. Just a week prior they'd noticed a family of wolves in the area; it was the whole reason they set the traps up. He had a buyer lined up who wanted wolf pups for their kids. To be honest Greg didn't care, as long as the money was good.

As they crested a hill, his worst fears were confirmed. Off in the distance was the cave they had found with a few of the traps scattered outside and what looked like Josh face down among them.

"Goddammit! Get yer gun, Andrew."

"No! Josh! Jooooosh!!"

Andrew took off like a bolt causing Greg to swear loudly as he called after him.

"Get yer fuckin' ass back here! They could still be around, you moron!"

He had his rifle at his side as he tried to keep up with the younger and faster boy. All he could think of, however, was how his sister was going to murder him for getting her boy hurt. If they were lucky the wolves didn't actually kill the sorry son of a bitch. It was a long shot but it was all he had at the moment.

"Andrew! Shut the fuck up right now!"

He hissed out the words, trying not to yell, but it was just no use. Andrew had already closed the distance between them and Josh and dropped down to his knees next to his brother, quickly turning him over.

"Don't move 'im!" Christ, he was gonna do more harm than good if the kid was still alive.

Andrew suddenly dropped his brother and scooted back, uttering a cry like he'd just been scared shitless. No other reason to do that other than Josh was fucking dead. This went from bad to worse real quick.

Greg finally caught up, and, between gasping breaths, managed to belt out "Fucking moron! You could'a been killed too! Get your damn gun ready and keep an eye out!"

The young man made no motion other than sitting there staring horrified at his brother. *Shit, he's gone into shock,* Greg thought as he made his way over to Josh. Of the two, Josh really was the stupider one, but he was still a sweet kid. Greg felt a tiny pang of guilt over him getting killed, but would blame it on Andrew anyway. He reached down, and gingerly turned him over.

It was in turning him over that Greg noticed the wounds on his back, probably from getting mauled, as well as the blood pooled around the body. He'd been wearing a dark red coat so it didn't look as bad as it probably was. Looked like Josh had bled out.

"Shit, they got him goo-"

His words stuck in his throat as he saw the boy's face.

"Jesus..."

Josh's face was frozen in terror and his eyes were bloodshot from the strain and wide in fright. His crooked teeth looked like something right out of a horror movie, the way his mouth was contorted in an eternal silent scream.

"Wh-what did this, Uncle Greg?"

"Like I know?! Could be anything really. Kid must'a just been piss-scared is all. Poor bastard."

"We can't leave him, we gotta take him back. Get him buried proper."

Greg turned to his nephew, stormed over to him, and brought him roughly to his feet.

"Bury him proper? What the hell did I tell you about this business we're in boy? We don't get no proper burial unless we want to be caught. You want to go to jail for your brother's stupidity?"

"I'm the one who sent him, though!" Andrew wailed, tears beginning to stream down his face.

"And his fool ass listened! We're gonna tell your mother a bear drug him off and leave it at that!"

He turned back to the body on the ground and then to the traps. A few looked like they'd actually been broken into, not out of, which was strange. The amount of blood and fur stuck around the wire edges was also concerning. He'd seen animals try and free their kin before, but the amount of blood near the traps looked more like something had been butchered. Not to mention there hadn't been any bears in the area for years and there was no way a wolf could do that much damage. Counting, he noticed at least one trap was missing.

"Oh you have got to be shitting me."

"What? What is it, Uncle?"

Realization dawned on him. Luke and Jeff hadn't been caught; they had taken the prey for themselves! Those two-faced cheats.

"We've been had! Luke and Jeff stole our catch."

Andrew didn't seem too interested, his focus squarely on the corpse of his brother. Greg however, was fuming. He paced back and forth, spewing all manner of curses, and swore to gut the both of them if he ever laid eyes on them again.

He was fully ready to continue his little tantrum for the rest of the afternoon, except a sound caught his attention when he paused to take a breath. It had come from the cave and sounded like a cross between an unusually harsh honk and a squawk. Like someone squeezed a bird, hard. Maybe today wouldn't be a total goddamn waste after all.

"Come on. Those two screwed us, but it sounds like they forgot something in the cave. We need to check it out."

"We gotta get outta here! What if whatever killed Josh comes back?!"

Greg got in very close to the boy, looking him dead in the eye as he spat the words through clenched teeth. "Then use your fuckin' gun and cover me. Come on."

Andrew looked like he was gonna topple over at any minute and Greg didn't give a damn. Those two fuckers took what was rightfully his and if there was anything in that cave he could either sell, or skin, there wasn't a force that could stop him.

Standing at the mouth of the cave, he tried to peer in, but the sun was at just the right spot in the sky to catch the lip of the cave opening. A dark shadow was cast down that stopped him from seeing more than ten feet in. Again the squawking sound happened, only this time it sounded louder.

"Get out your flashlight. Shine it in over there."

Whatever it was, sounded like it was injured, maybe. If something got free and managed to crawl into the cave this wouldn't be a wasted trip after all. Andrew fumbled with his light before finally managing to click it on and pointed it in the direction his Uncle had indicated.

"Oh my god..."

Greg was expecting some wolf or even a bear cub to be in a trap inside the cave. What he got was something he couldn't fully wrap his mind around. Inside the cave were three lizard-like creatures, guarding what looked like a bunch of eggs surrounded by bones. Their neon blue eyes shone in the light, and once the light passed over them they started squawking and honking like crazy.

The way they moved their tails reminded Greg of a video he saw once of a King Cobra. They raised them high over their heads and swayed them rhythmically back and forth in a hypnotic fashion. Greg's eyes focused on the bulbous tips that ended in what looked like an ice pick, and he almost didn't hear when Andrew called out.

"Uncle Greg! Over there!"

The shot caused his ears to ring and he whipped around to find his nephew had shot a fourth lizard creature that somehow managed to sneak up on them from the side. The kid was a lousy shot, even from close range, and somehow only managed to give it a graze on the leg.

Taking aim, Greg was ready to finish the job when he felt a stabbing pain in his shoulder. Glancing down he saw the tip of one of those stingers poking through his shirt with a white thick fluid gushing out of it. He'd stupidly turned his back on the other three, and, with the nest threatened, they attacked.

Another stinger hit him in the leg, burying deep into the meat of his thigh, and he felt the liquid spurt in. His knees began to buckle and give way as he started to lose control of his body. The creature Andrew had shot limped over and gave two squawks at the smaller ones he was being attacked by, causing them to back off.

Acting purely on instinct he grabbed at his pistol in the holster at his side. Heavy fingers gripped the hilt and it took all his effort to raise his arms to try and shoot the beast. His arm felt like lead as the toxin began to fully paralyze him.

The injured creature's tail whipped out and struck his hand, causing his arm to fling back. Somehow he managed to keep a grip on the gun, and his trigger finger convulsed. The gun went off and killed one of the three advancing.

Greg could see Andrew take aim again and hoped this shot would ring true. Andrew would finally take all his words and teachings to heart and save the day. They could laugh about it as he got stitched up over a beer. The shot rang out and fire bloomed in Greg's other leg. Andrew had shot him by mistake.

"YOU FUCKIN' RETARD!"

Any hope of salvation instantly disappeared and was replaced with white hot rage and pure fear. Andrew cried out when the large one turned to him and hissed. The fool boy actually threw his gun at it and ran. Satisfied that the other threat was gone, the beast turned back to Greg with its blue eyes full of malice.

He had never been a man to know fear. Greg had lived life by his own terms, and faced the consequences of his actions head on. He knew he was going to die, and had mentally prepared himself for this day. Somehow, though, he found himself weeping like a baby; his heart speeding in fright and peeing himself at the mouth to the cave as the large one straddled him.

The sensation of pure terror was so foreign to him that it actually frightened him more than what was happening to him in that moment. Whatever toxin they'd injected into him was causing his body to go into overdrive and all he could think about was getting away. Running for cover and never looking back.

These were not animals. It was a den of demons. Horrible things sent right from hell to punish the wicked. He began to blubber in what seemed like tongues, praying for forgiveness, for Jesus to help him, God to deliver him. Neither came to his aid as the large one bit down into his shoulder and ripped out a chunk with the others soon following suit.

The last thing he ever felt was his belly being sliced open and the sensation of clawed hands rooting around inside. The last thing he heard was a pop as something came loose with a sharp tug.

VI

Jeremiah pulled another thick book from the shelf and began thumbing through the pages. While he had promised to keep his mouth shut for a time, a find this large begged to be documented precisely. Once he either got the go ahead, or felt enough time had passed to avoid any culpability of blame, he fully planned to release his findings. It would all mean nothing, however, if he were unable to produce a creature.

While the machines hummed and processed the molecules of the various samples Julie had brought, he thought how to get his hands on a specimen. At best right now all he had was a very loose hypothesis. Hypotheses don't garner fame and fortune, they don't get new species named after you, and they certainly don't get your name placed as a leader of your field.

He hadn't originally gotten into biology, and more specifically Comparative Anatomy, to make a name for himself. His interest in animals and how they worked was of genuine interest to him. If this creature was some sort of genetic hybrid, his interest in that very field, Nothology, would be a great boon. There wasn't anything even close to it in the books, and it seemed to have evolved to use some of the best aspects of other reptiles and even some insects.

The desire for more than the day to day came more out of boredom with his position than anything else. He enjoyed working for the University, but it didn't offer him the kind of life he craved. While he was still in school, he envisioned himself going on expeditions into the heart of the rain forest, or some other remote corner of the globe, to document and discover new and exotic creatures. Instead, he ended up as a research assistant and began the somewhat soul-crushing climb up the academic ladder.

Being a smart man, he knew his lofty goals were mere flights of fancy and tried to push them to the back of his mind, all but forgotten over the years. However when Julie called him and told him about a new creature in his own backyard, those dreams and aspirations flared right back up to the forefront, like when he was a first year student.

If they captured the creature, he was sure he would have first claim to examining it. Even if they brought it in dead, he could dissect it. Plus, where there was one creature, there were sure to be more. The chances of finding a group of specimens was low, but even so he was sure, one way or another, there would be something to use as concrete proof.

He was lost in thought as he moved to the centrifuge to extract the second sample. The first pinkish sample was easy enough to separate the blood from the white compound. Venom didn't seem quite the right descriptor for it, so he held off on calling it anything more concrete until the spectrometer did its work.

The dark red, almost black, fluid was curious. He had a gut feeling he already knew what it was, despite Julie's assurance to the contrary. His hunch was confirmed as he pulled it from the centrifuge and held it up to get a better look at it.

"Blood."

The three layers in the tube looked exactly as he had expected them to: the plasma on top, the thin 'buffy coat' full of platelet cells in the middle, and the red blood cells filling the bottom of the tube. What surprised him was the amount of each in their respective layers.

Normally, the tube should have been mostly even portioning, with slightly more material in the plasma section. In *this* tube, the plasma accounted for a very small portion with the red blood cells accounting for almost eighty percent of the total volume in the tube. Rushing over to a microscope, he extracted a small sample of the red blood cells to see if this was the blood of the creature.

"Come on...show me your secrets little ones," he whispered softly to himself as he adjusted the dial on the side of the device and looked in.

His disappointment was palpable. Instead of finding some sort of reptilian blood cell, it was actually human. Sitting back in disbelief he double checked everything to ensure he had, in fact, used the sample Julie brought him and not gotten mixed up somehow. Looking at it again under the microscope, it was undeniable: the blood was human.

Human blood like this presented two interesting predicaments for Jeremiah. The first, was the fact he'd been lied to. His guess was the creature had attacked a human, possibly killing them, and gotten away. Hank and Julie's demeanor, and their insistence on discretion, made far more sense now.

The second issue was why were the levels so drastically off? Curious as to what secrets this sample could hold, he decided to analyze it further. He would find whatever information it was hiding.

A beeping noise caught his attention; the spectrometer was finished with its analysis. He moved over to the machine and clicked a few buttons on the computer next to it, displaying the read out.

"That...can't be right."

He re-read them. Apparently tonight seemed like it was going to be full of unbelievable things. The over-all chemical make-up wasn't like anything he was expecting, not to mention the specific compounds of the fluid. It wasn't venom, but it *was* highly dangerous for entirely different reasons. Jeremiah now knew exactly what to look for in the blood.

***

Julie was running through a field of flowers just after a sun shower. Her legs were soaked from the knees down as she ran without a care in the world. Nothing else mattered in those moments except the sound of her own laughter and the fresh air filling her lungs. God, how she missed her parent's farm.

Looking over to her left, the horses she'd grown up with were gently grazing, enjoying the treats spring brought with the new blooms. To her right was the barn her father built before she was born. Ahead of her was a giant ringing telephone.

Awaking reluctantly, she blinked several times to get her bearings in the dark. The glow of her smart phone as it went off on the bedside table made her regret not setting it on silent. She loved that dream.

"Someone better be dead," she said groggily into the receiver, then winced at her choice of words. What if there was another attack? What if someone actually was dead? *Oh god*, she thought, *don't be Hank on the other end*. Jeremiah's excited tone relieved her, but also brought more questions.

"No, at least no one new."

He knew. She wasn't sure how he figured it out, but that choice of words was too odd to mean anything other than he knew that the creature had attacked a person and not some cow. What she couldn't figure out was how on earth he'd managed to figure it out. *None of the samples I gave him were taken from the victims except the ven-*. She slapped her forehead. He must have done a far more through analysis of the initial sample and determined it was mixed with human blood.

"What is it, Jeremiah? And why couldn't this wait until morning?"

"The samples you sent. Those were all taken from the victim I assume?"

Her face contorted into a grimace as she debated trying to lie her way out of it. If any of this got out...Hank was right: it'd be both their hides. On the other hand, if she were honest with Jeremiah, right here and now, she might convince him to remain quiet longer. She hesitated a bit too long and he spoke again.

"It's ok, Julie. I understand why you and Deputy Murphy wanted this kept quiet, now more than ever. The agreement we made still stands, as long as you keep up your end."

That flirty tone. Ugh. Why had she agreed to a date? He was attractive enough, and his intelligence kept her attention more than most men, but she really didn't see him as a suitor. Her thoughts turned to Hank, but that was a whole other can of worms she didn't want to deal with at...she glanced at the clock...one in the morning.

"Yes, Jeremiah. You may still take me to dinner. On your dime of course."

His laughter eased her tension a bit and she spoke again.

"So why the call?"

"Answer my question first: where did you get those samples? The victim?"

He may know, but he doesn't need to know it was a deputy, or how many others there were, she decided.

"Yes. The pinkish fluid came from a puncture wound on the abdomen of the victim. The darker fluid was found in a puddle at the scene."

"I thought so. Julie you aren't going to believe this. The reason I found out it wasn't a cow was because the dark fluid is actually human blood. Well, it was."

She sat up in bed, clicking on her bedside lamp.

"What do you mean 'was'?"

"It's been digested. It looks as if it went right through the creature's digestive system and only certain enzymes and hormones were extracted."

"You've got to be shitting me."

"First, however, let me tell you about the other fluid. It isn't venomous, like you first thought. It's actually a neurotoxin."

"You mean to tell me it paralyzes the victims? How powerful is it exactly?"

"It looks to exhibit a combination of tetrodotoxin and chlorotoxin, but neurotoxins themselves were never my strong suit. From the analysis I've gotten, I'd even guess it keeps the victims fully aware as it paralyzes."

Julie felt her heart sink as she realized why the men had those looks on their faces. They felt every moment of their deaths and were powerless to stop it. Jeremiah continued.

"Look, that's not the most fascinating part. It's what else I found in the compound. Are you familiar with adrenocorticotropic hormone?"

"ACTH? Do I look like a first year flunky to you? Of course I know what causes adrenaline to be produced!"

"Along with the neurotoxin there was a form of ACTH I've never seen before. I'm even wondering if we should be referring to it as such."

"What do you mean? Why would ACTH traces in the toxin be worrisome?"

"These aren't traces, Julie. The amount of ACTH of this type would ramp up the adrenal glands in anything they were injected to. I'm talking burnout amounts. Not only would the adrenal glands fail under this amount of stress, it wouldn't matter, as the heart couldn't withstand this much adrenaline in the bloodstream."

"Good god. This thing is literally scaring people to death?"

"People?"

Julie swore at herself for letting another bit of information slip. After this conversation she swore to herself never to answer her phone in the middle of the night again. Sighing, she answered his question.

"There were two victims."

"My god, Julie. How long were you going to help keep this quiet?"

She didn't like the accusing tone in his voice and tried to keep the conversation under control.

"Stay focused, Jer. What does this have to do with the blood? You said that it looked digested?"

"Yes. When I analyzed the white fluid, that's where I first found evidence of the ACTH. This is what caused me to analyze the blood in the same way to corroborate my theory. Thing is, there was no evidence of adrenaline, or any other adrenal gland produced hormone, in this blood whatsoever, which leads me to believe-"

"-it's extracting the hormones?" Julie couldn't help but finish his sentence.

"It would appear that way, yes. The creature subdues its prey by injecting it with the neurotoxin, which also ramps up adrenaline production. It then feeds off the blood and extracts what it needs right then and there. It's fascinating how quickly the process takes, if Deputy Murphy was honest about how quickly he happened upon the attack."

"Of course he was honest! Don't you dare question his integrity!"

There was a pause. *Good*, she thought.

"Sorry. Julie, I'll be blunt: you need to have them bring me a specimen I can examine. I have ideas as to how it feeds, and why, but I need something in front of me to tell one way or the other. Do you think that's possible?"

"I dunno, Jeremiah. Can we talk about this in the morning?"

"Sure. I'll call you first thing. Get some rest, and tell Deputy Murphy I want him to give me a call as well. I need to know exactly what this thing was doing when he found it. Oh, and, Julie?"

She yawned. Despite his shocking revelations she was still exhausted. "Yes, Jeremiah?"

"Were there any other markings on the victims, besides the initial puncture wound? Bite marks? Anything?"

"On one there was nothing. On the other there was strange bruises on the back with smaller puncture wounds within them. Why?"

"Just an idea I've got. Thanks, Julie. I'll talk to you later."

He hung up and she sat there. Part of her wanted to call Hank and tell him the update. Chances are he'd still be awake, even this late at night. She wondered if he ever actually slept or if he simply subsisted off bad coffee and police work.

No, she decided. Tomorrow was another day and she had a feeling in her gut it was going to be just as exhausting as the past two were. Better to get her rest now and be somewhat prepared for it. After all, her parent's farm awaited. She was asleep before she even hit the pillow.

***

Hank poured himself a cup of cold coffee wondering how he managed to let this happen. He distinctly remembered telling the sheriff he was taking the day, and Dragert agreeing, but apparently that didn't include the night as well. He got a call around five to come in and turn in the report he'd done so that the sheriff could have it first thing in the morning.

Hank promptly forgot, until he was getting ready for bed around midnight. The last thing he wanted was the sheriff chewing him a new one for something so trivial, so he got dressed and headed down to work. Dorris, who manned the switchboard on the graveyard shift, and some deputy he only knew as Jefferson, were the only two on duty in the station by the time he got there.

Sitting down at his desk with coffee in hand, he booted up the system and waited for the login screen. At least it had been far easier to type out the report than to write it out. Some things he was appreciative of technology for. Others not so much.

After the system was fully operational and he was logged in, he began to re-read the report. After finishing he moved the cursor over the print button and his finger hovered over the mouse.

"Jesus...what am I doing? No."

He shook his head, took in a deep breath and sighed. No, this was horseshit and it didn't feel right. He didn't care if it looked stupid on the report. He deleted everything he wrote that morning and went about describing everything exactly as it occurred, right down to the blue eyes of the damned thing.

"There. Spin that you son of a bitch."

Once he saved the file and printed a hard copy, he went and placed it on the sheriff's desk and got ready to leave. It may piss Dragert right off, but Hank felt good. He valued integrity, and covering anything up, even with 'public interest' at heart, didn't feel good or right to him. Even if it cost him his job

Grabbing his coat, he even started to whistle a little tune. His attitude had changed for the better, he realized, after getting something so dreaded done, and done right by his books. He was heading toward the entrance to leave when the door burst inward and a scrawny, dirty kid of no more than eighteen burst in, gasping for breath.

"I need a cop! Something killed my brother and uncle in the woods!"

Fucking hell. There goes my good mood, Hank thought to himself as he ushered the kid over to his desk. The other deputy on duty got the kid a glass of water while Hank got him to calm down and take a seat next to his desk. As he gulped, Hank got a good look at him. He was young, his eyes were red and puffy, probably from crying, and his face was flushed. The kid looked like he ran the whole way from the forest to the station, which was no easy feat.

"Ok, son. Tell me your name and what happened."

"Andrew...Something in the woods killed my Uncle Greg and my brother Josh."

"What exactly happened, though?"

"I just told you! A monster killed 'em!!"

He was shaking like a leaf, wringing his hands together and bobbing his knees like he had all this pent up energy and no way to get it out. Hank felt for the kid, but tried to get him to focus. He had to know for sure it was the creature.

"Ok. What did it look like. Do you remember that? Or maybe where you saw the attack?"

"It was up in Conner's Woods, near Sasakwa River. We'd been checking our traps to see if we caught anything, and that's when it happened."

"Wait, traps? What the hell were you trapping, boy?" Hank suddenly got a knot in the pit of his stomach.

"We were out there trying to catch wolf pups, on account of us seeing a family earlier this week. I sent Josh to look at the traps alone and that's when they got 'im. Uncle Greg and I found that other traps were missing and he was right pissed."

"What did these traps look like?" Hank already knew the answer.

"Standard traps, steel wire cage. One was missing so Uncle Greg went into the cave to see if there was anything worth selling."

"Son of a bitch." Hank muttered under his breath.

"What, sir?" Even under duress, he still used his manners when speaking to an elder. The notion amused Hank slightly, as he continued to press for more information.

"You all were poaching up in those woods, weren't you?"

Andrew hung his head in shame and simply nodded.

"It got Josh killed. Shoulda never gone with Uncle Greg. But he said we'd get lots of money for little work!"

Suddenly he changed his tune, pushing more and more blame onto his Uncle Greg. Hank had never heard of the name before in relation to poaching, but he guessed these three were connected with the two who died in the crash. He didn't mention it though; he didn't want the kid to go off on a tangent again. Also, the department hadn't released the names yet, and he was certain there was no way for anyone else to know they had died.

"Back to what happened in the woods. You need to tell me what attacked you and why."

Andrew sniffed, nodded, and went into his tale. He recounted everything, right up to the moment he accidentally shot his uncle. Hank had to bite his cheek, hard, to keep from snickering. It was a tragic story, and he was certain the other man was dead, but the fact the kid had actually shot his own uncle, and then just threw the whole damn rifle at the thing attacking him...well, it was hilarious no matter how you looked at it.

"Alright. I'm sorry about your brother and uncle. The important thing right now is to make sure you stay safe and get some rest. And we need to let your mom know what's happened. Have you been home yet?"

"No, sir, I was afraid of what my mom would say when she found out...what happened..." His voice trailed off and his eyes welled with tears again. In a few seconds he was sobbing into his hands and Hank did his best to console him.

"It's alright, son. Just let it out."

What worried Hank the most right now wasn't the fact two more were dead but the fact there was more than one of those things.

"I'll go call your mom. I'm sure the sheriff is gonna want to talk to you as well. You gonna be ok for a few minutes?"

Andrew managed to nod weakly in between sobs.

"You need anything just ask Deputy Jefferson or Ms. Dorris, alright? I'll be back soon."

He needed a bit of privacy and headed into the sheriff's office. He dialed the number and waited. After three rings the other end picked up.

"You better have a good reason for calling so late, Dorris!"

"Sheriff, we got an issue."

"...Hank? Wha...? I don't think I like that tone. What's the issue?"

He sounded half asleep and heavily annoyed. Hank could swear he heard the sheriff's wife in the background, telling him to keep it down.

"Kid just came busting into the station. He says his uncle and brother were killed by more of those things."

"Did you just say 'things'?"

"Yep. I think keeping this under wraps just went out the window. It's too late tonight, but we need to form a group to go and check this out at first light."

"Hold up now. We even sure he saw the same thing you did?"

Now it was Hank's turn to be annoyed as he hissed into the phone.

"Right down to the goddamn scales, John! If we don't get ahead of this we may have more than just a few poachers and a deputy dead!"

"Fuckin' hell...Keep 'im there. I'll be right down."

The sheriff hung up and Hank replaced the receiver. The sheriff had always been a bit pig-headed but his outright stubborn attitude towards this was downright infuriating. He headed out of the office and back towards Andrew.

"Think you could show me where it all happened?"

"You think I'm going back into those woods yer fuckin' crazy!"

Hank shot him a look.

"Uh...sir."

"It ain't ideal. I get that. Right now, though, you're the only one who knows exactly where you were trapping and where the attack took place. Without your help we're looking for a needle in a haystack."

Andrew, who still looked scared out of his mind, went back to wringing his hands and bobbing his knees. It couldn't have been easy on the kid, with all that he experienced today, and Hank was asking him to head right back into the lion's den, of all places.

"I lost my brother and uncle today. I just wanna go home."

Hank nodded, "Alright. There's a couch over there. You can rest there while I get a hold of your mother. Give me her name and the number, and I'll make the call."

He recited the number almost mechanically before he moved over to the couch in a zombie-like trance, sat down, and just stared at the floor. Part of Hank really felt for the kid. He'd lost his brother in Vietnam, but he didn't witness it, or see the body after. The kid really had been put through his paces.

Picking up the phone on his desk he dialed the number, took a deep breath, and let it out slowly. Nothing really prepared him for these calls.

"H...Hello?"

"Hello Mrs. Fosley? I'm Deputy Murphy with the Stonesworth Sheriff's Office. I'm afraid there's been an incident with your brother and your sons, and we need you to come down to the station right away."

"Oh, oh god! What happened?! Are my boys alright?!"

The panic in her voice was palpable even over the phone.

"Ma'am, it's best you get down here right way."

He just heard the phone hit the floor and then muffled sounds of someone moving quickly about the room. After hearing what he assumed was the jingle of car keys, he quietly hung up the phone and looked over at Andrew. His face was back in his hands and his shoulders heaved as he was wracked with another set of sobs.

Things were going from bad to worse.

VII

Julie bit her bottom lip as she pulled into the station parking lot early the next morning. What looked like a small mob had formed outside the station and the sheriff seemed like he was on the losing end of a shouting match between himself and two women. Getting out of her car, she was glad to see Hank off to the side, doing his best to look inconspicuous. When their eyes met he made a quick 'get over here' motion with his hand and headed inside.

She followed, barely managing to push through the crowd of people. Trying not to pay too much attention, she couldn't help but overhear them demanding justice for those who were killed. Her stomach sank as she pushed through and went inside to meet up with Hank, who just shook his head.

"It's bad. Not full on nuclear, but it's gotten significantly worse."

"Oh my god, did Jeremiah talk?! Is that why all these people are out there?"

"No, for whatever his intents are in this, he's stayed true to his word. Had a kid run into the station last night. There was another attack deep in the woods. The group outside wants to mount a search party for the bodies. Sheriff is trying to defuse it but he's getting less than stellar results.

Deputy Wilk's wife is back out there as well, demanding to know what really happened to her husband."

Julie didn't know what to say. She'd never seen a situation get quite this worked up. Hank had told her about a time, a few years before she moved to the town, where a kid held up a corner store and ended up taking hostages. No one was hurt, thankfully, but as far as major crime and incidents, that was the top of the list. Until now that is.

"So why did you call me in?"

"I'm hoping you can get through to the kid, honestly. Only he knows where the attack took place, and he refuses to head back out there. Scared witless. I tried everything: bribing him, threatening him, the works. I think it needs a gentler touch, and you and I both know that is something I am sorely lacking."

Feeling both honored and a little overwhelmed by his request, she cleared her throat before biting her lip again.

"Nothing to be nervous about, Julie. Either the kid talks or he doesn't. I'd feel a whole lot better if we didn't have a whole crowd of people eager to go out into those woods half-cocked. It would be preferable to go in with at least some basic intel."

"I can give it a shot, but this isn't really my thing. Why not get one of the female officers to handle it?"

"Ha! I said a gentle touch, hun. Just give it your best, and I'm sure it'll turn out alright." Hank said as he led the way to one of the interrogation rooms.

"We've managed to avoid it devolving into a legal circus with his mother by dismissing any and all possible charges we could have laid against him. Only way we were able to keep Andrew here so we could question him. She's just wanting to find out where her other boy is."

"Hank, I don't know shit about what happened. You expect me to head in there blind and somehow get something out of a kid who's been through an obvious trauma? Are you high?"

Her demeanor was deadly serious but for some reason Hank found her rather amusing and just smirked. It pissed her off to no end.

"Fuck you, Hank. I'll figure it out as I go then."

"Now, Julie, wait, I–"

She had already let herself into the room and shut the door in his face. Sometimes he could be more of an oaf than the sheriff. As soon as she entered, Andrew looked up. Poor kid looked like he'd been through hell and back.

"Hello, my name is Julie Black. My friend, Deputy Murphy, thinks you might talk to me, more than you would any of the other officers."

She took a seat across from him, and noticed the Styrofoam container on the table that looked like it hadn't been touched yet.

"Not hungry?"

He made a sniffling noise and shook his head before coughing lightly and looking away from her, fidgeting slightly in his seat as she watched him. *Goddammit Hank*, she thought, *what the hell am I supposed to do now? I'm not a damn shrink.*

"Well, Andrew...It's Andrew, right?" He nodded slowly without turning to face her. "Alright. I'm just gonna cut right to the chase. Why don't you just come with us out to the spot it happened so we can get your uncle and brother back and give them a proper burial, huh?"

The word burial must have triggered something, because he started to blubber and breathe raggedly as a large sob welled up in his chest.

"N-No! I'm not gonna end up like them! I can't go back!"

Ok, time to switch gears then. She waited until he managed to calm himself down. After a few moments of silence between them she reached over, and popped open the container.

"Huh. Bacon and eggs. Not the most imaginative breakfast, but it'll do I suppose."

Grabbing one particularly crunchy piece, she bit it in half and started to chew, watching his reaction. As the smell started to waft out of the container and hit his nostrils they flared a bit and he turned to look right at the food.

"It's cold, but still pretty good." She pushed it back over to him. "Go ahead, have a piece."

Hesitating for a moment, as if he were trying to make the hardest decision of his life, he finally reached out, took a piece, and devoured it. Within seconds he was digging into the food like it was his last meal. *There*, she thought, *maybe that will keep him a bit calmer now.*

"I understand you don't want to go back out there. I really do. There was an attack a few days before your brother and uncle were killed. I may not have seen the creature, but I saw what it can do."

"They."

"...Excuse me?"

"There was three, maybe four of them. And a whole mess of eggs."

Julie's eyes went wide. If there was more than one, and they were multiplying, the town had a lot more to deal with than a few isolated incidents. Rushing out of the room, she nearly ran into Hank who was still waiting right outside.

"Whoa there...did he talk?"

"No, but we have a major issue."

"What do you mean? Can't be worse than more than one of those damned things."

"EGGS. They're laying eggs Hank!"

The color drained from his face as he turned around and ripped a map from the wall, then headed into the investigation room with Julie hot on his heels.

"Alright. If you aren't going up there someone else needs to. You never said anything about eggs last night, kid."

"I didn't?" He looked genuinely dumbfounded by this revelation.

"No, you did not. You need to show me on this map, right now, where it happened. I may not be able to drag you out there but you can sure as hell show me right the fuck now."

Julie could sense that Hank's anger was causing Andrew to withdraw again and close himself off. Even she wanted to yell 'man up!' at him. She moved to his side and leaned in close, placing a hand on his shoulder.

"I know it's difficult. It was difficult when it all happened, wasn't it?"

He nodded doing his best not to look at either of them.

"Do you want that to happen to anyone else?"

When he turned to look at her, fear in his eyes, she knew she had finally gotten through to him.

"If you don't at least show us exactly where it happened we can't help to prevent it from happening again."

Pushing the map in front of him, she urged him on.

"Your uncle was a poacher so he knew the land really well didn't he?"

Andrew nodded, looking from her down to the map.

"I'll bet he taught you everything he knew, didn't he?"

Andrew didn't respond but simply stared down at the map. Even from this angle she could see the tears welling up in his eyes. Hank pushed over a pen, and after a tense moment, Andrew took it in hand and circled an area about half a click east of the Sasakwa River, right near the heart of Conner's Woods.

"Thank you, Andrew. If you're still hungry, I'll have Deputy Murphy get someone to get you some more food, and maybe let your mom in here, ok?"

He nodded as he turned back to the food. Instead of finishing it off, he just sort of prodded a few bits of egg with the last piece of bacon. Once they were both outside the interrogation room she turned to Hank angrily.

"I don't know what you thought you were doing in there, but you almost blew it."

"He was being a little shit! There's more than one of those things and they're laying eggs. We need to get out there *NOW*, Julie. You can be mad at me later. Come on."

Walking quickly, they exited the station and went right over to the sheriff. Wilk's widow was wailing on again. A woman Julie assumed was Andrew's mother was at the head of a mob that was looking angrier by the moment.

"Something killed my son and brother and you can't stop us!"

"Now look here, everyone, I know you're all upset-"

"Upset?! Four men are dead and you think we're just upset?! How dare you!"

Julie cringed as the arguing went back and forth. Hank was trying to get the sheriff's attention, as well as the rest of the crowd's, but it didn't seem to be working all that well. Once, he managed to get the sheriff to look in his direction, but someone else shouted something that pulled his attention away again. Julie was fed up.

"Everyone! SHUT. THE. HELL. UP."

Her voice echoed slightly in the parking lot, and all eyes fell on her, most with either a surprised or dumbfounded look. Suddenly incredibly self-conscious, she cleared her throat as her face turned crimson.

"Deputy Murphy has a development."

Hank gave her a grateful nod as he turned to the crowd.

"That's correct. We now have solid information on where to begin the search."

The crowd started to act excitedly with men rushing to their vehicles.

"Now hold it! We're not all gonna rush off, especially when there's some sort of dangerous creature out in those woods. This is exactly why we didn't come public in the first place!" He shot an obvious glance at the sheriff before continuing. "It was in the interest of public safety and we wish to continue to keep public safety at the forefront. We will be heading out to the site with professionals trained to handle these situations."

"Ain't no situation I can't handle without a gun!" someone yelled.

"Yeah! Just tell us where, and we'll do your fuckin' jobs for ya, ya cowards!"

Julie wondered who was getting more upset: the crowd or Hank. He sneered slightly at the last comment, but managed to keep his cool

"Any one of you who heads off into those woods is not only taking an unnecessary risk with your life but you're also breaking the law. As of this moment, those woods are off limits until we get a handle on this. Are we clear?!"

"Fuck you! I'm going! Who's with me?"

A rather meaty looking man stepped forward, directly challenging Hank's control of the situation.

"Now, let's not be-" The sheriff tried to defuse the situation but what happened next shocked even Julie.

Hank moved through the crowd, making a beeline for the man. The man crossed his arms and puffed out his chest, an air of defiance around him.

"Whatcha gonna do, old man? Arrest me?"

"Yep."

A simple reply which Hank followed up with a simple action. He headbutted the man, causing him to stumble back. While he was disoriented, Hank's nightstick came out and he cracked him, hard, across the back of the knee. The man uttered a high-pitched whine as he went down. Hank got on top of him and quickly pulled his arms behind his back, placing them in cuffs.

Looking up at the rest of the crowd, he spoke evenly but with force and power behind his words. Julie had never seen him quite like this and was impressed.

"I swear to God, I will lock every last one of you up if you push me on this. These things have killed four men. They killed my partner. And I'll be damned if I let another person die needlessly."

Everyone remained quiet as Hank stood, helping the man he had subdued to his feet. Calmly, he walked him past the sheriff and into the station. The crowd's attitude had changed to a more docile one and the sheriff tried to place himself back in charge again. The last thing Julie heard as she followed after Hank was, 'Shoulda made *him* Sheriff' from someone in the crowd. It caused her to grin.

Hank had already dumped the man at his desk and was fixing up a fresh pot of coffee as if nothing had happened. Julie walked up next to him, placing a hand on his arm.

"That got some results."

"Maybe." He motioned over towards the man he'd cuffed at his desk. "I know him. Not well, mind you, but his reputation as a hunter gets around. Thinking of offering him a deal. He helps us, I don't throw him into county lockup."

"What about animal control, or the other deputies?"

He scoffed as he finished scooping the grounds into the filter and closed the machine, waiting for the water to percolate.

"The sheriff isn't gonna send shit out, and you and I both know Animal Control in Stonesworth can barely handle a lost dog, let alone a group of devil lizards."

"Is it really wise to bring a civilian?"

"We're scraping the bottom of the barrel already, Julie. We'll need Jeremiah as well. He wanted a live specimen, so now's his chance. Figure he'll come?"

"I'd be surprised if he wasn't already looking for those things in the woods."

"Good. While the sheriff worries more about his political standing, I'll be looking for more volunteers here in the department. Give Jeremiah a call and tell him to meet us here at the station. I'd rather we all head off as a group, rather than meet up somewhere else. There's no telling where those things are by now."

"You're not heading up there without me, Hank."

"As much as I'm sure you think you need to go, what skills exactly are you bringing to this table? The hunter is our tracker, if he agrees. Jeremiah will help us identify the creatures, and maybe their movement patterns. As for myself? The firepower."

"Moral support?"

That got a genuine laugh from Hank which was quickly followed by Julie's own. It felt good to laugh in spite of everything that was going on.

"Can you shoot?"

"Of course. Besides it's my day off. What else do I have going on today?"

After a moment of mulling it over, Hank nodded. "Alright. Go call Jeremiah, and I'm gonna get to work getting the rest of the party together. Shit, this better not be a bad idea."

"I think no matter what we do right now, it'll end up being a bad idea, Hank."

VIII

Hank already regretted the whole outing. Since the sheriff hadn't officially sanctioned the group, none of the other deputies had volunteered. Nothing like unpaid civic duty to show someone's true colors. That left just Hank, Julie, Jeremiah and the hunter, whose name was Chuck. Turns out, Chuck was an excellent tracker but also an arrogant son-of-a-bitch who got under Hank's skin immediately.

It hadn't taken them long to reach the section of Conner's woods they would need to hike into to find the spot Andrew pointed out, and about two hours later they were cresting the hill and could see the cave that he described in his initial account.

Except, there were no bodies. Hank rubbed his beard as he stood on the ridge, the soft sound of the nearby river the only noise as he took in the scene. Maybe another animal had dragged off any bodies. The creatures themselves may have brought them deeper into the cave. Either way, he got an odd feeling in his gut about it all, and headed back to the rest of the group.

"Alright, I don't see anything that could be of concern, so just stay close, and holler if you notice anything out of the ordinary."

"Whatever, old man. I know these woods like the back of my hand. Follow me and we'll be fine."

"Goddammit, Chuck. What did I tell you?"

The man shrugged and pushed past Hank. It took everything in him not to just drop him to his knees again. If they had other trained professionals to choose from, this ass would still be at the station rotting in a cell for a bit.

Slowly and cautiously, the group made its way towards the cave, keeping an eye out for any unusual movement. As they got closer, Hank pulled out his revolver and Chuck got his rifle ready. About ten feet from the cave's opening, they decided to look around a bit for any sign of the two men.

Hank immediately saw the large blood stain on the rock near the entrance, and the second about fifteen feet from that. The drag marks from the spots confirmed his initial suspicions of the bodies being drug off. He eased towards the cave and shined his light in. Something caught his attention so he focused on it, moving the light slowly to the object.

It was one of those things! He cried out despite himself, aimed, and fired. Everyone else jumped with fright, and Jeremiah was the first to run up next to him.

"I thought we were to observe and only engage when necessary!"

He actually has the gall to get mad at me, Hank thought as his heart pounded in his chest. He focused the light on the creature again and instantly felt like an idiot. There were two bullet wounds he could see clearly. One had killed it and the other was the one he had just added by going off on instinct.

"Never mind. It was already dead."

Giving the rest of the cave a quick run over with his light, he actually found it only went about twenty feet in, and left little in the way of hiding spots. Satisfied that there were no more creatures inside, he turned to Chuck.

"Keep an eye out. If any of those things shows up, holler."

"Whatever."

Hank didn't like his tone, and part of him worried if he should be turning his back on the guy he had brought to his knees earlier that day.

"Looks safe in there, Jeremiah."

Jeremiah brushed past him and quickly made his way toward the fallen creature. "I would have much rather preferred a living specimen but this will do nicely! Julie! Help me get this into the bag I brought."

"Wait...how the hell are you gonna get it out of here, Jer?"

"In the bag of course."

"I mean...shit, are you gonna carry this thing the whole way?"

"Of course! This is the find of a century! It's even more fascinating than I imagined."

He ran his fingers along the leathery hide of the creature, all the way down its tail, almost to the spine that jutted out of the bulb on the end.

"Amazing. It really does have a stinger delivery system for its toxin."

Reaching into his pocket, he pulled out a large rubber cork and placed it firmly on the stinger before getting Julie to help him lift the carcass and place it into the large duffel bag he'd brought along.

While they busied themselves, Hank was more concerned with what he saw on the other side of the cave. A crude nest had been built there, out of mud, sticks, and bone. Inside were several egg shells, signs that all had hatched. He poked around a bit and took in a sharp breath as he managed to find one that was still whole.

"How big is that thing you got there, Jeremiah?"

"I would wager about two feet in length, not counting the tail. Why?"

"Could something that small lay an egg this big?"

He reached down and gingerly picked up the still intact egg, and held it for all to see. It was the shape of a football, only about half as big. Jeremiah's eyes were as wide as saucers.

"Be careful!!"

He rushed over and took the egg, holding it even more gingerly in his hands than Hank had. The horror of its size, compared to the creature they had, suddenly washed over him and he placed it back into the nest.

"I...I honestly don't know. Some creatures can lay rather large eggs but most lay relative to their size."

"Which means?" Hank didn't like where this was going.

"Meaning the creature you encountered and the one here may only be juveniles."

A low whistle emanated from the edge of the cave. Chuck was looking at the creature then back to the egg.

"Imagine one of them suckers stuffed and mounted. Hot damn, that'd be a sight!"

Hank definitely did not like that guy.

"Fan out a bit everyone. We need to search for any signs of those things, or of the two bodies."

They spent the next hour searching the immediate area, heading all the way down to the riverbed. The only things of importance they managed to find were some scraps of clothing and what everyone agreed was a femur, broken in two. Jeremiah surmised that, since it appeared all the eggs had hatched, and the nest had been compromised, the lizards simply went to find a more secure lair.

Hank wasn't all too thrilled to hear that. He had hoped to find more than an egg and a dead creature. Jeremiah also said it was hard to tell just how many had hatched without analyzing all the eggshell fragments, but he guessed at least five more. According to Andrew's story, and accounting for the dead one, that made at least eight creatures.

"Ok, let's pack it in. It's starting to get late and there's no telling if they might return or not. We'll take what we found back and write up a report for the sheriff."

As they packed up their finds and started to head out, Hank could swear he saw something off in the distance. Squinting against the setting sun, he tried to make it out. There was something moving slowly along the riverbed and there was more than one. From this distance, and with the sun in his eyes, he couldn't tell if it was a gang of elk or something far more sinister. Deciding not to wait to find out, he vowed to return with greater numbers and firepower.

Whatever the hell these things were, he sure as hell didn't want them multiplying any more than they already had.

IX

As much as Chuck had demanded to be included in the examination of the creature, the other three all agreed he should just head home. After dropping him off at the station, they headed inside to report to the sheriff.

Hank turned to Julie and Jeremiah and stopped them at the door. "Look, after I speak with Dragert we'll take that thing and figure out what makes it tick. The more we know about them, the easier it'll be to stop them."

"You mean study, right?"

"Sure, Jer. Study."

Hank looked weary, tired, and about ready to collapse into a deep sleep. Julie knew he'd want to be there for the autopsy, but she also knew he'd just as soon fall asleep on the couch in her office.

"Do you need us when you talk to the sheriff?"

"I suppose not..." Curiosity spread over his face slowly, replaced with realization.

"Then go home and get some rest. Whatever we find can wait until we're all a bit more refreshed."

"Julie."

The word hung in the air, as if waiting to be followed by all manner of excuses as to why he had to accompany the two of them. Finally he just let out a short breath, shrugged, and went to go talk to the sheriff.

"I better get a call first thing in the morning, Julie."

Smiling, she nodded and she and Jeremiah went back out to transfer the creature to her car.

"Right, now that we've gotten that done, back to the University?"

"If you think I'm driving over an hour to get to your lab and find out what I already know, that it is woefully under equipped for a proper autopsy, then you're crazy, Jer."

"What are you talking about? I have some of the best diagnostic equipment in the country!"

"Exactly. Diagnostic equipment. Even if you could do an autopsy, I have everything we need right in town."

He seemed like he might argue the fact further, but Julie cut him off by putting her hand up before getting into the vehicle.

"Unless you want to walk back home, we're doing this my way. Besides, I highly doubt the police will want you carting potential evidence out of the county."

She had him there. Even if he wanted to argue the point further, which it seemed he did not, the corpse was still a piece of evidence. Evidence that, for the moment, was property of the sheriff's department.

About twenty minutes and a quick bite later, they were ready to get to work. Jeremiah had been very specific about how he wanted this done and Julie just didn't have the energy to argue with him. It was already getting rather late and, like Hank, she'd not gotten much sleep in the past few days. Add in the hike today and she thought that if she let herself slow down, even a little, she'd simply pass out.

Jeremiah prepped the body, but Julie had insisted the face guards. After his discovery of what the toxin could do, she didn't want to take any chances of even a drop of it being absorbed through skin or membrane. There was no telling how much could be enough to send the heart into arrest, or how much toxin could result in major bodily functions being paralyzed as well.

Part of her knew he was excited about cutting into the creature and learning more about it, just as she was, but the fact that he was too excited to remember basic safety protocol made her glad she was around to keep an eye on things.

"Alright. Here we have an unidentified new species which we will be cutting into in a moment to view the organs and internal structure. For the remainder of this video, since it has not been officially named, I will refer to it as 'the reptile'."

He decided to record the procedure so they could revisit and review anything they may have missed in the initial autopsy. She hated using the damn thing but Jeremiah insisted, claiming it was necessary for record keeping. *It's also necessary for exclusive television clips for the nature channels he'd want to sell this to*, she thought. Julie went along with it after getting Jeremiah to agree to show this to Hank and the sheriff after.

Playing the part of assistant to Jeremiah, she stood by and waited for when he'd need a tool or an extra hand as he continued to speak to a phantom audience.

"The reptile is approximately two feet tall and bipedal. While not uncommon for other species of reptile to occasionally stand on their hind legs, it is unusual for that to be their primary form of locomotion."

It took everything in her not to roll her eyes and scoff at him in that moment. She hadn't taken him for pompous and full of himself, but he was clearly trying to sound far more intelligent and worldly. This wasn't a medical documentary they were making. It was a tape for the police. Julie was fairly sure Sheriff Tusk wouldn't care how scientific it all sounded.

"There appear to be either rigid scales or bony protrusions near the eye sockets, knees, and elbows. Whether they are there for protection or simply a throwback to some other use forgotten by evolution is unknown."

He moved around the creature as he spoke and sometimes looked directly at the camera. *What a goddamn ham*, Julie thought.

"While the skin seems to resemble that of a scaled reptile, it is in fact more like a tough leather hide; one solid piece with ridges and bony protrusions all throughout. Julie, can you please zoom in, and focus on this area here?"

Knocked out of her little daze as he continued on, she moved over to the camera and kept her mouth shut. No sense egging him on. The sooner he was done with his little shot at fame, the sooner she could go home and crawl into bed.

"As you can see, the eyes resemble those of a gecko. Notice the shape of the iris. This could indicate the reptile has superior night vision, and certainly leads one to speculate that it has better vision than humans. I will be sure to analyze the eyes, to determine the amount of cones, at a later time."

He motioned her to move the camera down to the tail.

"It has a cloaca which is unsurprising. What makes this reptile unique, and altogether special, is the tail."

Being careful of the stinger on the end, he held it up by the bulbous part, and turned it slightly for the camera's sake.

"The tail itself, including the stinger, is about two feet longer than the entire body of the creature. The musculature also appears to be prehensile. At the tip is a bulbous growth, possibly a gland for producing the toxin that it injects into its prey with this."

The stinger was something that evoked a sense of dread in Julie. About four or five inches in length and ending in a slightly curved pinpoint, there was nothing subtle about it.

"...resembles a scorpion's stinger in shape. As stated previously, it is possible this bulbous growth at the end of the tail is responsible for the neurotoxin it injects as it feeds."

Jeremiah gently placed the tail back down and moved to the side of the creature. It was secured spread eagle, to allow him to more easily cut into the skin, and he looked like he was finally ready.

"I am now making the first incision. Who knows what wonders we will find just beneath the surface?"

"Jeremiah, do you really need to act like this is going on TV?"

"You never know, Julie."

He placed the edge of the scalpel right under the throat, and started to cut. Tried to start the cut was more appropriate. The initial attempt barely got through the skin so he repositioned. This time he put a good deal of force into it and managed to get a good cut going. It took a bit of tugging but soon he had a line running the length of the beast.

"Even the skin on the belly region is tough, like the rest of the exterior. Perhaps it developed such a resilient underside because of its being bipedal."

Making several more difficult cuts, he then splayed open the skin, and exposed the organs underneath. It made some sense to Julie, but there were several of the organs she couldn't identify. She went to school for people, not animals. Jeremiah, however, looked a little disappointed.

"At first glance it would appear to have the standard assortment of internal organs on first glance. Esophagus, stomach, lungs, intestines..."

He let his gaze move slowly across the creature's inside, until something caught his eye and his mouth widened into a grin.

"Hold on, we may have something here. Julie, please?"

She followed where his hand was pointing to something on the side of the creature. It looked like a tube of some sort, extending from the arm. There was an identical one from the other arm, which caused Julie to follow it up to the hand. Somehow she had missed it before, but there, plain as day, were several sucker-like nodules all along the palm of the creature's hand.

"My god...are those..."

"Suckers. The reptile actually consumes by drinking from its hands!"

Jeremiah was ecstatic. He followed the tubes as they joined and then fed into what looked like a single giant kidney. He extracted it carefully, documenting its size and weight, before noting there were two more tubes that had led from it. One fed directly to the cloaca and the other into other systems of the body.

"That explains the blood pools. They weren't from injuries but simply were what its body couldn't or wouldn't filter out."

That left a very troubling question in her mind; one that must have troubled Jeremiah as well as he vocalized it soon after it crossed her mind.

"Because of my earlier analysis of those samples you gave me we can now confidently speculate that they are extracting the adrenal gland hormones from the blood and discarding the rest. Why?”

A few seconds of silence, and then his eyes went wide.

“They can’t produce their own!”

A few moments of him rooting around in the guts of the creature and he nodded to himself.

“Nothing that even remotely resembles an adrenal gland. While that explains why they extract it from other creatures it still does not answer what they do with it once they have it.”

Jeremiah continued to poke and prod among the organs, paying special attention to what appeared to be a gland or lymph node right under the stomach.

“If I had to wager a guess, I think this organ here is where they store the siphoned hormones.”

Taking the scalpel and cutting carefully, he tried to extract it, but accidentally nicked it. A clear fluid leaked from the tiny cut and he frowned.

“Dammit. Julie, can you please get me a container, quickly? I want to get this before it all leaks out.”

Putting the camera back onto the tripod, she rushed over and grabbed all she had available, a small glass flask, and rushed back over. Jeremiah lifted the organ out and plopped it into the glass with a wet slap. It continued to ooze the clear fluid until it seemed empty and slightly deflated.

“If I were a betting man I’d wager that fluid is full of adrenaline and other hormones. I can’t wait to get it back to the lab for analysis.”

“Jeremiah, I dunno if I can keep acting like a glorified camerawoman. To be honest, I think I need a breath of fresh air. You mind?”

He seemed slightly annoyed with her disinterest, but simply nodded curtly and motioned to the tripod.

“Alright. Just please set up the camera to get as much of the reptile as possible as I continue.”

“Thanks.”

Resetting the camera was a cinch. She moved it slightly to get both Jeremiah and the creature into the frame, with a greater emphasis on the corpse. She made a motion to him that it was done and he continued.

"Right then. We have already removed several organs having to do with the creature's hormonal system, or for lack of a better term, borrowing of a hormonal system. Now I will be extracting the stomach to examine the contents. Here I will..."

She had no wish to be there when he started to look at the thing's last meal. Even if it wasn't human, the one thing she hated the most about her job was digging through a stomach's contents. Not only was the smell atrocious, but the consistency was usually enough to make her own stomach turn. She quickly removed her gloves and face shield, and headed out of the morgue, after making a quick detour to grab the pack of cigarettes in her desk.

*****

Andrew hadn't been able to sleep at all that night so he paced his room. His thoughts kept going back to the look frozen on his brother's face and his uncle's last words as he ran. He was scared and frightened...of course he was going to miss the shots! At least he tried...that had to count for something, right?

Problem was, he just couldn't seem to convince himself that he had tried hard enough or did everything he absolutely could. His mother's attitude once they got home, and away from prying eyes, hadn't help his mood either.

She had basically blamed him, not only for Josh's death, but for her brother's as well, saying he was a coward for the way he left him to die. Didn't matter how much Andrew tried to explain that the things already had Uncle Greg on the ground and were feeding before he even started to run, she had made up her mind. Her surviving son was a coward, and she could never forgive him for what he'd done to their family.

His grief slowly festered into anger over the way his mother had treated him after all that had happened. It's not like he tried to get Josh and Uncle Greg killed. However, when he thought about getting revenge, he remembered exactly what those things looked like and what they had done to his brother and uncle.

Maybe he was a coward, but he was alive. Shouldn't she be grateful for that? He kicked at a soccer ball that was on his floor and missed, causing three of his toes to crash into his bedpost. Crying out in pain, he plopped down onto his bed and rubbed his foot.

"Fucking hell!" he yelled, his anger getting the better of him as he picked up the ball and threw it across the room. It bounced off the wall and came rocketing back at him, narrowly missing his head and knocking a few things off a shelf behind him. Groaning in aggravation, he moved to go pick up the items.

Just as he was putting the last piece back, his mother burst into his room, screaming and carrying on.

"What do you think you're doing?! It's not enough you killed your brother and uncle, but now you carry on like a bull in a china shop? Let me grieve in peace, you stupid sack of shit!"

Andrew flexed his hands into fists, took in a deep breath, then let it out slowly. He did this again and his mother just stared at him. He almost laughed at how much she reminded him of a cow standing there; her mouth half open and her eyes glazed over with stupidity. He wasn't stupid and he wasn't a retard like Uncle Greg had said.

"Ma, I'm not stupid sack of shit and I'm grieving just as much as you are! What happened was an accident." He tried to speak calmly but he couldn't help the level of his voice as it raised in defiance against his mother.

"Boy, don't you dare raise your voice to me in my home!" Before he could react she closed the distance between them and gave him a hard slap across the face. "You will respect me in my home and you will accept your blame in this!"

He could feel her hot breath, accented by the scent of alcohol, on his skin as she yelled at him. Flecks of spittle hit his face, causing him to wince instinctively, and, as she continued to berate him, something inside of him finally snapped. He didn't slap his mother but reached back, clenched his fist even tighter, and struck her. He was done being afraid. He was done being the scapegoat for something outside his control.

His mother was dumbfounded as she fell back and collapsed onto the floor. Holding a hand to her face where he had hit her, she looked up at him with those same damn cow eyes and it made him even angrier.

"Y-you piece of shit! I'll call the sheriff! Tell them you made it all up and killed those two! You'll burn for this! I should have aborted you!!"

The thought of being officially blamed, and not just emotionally berated, for the deaths of his uncle and brother sucked all the bravado and moxy out of the young man. His eyes went wide with fright and his mother stood, smirking as she did.

"I always knew you were a hell child. Josh was so sweet and innocent and my brother Greg was a good man. Then you came around with your wicked ways and killed them! I'm calling the sheriff right now!"

***

Inhaling deeply, she felt almost intoxicated by the smoke. Julie was leaning against the wall of the hospital, the heel of one foot holding the emergency exit open as she took another puff of her cigarette. Quitting be damned; when giant lizards that can make your heart explode show up, that's reason enough to fall right back off the wagon, she surmised.

She looked at her phone. It was a little past 1AM, which shocked her. Her body felt like it was much later than that, and they'd spent a good deal of time already that night getting the thing ready for the examination. Wracking her brain she tried to tie certain events of the day to certain times.

"Coulda sworn we came into the morgue at midnight..." she whispered to herself. Then it hit her and she slapped her forehead, laughing at her own brain fart. Daylight savings time had taken effect and her phone automatically updated. Mystery solved.

Finishing off her cigarette, she wished the mystery of these creatures would be solved just as easily. However, she knew that things had a habit of getting worse before they got any better. She just hoped more people wouldn't get hurt before they could figure out a way to contain or stop them.

She tossed the butt to the ground, crushed it with the tip of her shoe, and then headed back inside.

***

"Look, I can appreciate your concern, but unless your son is also the one who killed another man and one of my deputies you're placing blame on the wrong person."

Sheriff Dragert wished to God he hadn't given her the business card with his personal cell number on it. In fact, he swore he hadn't. Maybe Dorris had given her the number simply to spite him. Between all the problems facing the department with the strange animals and Hank questioning his authority at every turn, he'd started to drink almost a full bottle of milk of magnesia every night, just to get his stomach to settle.

His wife told him to see a doctor, but 'the sheriff of the town needs to look strong,' he told her. Any sign of weakness and the vultures would descend, fighting over the scraps of the corpse that was his career.

Now he found himself eyeing the bottle on his nightstand as he sat up in bed. His wife turned over grumpily and put a pillow over her head as he continued to talk to the woman on the other line.

"Ma'am....yes....ma'am....MA'AM, please let me speak."

No matter how much he tried to get a word in edgewise, it was like speaking to a brick wall. Except the wall had the good sense to keep quiet. Standing and walking out of the room, he made his way to his study, sat down at the desk, and continued to wait for his opportunity to get a word in. He placed the phone on his desk and hit the speaker button.

"...will you do about this?!"

Finally she'd shut up enough to let him talk.

"First of all, is your son threatening you at this very moment? Is your life in danger and can you not leave the premises?"

"He killed my son and brother! I know he did it, and he lied about some sort of creatures doing it! He must be on marijuana!!"

The sheriff snorted at that, which caused her to be silent. Probably offended the old bag, he mused.

"Ma'am, please answer me without going off on a tangent again. Are you safe in your home currently? If you feel unsafe, can you leave? Is your son threatening you this very moment?"

"...Not this moment no, but he-"

"Listen to me, please. While I do not condone what your son did, I can understand it. You both have suffered a traumatic event today, and he actually witnessed it. It's possible his emotions boiled over. I will be glad to take him aside in the morning and give him a good talking to about striking a woman."

"No! He needs to leave this house, now! I do not feel safe! I feel threatened right this very moment!!"

He closed his eyes tightly and took a small short breath. His face started to grow hot and his mustache started to itch. It always itched whenever he started to get angry.

"I will not repeat myself in this matter. I am off duty, and if this is a true emergency then please dial 911, and they will direct you to an officer who can help. However, given your tone, I believe the immediate danger has passed and you both need to sleep off your tempers."

"I can't believe I voted for such a sad sack of a man who can't even protect his own citizens from harm!"

"I probably woulda hit you too! Now go to sleep or call someone else. I'm going to bed!"

Bringing his finger down on the red phone icon wasn't as satisfying as slamming a receiver down, but it got the job done. His phone immediately began to ring again, but he simply turned the damned thing off.

The comment would probably come back to bite him in the ass, but he only had another two years before he could retire from the position with full pension. The idea was to head into private security work, consulting, that sort of thing. He'd had enough with headaches and people like that woman to last him a lifetime. Being a public servant wasn't at all what it was cracked up to be.

***

His mom looked flustered and her face was a shade of red he'd only ever seen when she got off the phone with his father. She was a special kind of pissed and he wondered if he had time to leave before she directed her wrath at him. As she turned and stared right at him, he knew it was too late.

"Get the fuck out of my house!"

She bellowed and started throwing things at him, whatever she could get her hands on. Silverware, plates, and books all flew through the air at his head, and he ducked to avoid most of it as he backed away from her.

"Come on Mom, I didn't mean to hit you! You just pushed me!"

"Pushed you?! PUSHED YOU?!"

The woman stormed over and gave him a huge shove, causing him to land on his ass. Andrew gave out a yelp of fear and pain as she towered over him.

"I wish it was you that died out in those woods!! GET OUT!!"

Her hands came flying, slapping at him wildly and furiously. Holding up an arm to try and defend himself, he stumbled out the back door and into the yard. She even picked up a lawn chair on their deck and threw it at him, which forced him further away from the house.

"Don't ever come back! EVER!!"

"Fuck you, you bitch!"

Her eyes went wide, and she uttered a sound that was kind of a mix between a cat getting hit by a car and a goose honking. She started to chase after him, but he ran out of the yard and into the street. Fuming, she gave up after just a few feet and went back inside, slamming the door so hard it didn't shut fully and creaked back open again.

Now he really was out on his own. *Whatever*, he thought. *I hated living with her, anyway.* That was most of the reason he went out so much with Uncle Greg. While he was almost as verbally abusive as Andrew's mother, at least he didn't go on and on about how he and his brother had 'destroyed her body' and 'caused your dad to run off'.

Mom was a vile, bitter woman, and this just cemented it. Thinking about Greg and Josh started to get him down, so he started to walk along the road into town. His mood and demeanor started to calm down as he felt the cool air on his skin, and, checking his wallet, he decided he wanted to go get a slice of pie. He had some friends he could crash with for a few days, or he still had a key for Uncle Greg's cabin outside town.

Wondering if that would be breaking-and-entering, he never noticed the rustle in the bushes behind him heading back the way he came.

***

Walking back into the morgue, there were far more containers with all manner of organs in them than when she had left. She looked at the clock and then back to Jeremiah and just shook her head.

"You may as well have taken the whole thing back to the University at this rate."

He shot her a glance that basically said 'told you so' as he turned his focus back to the creature.

"I'm still recording. I've found a number of other organs I can't quite explain, especially an odd one around the lungs. Come take a look at this."

Making a face, she put the face shield back on and a new pair of gloves. She marveled at the fact that the body cavity was nearly empty except for the heart and lungs. One of the legs had been cut into as well, with the skin and some layers of muscle peeled back to expose bone. He motioned towards the lungs.

"At first I thought this may have been a tumorous growth around the lungs, but it actually seems to be incorporated into them. I'm completely unsure of its purpose at this time, however."

"Could it be gills?"

When his immediate response was laughter, she knew she'd said something stupid.

"Not everyone is an animal biologist, Jeremiah," she shot back

"I suppose not. But no, they aren't gills. They could be some sort of system to help filter the air the creature takes in, perhaps making it able to survive in harsher conditions. Given their increased night vision, it makes sense that they may come from underground environs, near pockets of methane and sulfur. But this is all purely speculation."

"Fancy way of saying you don't know."

"Ok, I deserved that. I did find something interesting, though. These creatures appear to be mesothermic."

"Jeremiah, I'm not even going to attempt a guess at what that means, as I'm sure you will simply laugh again at my lack of knowledge in your chosen field of study."

"Let me break it down a little, into more colloquial terms. Most people, erroneously, refer to creatures as either warm-blooded or cold-blooded. Lizards would fall mostly under cold-blooded. However, there are some creatures that could be considered lukewarm-blooded. That is, to say, they get their heat both from their environment and are able to regulate it somewhat on their own."

"I'm guessing that's why they're still so active, even though the days are getting colder?"

"Precisely. It's got rete mirabile along its leg muscles."

"That term I know. I thought only warm-blooded animals and humans had arteries so densely packed together."

"Yes and no. Tuna and leatherback turtles have them but I've never heard of a land lizard with them before. The way these are situated, so close to the bone...I can only assume it's to help regulate body temperature during times of stress, and to help conserve heat when they are more dormant. In fact we may see an increase in activity as it gets colder, simply to keep their core temperature up."

"Christ, Jeremiah. The last thing anyone wants to hear is that these things are becoming more active. That puts a kibosh on their slowing down with cold then, doesn't it?"

"It would have to be extreme cold. And even then they may act like humans and still function until death. It would be more effective to simply shoot them, assuming we're going for killing instead of subduing them."

"Heh, Hank would like that option, for sure."

Jeremiah frowned a bit as he pulled a sheet over the creature, pulled off the gloves, and then turned off the camera.

"I'd think you, of all people, would understand and appreciate the importance of trying to preserve and protect a new species."

"One that's managed to kill four people in the past 48 hours since it was discovered. Not looking too good, Jer."

"I'll give you that. We should definitely proceed with caution so no one else is hurt, but these creatures are far too significant to simply hunt down to extinction! We need to preserve them! Possibly relocate them to a much more remote area."

Julie shook her head.

"Four people are dead, and you want to propose the town pays for their relocation? Even endangered animals that attack people are usually put down, Jeremiah. I'm sorry, but you know there's only one way this is going to go."

"We'll see."

The way he looked right then, with a self-assured smirk on his face, wasn't doing much to put Julie's mind at ease on the subject. Part of her wanted to continue to argue with him about it, but a yawn came out of her mouth before she could stop it and betrayed her exhaustion.

"I was about to call it a night as well," he said, as he started to place the organs and biopsies he'd taken into the medical refrigerator. "I can continue my analysis of the lungs tomorrow, and then we can take the samples back to my lab so I can get down to what really makes this thing tick."

"Sounds good."

Both of them finished cleaning up the items, and then gingerly placed the creature into one of the positive temperature cold chambers on the wall. It wasn't until after she shut the door that she realized they'd placed it right next to the one for Deputy Wilk. The funeral home hadn't sent for the body, and she'd been in no rush to follow up with it either.

A tiny pang of guilt went through her as she looked at the two small doors. This could even have been the creature that killed Wilk initially. There was no way to know for sure, unless Jeremiah found something specific in its stomach. She decided not to ask him what he had found when he cut into it. Some things you were better off not knowing.

"Since it's so late, you can just crash at my place tonight."

"Julie, so forward of you! Do I get the left or the right side of the bed?"

Rolling her eyes at him, she was in no mood to flirt. She smirked a little and shook her head.

"Whichever side of the couch you can fit on."

"Fair enough. You still owe me a dinner date, by the way."

"I think I've got some hot pockets in the freezer. Will that count?"

"Only if they're by candlelight."

The absurdity of their conversation, coupled with how late it was, must had addled their brains, because both of them started to laugh hysterically at that. They made their way out of the morgue.

"So, what do you think that was on the lungs?"

"I haven't a clue. I'd need to take some more samples, but that is a task for tomorrow though. Tonight, I'm far more concerned with sleeping, and partaking of your delicious hot pocket."

"Don't make me turn the hose on you."

As the lights clicked off and the door shut the morgue fell silent. The forgotten egg, still nestled inside the bag, jostled with a bit of movement. It shifted an inch or two inside the bag and then lay still again.

***

Andrew's mother, Cathy, was still fuming some twenty minutes after she kicked him out. A tiny, very tiny, part of her felt that she had over-reacted. Should she really have blamed the possible deaths of her son and brother on her only other son? Maybe not. There hadn't been any bodies found, and it was more likely Greg had just high-tailed it out of the county.

Her brother hadn't always been the kind to go against the law, but when he did, he made good and sure his ass was covered in any eventuality. It was that knowledge that gave her hope Andrew was wrong about their deaths and the two would turn up.

Thinking of Andrew's actions still made her mad though, no matter how much she may have regretted blaming him. The boy had some nerve striking her. Actually striking her! No, any thoughts of regret or sorrow for her boy went right out the window the more she thought of how he treated her.

Then there was the sheriff. She planned on launching a formal complaint with the mayor's office. Andrew could have killed her, and that fat oaf couldn't be bothered to come to her rescue. Already a bit tipsy from drinking that night, she went and poured herself another glass of wine. Drinking most of it down in a single gulp, her thoughts strayed to the sheriff again.

Even as stupid and oafish as he was, he sure had something about him that she found quite alluring. Either that, or she found authority attractive. She'd even take Deputy Murphy for a good solid fuck, if she weren't so sure he'd throw out a hip or die in the middle of it.

Christ, she thought, this line of thinking wasn't doing her any good. It had been years since she'd known the touch of a man in a more intimate sense. She wasn't an ugly woman, at least she didn't think so. She was just very guarded with her heart, she told herself. A good woman like her wouldn't just spread her legs for anyone, no sir. You wanted a ride with this majestic creature, you earned it!

Many mixed emotions flooded her mind. Guilt over having lustful thoughts when her son and brother were probably dead, anger at her other son, more lustful thoughts about any man that happened to wander into her mind at the present, more anger at the stupid ineffective sheriff, and a whole host more. Thinking more and more about it, she felt the need to release all the pent up stress. A nice hot bath would do the trick.

Heading upstairs to her room to grab a few 'necessary' items to help with the relief of her tension, she never did notice that the back door was ajar, nor did she notice, or hear, when it opened even wider and something slipped inside.

Now more than a bit tipsy, she moved into her room and checked herself out in the mirror. Not bad, she thought, as she went to her dresser and grabbed her special friend. Cooing slightly, she pulled it out of the drawer, clicked a button on the side, and giggled to herself as it came alive.

Feeling a bit naughty now, she stripped out of her clothing, slipped on a robe, and headed to the bathroom. Drawing her bath, she made sure the water was nice and hot, but not too hot; she didn't want to burn herself again. Last time she got a bit too drunk and tried this, she forgot to add any cold water. Looked like a damn lobster for days.

Steam filled the bathroom as she waited for the tub to fill. Knowing she was home alone, she didn't bother to close the door. Even if Andrew came back, she was certain she had locked the doors and he didn't have a key. He could bang on the front door for a spell while she enjoyed herself.

Once the water was the right level, she dropped her robe and slipped into the tub. Sinful thoughts took over as she let the warm and wonderful water soak into her skin. Closing her eyes, she let her hands start to gently explore her body, feeling the areas that had been so neglected. She reached over to grab for her little toy. Finding it and clicking it on without ever opening her eyes, she grinned and licked her lips.

She had made sure to get a waterproof model just for moments like these. The buzz filled her ears and made her whole body tingle in anticipation. She heard a click. Then another. It sounded almost as if something was walking on tile with nails. *Oh god*, she thought, *it's the fucking dog*.

Opening her eyes and starting to chastise the perverted beast, she stopped mid sentence when she saw it wasn't the dog but some sort of lizard thing. It looked at her curiously, cocking its head to one side. When she screamed, it screamed as well.

Then lunged.

X

Hank had managed to get a decent night's rest, for whatever it was worth. Looked like Julie had as well. When he called her, she said she had Jeremiah over but she'd drop him off at the morgue to finish studying the creature. Neither of them fully expected it to be a literal blood bath when they arrived at Andrew's home.

Julie had already done a preliminary examination by the time Hank arrived. Since other officers were on scene, he took his time. The body would still be there, he figured, and at least this way he could get a decent cup of coffee to start the day.

The first thing that popped into his mind when he went up the stairs and headed into the bathroom was Jackson Pollock. There had been definite signs of a struggle, and red water had been splashed against almost every surface. Andrew's mother was floating face down in the tub, which, if Hank had to guess, was probably half as full as when she had first started her bath. He noted the vibrator over near the door.

Julie must have noticed where his eyes went, because she cleared her throat.

"It was actually still going when I got here. Apparently, the officer on the scene didn't think he should turn it off, due to it being possible evidence. I had to bite my lip not to giggle like a schoolgirl. All things considered."

"Why the hell is it all the way over there? Think it...uh...moved that way?"

She did laugh a little at his comment and shook her head. "No, I think she threw it at the creature in self defense. It didn't do much."

Hank's shoulders slumped as he turned back to Julie, and then the body in the tub.

"Are you sure it was that thing? We're in town, Julie. On the outskirts, sure, but this is still a fair distance from the woods where those things were sighted."

"Positive. Just look at her back."

He stepped a bit closer and peered over the edge of the tub. Since she was in water, and they didn't have a bruise formed around them, it was easy to miss the small punctures on her back near the kidneys.

"Great. You determine the cause of death?"

"Are you serious right now, Hank? I'd say it's the exact same as the other deaths involving these things, but without actually getting to examine her it's anyone's guess."

Hank realized his mistake and apologized.

"Sorry. Guess I'm not firing on all cylinders yet. Where's the kid? I heard they only found the one body."

"Apparently there was a fight between Andrew and his mother last night. Didn't the sheriff tell you? Andrew struck her and she threw him out, after the sheriff refused to do anything to help her if she wouldn't call 911."

Hank smiled and shook his head. As spineless as John could be at times in dealing with the public he had to admire the man's tenacity when he felt he was right. Julie continued.

"Few of the neighbors heard the fight when it happened, but since they've been known to get into it late at night no one bothered to look. Back door was wide open, which I think is how it got inside. So far though, no one has been able to find Andrew."

"You're telling me we not only have one of those things loose in town but we're also missing the one kid who probably led it here? What if it was tracking him from the cave?"

"That's highly unlikely, Hank. If it was, why not attack him once he was outside?"

"You got me. None of this is making any goddamn sense."

Hank felt utterly confused by the whole situation and unsure of what to do next. If this was a regular suspect he could advise people to be wary, go out in pairs, stay in after dark, and so forth. Since this was some kind of hellish wild animal, he had no idea if staying indoors would keep anyone safe, let alone the other things.

"Julie, we need to get a handle on this, but first things first: we need to find the kid."

"Actually, no."

Hank spun around so fast he was afraid he'd slip on the bloody water on the floor. He had expected Julie to agree with him.

"Excuse me?"

"Andrew can wait. Last night it had a perfect chance to go for him. I put death around 2am, which is right after she apparently kicked him out. The creature was outside when he was and it ignored Andrew to come inside. Why it did that, I've got no idea, but I don't think he's in any immediate danger. As for getting ahead of this..."

She trailed off a bit as she moved past Hank into the hallway, and motioned for him to follow. Scratching his head, he wondered just what the hell she was up to.

"Sorry, just needed to get out of that room. I've been in there since I got here. So, I've already spoken with the sheriff. We're going to call in some experts from the zoo and from animal control to try and capture the things."

Hank's jaw dropped and his eyes went wide. He jabbed a finger at her, even though he knew she wasn't in control of this decision. Regardless, he was pissed.

"Fuck that, Julie! You and I both know they need to die."

Julie looked down at the finger he pointed at her, and pushed it aside. Hank withdrew it a little, sheepishly, a bit ashamed that he had let his temper get the better of him like that.

"I agree with you Hank. But, do you think the media and general public will share that sentiment? 'Small town wipes out new species.' Plus this isn't fully on the sheriff's shoulders this time. I caught Jeremiah calling in some favors this morning. Bringing in animal control and the zoo experts was actually his doing."

"That son of a bitch. I'll kill him!"

"He has a point, Hank, as much as I hate to admit it. These could be the very last of their kind. We simply don't know enough about them. What if humans encroached on their habitat and this is their response?"

"You sure it was Jeremiah who called, and not you? You sound just like him, Julie."

Hank had meant to be a little venomous with his words. As far as he was concerned, she was turning her back on him by agreeing to go along with this stupid idea. "If we don't shoot to kill, we put people at risk. If those idiots don't handle them properly, they're all gonna get killed.

"I realize you're upset, so I'm choosing to ignore the Jeremiah comment. Asshole."

"I'm serious, Julie. This is now the fifth person dead because of those things. When a bear goes rogue, we put it down. This is no different."

"Everyone is, at least partially, in agreement as far as that's concerned. From now on, any of the creatures get put down the second any human life looks to be in danger. The task force is forming at the station in about thirty minutes. Dragert told me to tell you to head there as soon as you were done here."

"Why would I do that? Might as well hand in my god-damn badge at this point. No one's listening to me!"

"They're going to have to now. Apparently, you're heading the task force."

Hank gave a dry chuckle. Shaking his head, he shrugged. "Of fucking course I am. You need anything more from me?"

"If it's going to be more jabs because you can't deal with the situation like an adult, no, I do not. However, if you want to get someone from downstairs to help me get her out of that tub, I'd appreciate it."

Hank nodded. He started to apologize "Alright. Look, Julie..."

"Forget it, Hank. I'm upset too. Maybe next time you won't take it out on your friends." With that, she turned and headed back into the bathroom to prepare the body to be moved.

He felt sheepish again. He kept lashing out at Julie simply because she was the only one there, and he felt a little guilty for it. Once he got to the station, if they really did put him in charge of a task force, he'd be sure to drum it into their heads that capture was not an option. Looking over at the body floating in the water only made him all the more certain that these things needed to be disposed of.

***

Hank counted a total of seven men and women, including Jeremiah and himself. Two of the seven, one man and one woman, had come from the animal control office, and didn't look older than about twenty. That alone annoyed the hell out of Hank. If they were going to send people, the least they could do was send *experienced* people. The other three he guessed were from the zoo, due to their lack of uniforms, and he was thankful they at least seemed to know what they were doing.

The only other woman was maybe ten or fifteen years younger than Hank, and she was probably a doctor of biology, like Jeremiah. When Hank entered the conference room they were chatting like two old friends over a cup of coffee. Probably swapping ideas about the creature, for all Hank knew.

The other two men looked just about as young as the two from animal control. This was going to turn into a circus very quickly if he didn't assert some sort of authority. God, he needed a drink.

"Hello everyone. I'm Deputy Hank Murphy. If you don't mind, I'd like you each to introduce yourselves, and maybe tell us what you'll bring to the table for this hunt."

"Expedition."

Hank glanced over at Jeremiah, who had interjected. He just stared the man down for a few moments, which made him fidget a bit. Hank smirked to himself and turned to the first person on his right, from animal control.

"Ok, let's start with you."

Clearing her throat, the young woman started to speak. She had short-cut hair, dyed a bright, unnatural red, and several tattoos along her arm and neck. Some sort of piercing that reminded Hank of a bull ring hung from her nose. When she spoke, her voice sounded timid and very mousy.

"Um, my name is Eloise. I've been with animal control for about two years now."

The next one to talk was the young man from animal control. He was clean cut except for his shoulder length hair, and didn't look a day over fifteen. He spoke with a slight squeak to his voice and ran his fingers through his hair to get it out of his face.

"Name's Ted. Only been with animal control for four months. I needed a job."

Hank bit his tongue. This was utterly ridiculous and he could tell from the reaction on his face Jeremiah had expected a bit more as well. Instead of dwelling on it, he decided he would call animal control after the meeting to see if there was anyone else more qualified than Ted.

Next to take a step forward was the woman from the zoo. She was not in any sort of uniform, and he was a little disappointed that she and her associates weren't dressed like the nature types he'd seen on television. Black boots, shorts, a button up shirt in a drab neutral color, something along those lines. Instead, she wore a pair of jeans and a blouse, with her dark brown hair drawn up into a bun on the top of her head. There was a streak or two of grey, just enough to make her look a bit distinguished. Had she not had that bit of grey, there was no way he'd peg her as being any older than Julie.

"My name is Miranda Hershey, and I-"

"Whoa, like the candy bar?"

Ted had spoken up, and he was looking far too excited at the prospect that Miranda may be the heiress to the candy empire. Hank sighed, quite audibly, which caused Ted's co-worker Eloise to snicker under her breath, and bite her lip to try and keep quiet. When all eyes fell on him, he looked around from one person to the next.

"What?"

"Get out. Just get the hell out. Tell your bosses I'll contact them later."

"Serious? But they told me I gotta be a part of this taser force thing, or I'll lose my job!"

"Did...did you just call it a taser force?" Miranda looked awestruck.

"Please, just go. It's for the best." Hank tried to sound polite.

Ted seemed like he was about to burst into tears. Frowning, he took in a breath and let it go in a huff as he turned to leave. "Whatever. This taser force is lame anyway."

Both Miranda and Eloise lost it at that, and couldn't help themselves from almost doubling over with laughter. Ted's face went a dark shade of crimson as he stormed out, slamming the door behind him. While it may have been embarrassing for the kid, there was no doubt in Hank's mind he'd have gotten either himself or someone else seriously hurt or killed.

"As I was saying, my name is Miranda Hershey and I run the reptile area over at the zoo. While I do not have a PhD in biology like Jeremiah here, I do have extensive experience and knowledge of reptiles and their habits. My two associates, Timothy and Elliot, work in different areas in the zoo, but are expert trackers in their own rights."

That was more like it, Hank thought. Timothy was a smaller man with dark ebony skin and dreadlocks. He had a bit of pudge around his middle, while Elliot looked to be sculpted from marble. Veins bulged as he crossed his arms, and his hair was a bit longer, cut in a shaggy style. Hank took a seat at the head of the conference table and gestured for the others to join him.

"Jeremiah I'm going to assume everyone here already knows you, unless you'd like to tout your own accomplishments."

A gentle laugh rolled through the room, as Jeremiah shook his head in response.

"Alright, then I guess we get started? I'll be perfectly honest right now folks: I have never run a task force before, nor do I really think I fully understand what that entails. However, the simply fact remains that at least one creature is loose in town, and needs to be stopped immediately."

All eyes went wide, at this revelation, especially Jeremiah's.

"Are you absolutely sure, Deputy Murphy?"

"What I am about to divulge does not leave this room, understood?"

All members nodded, looking a little apprehensively towards each other and then to Hank before he continued.

"There was an attack last night. We believe one of the creatures entered a home near the outskirts of town, and attacked and killed a woman. Her name was Cathy Ferguson, Andrew Ferguson's mother. The reason we believe it was one of the creatures is because the wounds match. Have you informed them yet, Jeremiah?"

"Actually no, Hank. I was waiting for you. I've made some discoveries during my autopsy of the creature that I thought you should be aware of. Namely, that it feeds off adrenal hormones. This explains the puncture wounds on the backs of the victims."

As Jeremiah began to describe his findings, and their significance, Hank noticed Eloise looking a bit green around the gills, fidgeting in her seat and looking down at the table. He started to think the sheriff had just phoned in animal control as a courtesy, conveniently leaving out how dangerous the creatures they were going after were. The other three looked positively enraptured.

"Care to elaborate, Jeremiah?" Turning his attention back to Jeremiah, Hank was honestly curious as to why the creatures did what they did. It might give a clue that could end up getting them a step ahead, instead of having another dead body to clean up after.

"Gladly!"

Jumping up, he went to go retrieve his bag and pulled out several photographs. Placing them on the table, it appeared he'd documented his autopsy of the creature rather thoroughly.

"Many of these are stills taken from the footage I recorded last night. I made a great number of discoveries that I feel are quite important."

"To catching them?"

Jeremiah seemed a bit hesitant to answer, and that alone gave Hank the answer he needed. A slight frown creased his brow as he let the scientists discuss the creature's 'finer points' at length. This task force was going to go nowhere fast if it delved too much into intellectualism without action.

Miranda and Jeremiah soon got into a heated discussion over some biological function, with Timothy and Elliot interjecting their own expert opinions here and there. They were in their own world now, and almost all the talk went over Hank's head anyway. He was never one for overly scientific babble; he preferred more frank words. He leaned over to Eloise.

"This all going over your head too?"

Without looking up, she nodded. Looking at her, he noticed that her left hand was fiddling with an errant string on her work uniform, constantly pulling at it, but never hard enough to break.

"If you aren't up to this, I understand. I can call your boss and figure out if there's anyone with more experience or-"

Eloise looked up at him and shrugged.

"The only other person besides Mr. Henderson is Mrs. Henderson and...Ted. We've never had to deal with anything dangerous like this before. I had no idea anyone actually died."

"One of the deceased was actually my partner."

"Oh, geez. I'm so sorry!"

When she looked at him, she reminded him a bit of a wounded animal. Big wet eyes, almost ready to burst into tears at any second.

"This is your out, kid, no questions asked. If you stay, you better follow my orders to a T, understand?"

For a moment she seemed deep in thought, her brow furrowing slightly as she mulled over the prospects. A second later she simply said, "Got it, sir."

"You, I like." He flashed her one of his big bright smiles, which got one out of her in return. He turned his attention back to the other four. They were still in the thick of some discussion involving the lungs when he cleared his throat. The conversation died down and all eyes fell on him.

"I realize this may be the scientific find of a lifetime. However, five people are now dead, and we're going to focus on *that* for the time being. While we may attempt to capture one of the beasts alive, I'm going to authorize lethal force. Shoot first and ask questions later. Understood?"

"Deputy Murphy, you can't just indiscriminately murder a species that has never been seen before simply because it's defending its territory."

"Miranda, had the fifth death not occurred last night, right in town, I'd be inclined to agree with you, and even try and see it more your way. But these things are doing more than defending territory from poachers. If what Jeremiah says is true, and they feed on hormones and then kill, last night may be their way of breaking out into a new hunting ground."

Miranda looked a little defeated, but nodded solemnly. "Unfortunately, Deputy Murphy is right. We may be lucky and this is a highly isolated incident. You said it was a Cathy Ferguson that was killed...is she significant to this situation?"

Jeremiah took the opportunity to fill in the rest of the group, giving them a bit of back story "Andrew witnessed his brother and uncle, local poachers, being attacked and killed by the reptiles after they happened upon a nest and disturbed it."

"Poachers got what was coming to them in my book," Elliot interrupted.

Hank may have agreed somewhat with the sentiment, but he didn't like how Elliot's eyes lit up when he heard who was killed. "Criminal or not, they deserved better."

Elliot remained quiet, and simply shook his head as Jeremiah continued.

"Andrew then apparently ran back into town. Is it possible one of the reptiles followed him that distance, in some sort of revenge attack?" Jeremiah turned to the three from the zoo for insight.

Timothy shook his head, a firm and solid no. "No way. If an animal like that was in danger, or its young were in danger, then attacking in the immediate would make sense. For them to actively follow him, through unfamiliar terrain, over a long distance, makes little sense."

"What if it weren't following him to defend the nest, but to simply hunt him?"

Miranda placed her elbows on the table and leaned forward into her interlocked fingers, looking from one person to the next. "It's been established they extract adrenaline from their prey, at least according to Jeremiah's preliminary findings. What if one, or more, followed him for his potential to deliver these hormones?"

Timothy shrugged and seemed to mull it over. His response was slow and deliberate; he seemed to be choosing his words carefully. "It is theoretically possible. There have been dozens of documented cases of animals tracking prey over miles before finally going in for the kill."

Hank brought up the next point from his conversation with Julie. "When the fifth victim was attacked, Andrew was already outside. Why kill the mother, instead of the son? He was available, but the thing went inside to attack her."

The room fell silent as no one had a plausible or believable theory as to why that happened. Hank sat back in his chair and folded his arms, regarding the room.

"We can sit here and try and figure out the whys of this thing until we're all blue in the face. The cold, hard truth of the matter is, we need to find it before it becomes a threat again."

"We may actually have a bit of luck with that part, Hank. When I examined it last night, I noticed that the eyes were exactly as you described. This leads me to believe that it has excellent night vision, and may have high sensitivity to light. It may still function during the day, but it will be limited to short spurts. It will more than likely have found a location nearby to wait for nightfall."

"Alright, then. Looks like we're going out into the field, people. Timothy and Elliot, I assume you're trained with firearms, and have valid carry permits?"

"Yes, we have both had extensive training, but we only use tranquilizers."

"Today, you're going to use lead. You will both be issued firearms from the station armory. These will be returned after our little hunt."

"Expedition, Hank. We have to try and preserve these creatures. Please."

Hank shot another glare at Jeremiah before shaking his head in exasperation and resuming.

"As I was saying, each day we go out, you two will sign them out and back in again after the 'expedition'. Now, let's go. We're burning daylight, and, if Jeremiah is right, we have the upper hand right now."

***

On the way, Hank briefed them on how important it was to avoid the press and simply state no comment if they were questioned for any reason. Hank was all for being upfront about the creatures, but he also knew that if the media got a hold of the story before they had a proper handle on things, it would turn into a circus. They'd not only have townsfolk traipsing about, and possibly getting hurt, but any amateur scientist wanting to make a name for themselves would show up as well.

Jeremiah agreed with him, at least on that much. Besides, this was going to be *his* big discovery. He and Miranda went way back, and she owed him a few favors. It was partially the reason he had called her in. Not only for her expertise, but her discretion and willingness to let him have all the credit. She also shared his opinion that, no matter what, the remaining creatures needed to be kept alive.

He still hadn't settled on a decent name, and he hoped one would come to him after observing a live specimen. Poking around the dead one had done little to inspire him in that regard.

Once at the scene of the attack, Hank seemed surprised that there wasn't a news van out front. He stopped, looked around, and even walked out into the quiet street and looked both ways. Satisfied that there would be no surprises, he rejoined the group.

Breaking the group into three teams of two, Hank insisted everyone be paired up with a gun. He went with Miranda, Eloise went with Timothy, and Jeremiah was paired up with Elliot. Hank pulled out a few maps and handed one to each group, pointing out different areas he wanted them to canvas.

"We'll need to focus on any heavily shaded areas. Out-croppings, sheds, dense foliage, crawlspaces...anywhere it may have found shelter for the day." Jeremiah interjected.

"What do we do if someone comes out of their home to ask us what's going on?"

"Good question, Eloise. Just inform them a large snake, a boa, escaped from the zoo. Non-lethal and you're merely acting on a tip that it was sighted in the area. If they ask about Ms. Ferguson, tell them you don't know anything and that would be an unrelated police matter."

"Hank, Julie told me you were wanting to go public with this in the beginning." Jeremiah goaded him a bit. His constant insistence the creatures be killed was short-sighted, and this was really the only way he knew to get at him.

"Jeremiah, I just wanted to be honest in my police report, not cry it from the mountaintops. Let's go. We've got a good amount of ground to cover."

Once the three groups set off in their different directions, Jeremiah waited until they were out of vision and earshot of the others before engaging Elliot.

"You brought your tranquilizer, correct?"

"Of course. The cop's dumb as fuck if he thinks I'm going to kill them. They're a brand new species and have every right to life, same as we do. It's not their fault man pushed them into a corner."

Elliot was a little more sanctimonious than Jeremiah was comfortable with, but he was a good means to an end. At least he was sure that if they found the creature there was no way Elliot would kill it. This feeling was new to Jeremiah, this hunger for prestige and renown. These creatures were his ticket.

The house where Ms. Ferguson was killed bordered a small wooded area, and that was where they were to begin their search. Hank had said an officer of the law snooping around the homes in the area was a bit easier to explain away than a few civilians. He muttered something about wanting more deputies as he and Miranda traipsed off, but Jeremiah didn't hear and he didn't care. Leading the way into the thick of it, he stopped just at the forest's edge as common sense took over.

"Since you have the only gun, why don't you take the lead?"

Jeremiah really wished Hank had let them all carry some form of tranquilizer gun, but he said it would take too long to get everyone fully trained on their use. Jeremiah didn't buy it for a second. You simply load the tranq gun with the dart, point, and shoot. Just more proof Hank simply wanted the creatures dead and any chance of Jeremiah's fame to die with them.

Elliot stepped in front of Jeremiah and took a few steps past the tree line before stooping down on his haunches to inspect something on the ground. He pointed to a few broken twigs and an odd looking print in the dirt. There was another about twelve inches from the first, and a third after that. They all seemed to be leading deeper in.

"Could be nothing, could be the creature. Worth checking out regardless. What are they called, anyway?"

"I've yet to name them, actually. Any ideas?"

Elliot took a moment to think, scratching his head and looking up into the trees as he did. Another moment, and he was looking down at the ground for more tracks.

"I'm horrible with names, Doc. How about...lizarpion?"

"...Lizarpion? Sounds a little B-movie. Don't you think it should be something more scientific?"

"You asked," Elliot replied over his shoulder as they cautiously made their way deeper into the wooded area. Jeremiah felt a bit giddy, despite the fact that someone else had died. Looking around them, this area closely resembled where they had originally found the nest. If the creature had sought refuge from the day's harsh light, it made sense for it to try and seek that solace in an environ that was so similar to what it was used to.

"Kinda rolls nicely off the tongue, too. Lizarpion. Lizar-pi-on."

Jeremiah just ignored Elliott at that point. To reduce the reptile to some sort of B-movie creature seemed almost a disservice to it. It was a magnificent beast, one that had evolved such specific traits that it almost defied logic and reasoning.

Then there was the organ that surrounded the lungs. He wanted to head back to the morgue to examine it further, but capturing one alive took precedence. Since it was his idea, he had no choice but to go along for the ride. Perhaps seeing a living specimen would help him understand the purpose of that organ. A nagging feeling started to grow however, the more he thought about the creature.

Every system seemed almost too perfectly assembled. What were the chances of it developing two digestive systems like it had? One for food, and one for hormones? The stinger and its cocktail of toxin and ACTH also seemed too perfect. A terrible thought crossed his mind as they continued onward. What if these creatures were not some missing evolutionary side-step, but the result of extensive genetic research and engineering?

What if they had been manufactured and not born?

He trembled at the thought, becoming more nervous with each passing second as that fear planted itself firmly in his thoughts and began to sprout. Were that true, then he wouldn't receive the accolades and acclaim he not only desired but that he believed he deserved. Dammit! Why hadn't he realize this possibility sooner?

No. He couldn't believe such a thing to be possible. There may have been cloned sheep in this day and age, but such a complex and perfectly crafted organism was well beyond the scope of known science. Even if such a feat *were* possible, there was no way those who created it would have let it not only escape but thrive in the wild.

The doubt subsided a great deal, but never fully dissipated.

"Hold up, Doc. I think I see something."

Jeremiah nearly walked into Elliot as the man stopped a few feet in front of him. He was going to question what he thought he saw, but then a thick patch of brush, some twenty feet off to their left, moved. Something was there.

XI

"Tell me, Deputy, was there a specific reason you didn't trust my assistants to accompany me? Or perhaps you didn't trust me with them?"

"I currently seem to be the only one in this whole goddamn town that would rather see them dead than take any chances. You'll forgive me if that makes me come across as a bit paranoid."

He was not a fan of the accusatory tone her voice had taken. The frank answer was, no he did not trust her, or her men, to kill the creature if the opportunity arose. Had they more time to search the surrounding areas he would have insisted they go as a single group. At least that way one of them would be ready to pull the trigger.

Miranda broke the silence between them again, her tone just as before. It was beginning to grate on Hank. "It just seems very backwards. If I had the chance to study and learn from a new species, my first act would not be to eradicate it."

"I'd love to see you hold onto that ideal after seeing the bodies."

She cleared her throat, and he could tell that sentence made her uncomfortable. Part of him wanted to continue to goad her, but he thought better of it. No sense reducing himself down to a juvenile level.

Crossing the street, they headed to a home that had a detached garage and a shed, both of which would be ripe for any creature trying to avoid bright light.

"Miranda, I can appreciate why you want to save them. I just hope you understand why I do not."

She made no reply as he went around the back, heading towards the shed first. Pulling out his service revolver he cocked back the hammer and eased open the door. It gave a groaning creak as light flooded into the small dingy room.

Nothing. Some tools hanging on one wall, and a half-taken apart lawnmower in the center of the small room. Closing the door behind himself, he headed over to the garage and peeked in the window on the side of the building.

There were no cars, just a pile of rags in one corner, which was far too small to hide a house cat, let alone one of the creatures. Cursing quietly he had turned to leave, when he saw the back door of the house open. He recognized the man immediately.

"You gotta be shitting me."

"Howdy, Deputy Hank! Whatcha up to this fine afternoon?"

It was Chuck, and he was looking like a smug son of a bitch too. He probably knew exactly what they were up to out there, but it seemed he was playing it close to the vest. This infuriated Hank to no end.

"Just out for a walk, Chuck. I noticed your shed was unlocked, and decided to make sure nothing looked missing."

"Oh, you can search my property all you like, Deputy Hank. I'm sure whatever you're looking for can't possibly be here."

There was something about the way he kept saying 'Deputy Hank' and how he kept pouring on the nice guy act. It made Hank's brain itch, and he felt something was grossly off about the whole situation. He couldn't place it, but it didn't feel like he or Miranda were in any immediate danger so he tried to ignore it.

"Mighty neighborly of you, Chuck, but as I said, we were just out for an afternoon stroll. Part of a new county watch program."

Giving a tip of his hat, he made a quick glance and nod over to Miranda, trying to get her to follow his lead and leave the property before Chuck changed his mind.

"Good luck, Deputy. I for one hope you find whatever it is you're looking for."

His eyes looked devoid of any real emotion, and that unnerved Hank quite a bit. Chuck was trying a bit too hard not to give off any signal that might betray whatever was going on. The last time he got a feeling like this was when he pulled someone over for a broken taillight and managed to find an unlicensed handgun and a pound of pot in the trunk.

Chuck was hiding something. But without any evidence to the fact, Hank couldn't do shit about it, which only served to make him even more upset. Once he and Miranda were back out on the street in front of the house he looked back. A curtain in the front window flopped into place.

"Why didn't you tell that man the story about the escaped snake?"

"Chuck was one of the original mob that wanted to go out and hunt the creatures. Personally, I don't trust him as far as I can throw him. I was trying to keep our true intentions vague, to judge his reaction. He kept talking about us actively searching, even though we made no mention of it."

"We were poking around his property. Perhaps he meant that?"

"Maybe. I'm going back."

"Do you think that's a wise use of time, right now?"

"My gut is telling me something is up, and we have two other teams searching right now. Come on."

Hank led the way back to Chuck's home, this time walking right up the path and up the stairs to the front door. Giving a loud knock, he waited. A shuffling sound and more than once voice filtered through, but was too muffled to determine who was saying what. Seconds later, the door opened.

"Deputy Hank. Thought you were moving on."

"I was, but your invitation to search your property was a little too inviting. Never know what ya might find. Mind letting me in?"

"Not right now actually, I've got company over, and, well, she's raring to go if ya catch my drift."

"Won't take a minute. After all you did invite me in, and I've got a bona fide witness to that fact."

Miranda looked like she was about to protest, but when Hank forced himself inside she shut her mouth and scowled.

"Goddammit, Chuck, what the fuck did I tell you?"

Inside the house were four other men with all manner of hunting rifles and equipment splayed out across a kitchen table in the back. They all looked like kids with their hands caught in the cookie jar. Hank just shook his head and fired an icy glare over at Chuck, who immediately became defensive.

"We ain't doing nothing wrong! We all got licenses and permits so you can just go fuck off, Deputy!"

"Chuck. I'm gonna say this once and only once. I see even so much as a tire track near those woods, I'm throwing you," he then motioned to the other four men, "and your cronies into jail and tossing away the key! This ain't no duck hunt, you daft son of a bitch. Those things have killed several times, and they are dangerous! Stay put!!"

Chuck started to jab his finger into Hank's chest to protest when one of the other men spoke up.

"Dangerous? Killed? Chuck, you said these were just big lizards, like crocs, and they would be easy pickings."

Hank turned to the four men, "These are highly mobile and venomous creatures that have killed four men, including an armed sheriff's deputy. If you all have got any sense you will stay home until this matter is resolved."

The men turned to one another and spoke quietly among themselves as Chuck rushed over to try and regain control of his group.

"Don't listen to him! He's just trying to keep us from gettin' our trophies! Some science quack thinks they're endangered, or some shit. We got a right to hunt them!"

"Forget it, Chuck. I got a wife and kids. This seemed fun at first, but if they're really that dangerous, then I'm out."

"Same for me. I can't be thrown in jail, man. I'd lose my job!"

The other two men added their own reasons for backing out of the hunting party and started to pack up their things. Chuck turned and glared at Hank, who merely tipped his hat again and flashed a smile.

"Have a great day, Chuck. And don't try this shit again."

He and Miranda left the house and headed off down the street in the direction they were originally going.

"How on earth did you know?"

"I didn't. I had a gut feeling something was up, and just went with it. Only makes sense he'd try to organize a hunting party under our noses to try and bag a few of those things. They might get one or two but a bunch of weekend hunters going after a pack of ruthless killing machines? They'd be like lambs to the slaughter."

Miranda nodded in agreement and added in a playful tone, "Perhaps you aren't as stubborn and pig-headed as Jeremiah said you were."

"He said what?!"

Before he could question her further, a scream rang out.

"What on earth?"

Hank didn't even bother to respond to her question, just headed off towards where he thought the scream came from: the woods behind the Ferguson's house. Even at his age, it didn't take him long to hit the house and then continue on towards the back. Breathing deeply from his sprint, he scanned the treeline for any sign of movement. He held his gun by his side and waited one second, then two.

There, deep in the woods, barely visible, were two figures. Taking off in another sprint he moved quickly through the trees to come upon Elliot and Jeremiah, both looking a bit frazzled, but no worse for wear. Puzzled, Hank looked at each man as he placed his hands on his knees, catching his breath. Miranda was a bit behind, running to catch up.

"What...what the hell is going on? We heard a scream."

Elliot started to look a bit sheepish, and pointed over to a dense cropping of bushes about 5 yards away. Jeremiah just kept taking in deep breaths and letting them go slowly, as if to prevent hyperventilation.

"Talk to me! What. Happened. Here?!"

Elliot broke the awkward silence first and continued to point at the bush. Not only had Miranda caught up, but Timothy and Eloise had arrived as well. All three were wide eyed and just as concerned as Hank, but Hank's patience was wearing thin.

"We noticed some movement in the bush. We both went to investigate, and when it lunged I shot it with one of the tranq darts. Jeremiah cried out, we both ran back, and you showed up a few minutes later."

"Did you even check to see if that was it?

Elliot sort of stopped and turned to Jeremiah who in turn looked right back at him. Both men then turned to look over at the bush.

"Jesus Christ. If that isn't a lizard then I'm gonna shoot both of you with the tranq gun!" Hank stormed over to the bush and pulled it aside.

A gasp escaped his lips as he saw what looked to be reptilian skin with one of the tranquilizer darts sticking out of it. Pulling the bush further back exposed the rest of the creature. There, in the dirt and dry leaves, was just a stray dog. It looked to be suffering from a severe case of mange which gave its skin a scaly, leathery appearance, not unlike that of the creatures.

Letting go of the bush he couldn't help but laugh at the absurdity of it all. Re-holstering his weapon he turned back to the group to find all eyes on him. He held up his hands, using them to reassure and calm the others.

"It's a false alarm. Just a mangy mutt."

The collective release of tension was palpable, as held breaths were finally exhaled and everyone started to ease up a bit. The group began to disperse but Hank corralled them back in.

"Hold it, everyone. We need to have a chat."

He was met with confused gazes as he looked from one person to the next.

"We need to be discreet while we're out here searching. The less attention we bring to ourselves the better. That means, more than anything, not screaming unless you are about to die."

Hank looked quite pointedly right at Jeremiah. He enjoyed that his gaze was making the man shrink back a bit, but didn't let it linger. Right now, he was chastising the group as a whole and trying to keep this operation intact.

"If you feel you cannot keep your emotions in check, then you're free to leave now. That scream probably got the attention of the whole neighborhood."

He waited for a moment to see if anyone bowed out. When no one did he, gave a quick and curt nod.

"Ok then. Get back to looking for it."

Almost on cue something fell from one of the trees behind them. Eloise started to scream but Hank shot her a glance to get her to keep quiet. The form shook itself, stood to a full height of about four or five feet, and gave a honking squeal. It was one of the creatures.

"Oh...oh my god." Hank wasn't sure who spoke behind him but every muscle in his body was on fire and ready for whatever might happen. This one was a good deal larger than the one he had seen that night or the corpse they found in the cave. The coloring was off as well; a good deal lighter than the others. Instead of lunging right for the group, it cocked its head and regarded them with a curious gaze. The tail swung lazily behind it, much like a cat that had caught a mouse and wasn't sure what to make of it. Toy or food?

"No one make a sound."

Hank slowly started to reach for his gun, but, just as he was about to pull it free, Elliot yelled out.

"Don't hurt it!!"

Running to the front of the group, he held his arms out wide and tried to seem bigger and more imposing than the creature.

"Quick! Someone hit it with a dart before he murders it! My gun is empty!"

"You goddamn fool!" Hank hissed between clenched teeth.

The creature gave a squawk and changed its focus solely to Elliot. The larger man moved from side to side slowly, keeping his arms outstretched, as the creature started to move its head to follow him. The tail, which Hank was fully focused on, continued to move lazily about in a non-threatening manner. Could Elliot be onto something?

Timothy moved slowly up next to Hank, holding one of the tranquilizer guns. Taking aim he fired once, but missed.

The creature didn't seem to notice, but Timothy immediately began to freak out.

"Oh god, oh god. Elliot, I missed! No no no..."

He was beginning to have a panic attack. Miranda tried to talk him down, "Timothy, remember your breathing!" but to no avail. He continued to freak out and crumpled to the ground in a fetal position, as his breathing became shallow.

The creature then did a curious thing as it turned its full attention to Timothy. It sniffed at the air, its nostrils flaring, then a gave a short burst of noise as it leaped over. What happened next occurred too quickly for Hank to react. The tail whipped towards him. Fearing he was about to be stung, Hank tried to block or deflect the attack, but instead it side-swiped him, sending him spiraling out of the way. The creature looked down at Timothy who was getting more and more freaked out especially with the thing towering over him.

"No! NO NO NO!!"

Elliot tackled the thing, flying past Timothy and almost into Jeremiah, who moved at the very last second. The creature cried out in pain and quickly got to its feet. Before anyone could react, it brought its tail around and stabbed Elliot, hard, right in the arm.

"Ow! Fucking bastard stung...me..."

His speech started to slur and he began to stumble as the toxin took hold in his system.

"Fuck!" Hank yelled as he finally got his bearings and aimed at the creature. A shot rang out, but it was muted and airy. A tranquilizer dart stuck out of the creature's side, and then another. It started to stumble momentarily, like Elliot, but then turned its attention to Timothy. Leaping past everyone, it descended on him, grabbed onto his back, and gave a guttural, disjointed cry as it began to feed.

Hank fired three times but only hit it twice. One in the tail, which exploded the bulbous growth under the stinger and completely destroyed it. The other shot hit it in the leg. Neither injury seemed to faze it.

Timothy thrashed on the ground, but to no avail. A few moments more and he either blacked out or perished, because his body suddenly went limp.

Hank took better aim this time, right for the creature's head. He pulled the trigger, but the creature moved just enough for the shot to graze it, and break one of the bony ridges above its eye. *This* it noticed, and its blue eyes filled with malice as it turned toward Hank.

But instead of attacking, it merely let go of Timothy and darted off into the woods, despite its wounds. Ignoring the fleeing beast he rushed over to Timothy. He placed two of his fingers just under his neck.

"He's barely got a pulse. Call 911!"

Eloise pulled out her phone with shaky hands and started to call. Even under pressure she still managed to keep it together. Hank was proud of her. He stayed with Timothy, but looked over to where Elliot had collapsed. Jeremiah and Miranda hovered over him.

"Is he ok?!"

Miranda turned to look at Hank, and she seemed lost. Jeremiah tried to help Elliot up but found him nearly unresponsive.

"Stay with him!" Hank commanded Eloise and rushed over to the other three.

Elliot had only been stung in the arm, but it had been more than enough. It appeared that since he was stung in the muscle, the toxin was taking a bit longer to flow through his body. There was still a degree of movement in him, but his face contorted into a look similar look to the other victims as he gasped for air. Hank had no idea the sting could affect someone this quickly. No wonder he hadn't heard a thing when Wilk was killed.

"Is there anything we can do for him?"

Jeremiah tried to hold Elliot down as his body convulsed. Miranda looked on the verge of tears. Placing a hand on his chest, her eyes went wide with fright.

"His heart is beating far too quickly. If we don't find a way to stop it, he may die from the stress!"

A feeling a helplessness crept over Hank. He looked off in the direction the creature had gone and wanted very badly to just go after it. The problem was there was no telling if there were more creatures deeper in the woods, and he was needed more here. Cursing to himself, he looked around for some divine inspiration as to what he should do.

"If we sedate him, will he live??"

Jeremiah seemed to be in a daze and didn't respond so Hank shook him out of it.

"Jeremiah! If we sedate him, slow his heartbeat, will be survive?!"

"I...I don't know. I'm not a medical doctor!"

"Fuck it. He's dead if we don't try."

Hank grabbed one of the tranquilizer guns on the ground and popped it open, thankful it still contained a dart inside. Pulling it free, he held it firmly in his hand and stood over Elliot. The veins on his neck were bulging and a froth was developing in the corners of his mouth as his eyes rolled back into his head.

"This better work," Hank said to himself as he brought his fist down on the upper left of Elliot's chest.

There were a tense few moments as Elliot's body accepted the tranquilizer. His seizing slowed and finally stopped, his breathing became more even, and finally his face began to relax. It seemed as if he were going into a deep and peaceful slumber.

"Oh my God, it worked!"

A sense of relief washed over the trio as Hank moved to the side and sat down in the dirt next to Elliot. Smiling and wiping away her tears, Miranda placed a hand back on Elliot's chest. Her face immediately filled with horror.

"His heart...it stopped!"

Relief turned to dread as Hank placed his hand right where hers had been. He then checked for a pulse and found nothing. The sounds of the approaching ambulance seemed to drown out everything else around him as he started CPR on the man, already knowing, deep down, it was far too late to save him.

XII

Julie hadn't known what to expect when she arrived. She was about to start on the official autopsy of Ms. Ferguson when she got the call about the new attack. All they said was that someone from the task force was killed but they didn't know who. Fearing the worst, she got out of her car and ran through the crowd that had gathered along the edge of the woods.

Seeing Hank sitting on a stump caused her to thank the powers that be as she rushed over to his side. "What happened?"

"The creature that probably killed Ms. Ferguson got the drop on us after a false alarm. It attacked Timothy and killed Elliot. They were both from the zoo, assistants of Miranda Hershey."

"How is everyone else?"

"Miranda went in the ambulance with Timothy, and Eloise from animal control went home after giving a statement. She did well under pressure, but I don't blame her for saying fuck it after this shit show."

"And Jeremiah?"

"He's pretty shaken up. I think seeing one of those things in action may have changed his mind about preservation. We'll see."

Julie turned to the body on the ground, covered by a tarp, and headed over. Dreading the look of fear sure to be on his face, she pulled back the covering and was suddenly confused. He looked asleep; nothing at all like the others who had been attacked and killed by the creature. It then hit her that he said the other man was still alive in an ambulance.

Hank must have sensed her confusion, because he came over, and was joined by Jeremiah, who kept glancing over in the direction the creature had run off in.

"Timothy wasn't stung and it still tried to feed off him. Damnedest thing actually. It stung Elliot, but then went after Timothy."

"Why doesn't he seem to be frozen in fear?"

"We tried to sedate him with one of the tranquilizer darts from the guns we brought. I dunno if we did it in time, as his heart stopped." Jeremiah responded to her question, but his eyes never left the area he was staring at.

"Fucking hell guys, you killed him!"

Both Hank and Jeremiah stared at her, dumbfounded.

"If these creatures affect the adrenal glands like we think, it's going to cause someone to go into cardiac arrest eventually. A sedative will just knock them out and kill them quietly. You need to perform CPR immediately, maybe even use a defibrillator unit if the rhythm isn't too sporadic."

"We didn't have much choice. If you hadn't noticed, there isn't much in the way of medical equipment out here, Julie."

"I know. Given the circumstances, it wasn't a bad guess. It just would never work, medically speaking. I mean, a heavy sedative just knocks someone out. That's pretty basic stuff."

"It doesn't matter. A man is dead and another is in the hospital."

Julie felt for Hank and Jeremiah, but they were reckless and may have acted too quickly on instinct and ruined any real chance at saving Elliot's life. Jeremiah seemed to be taking it a bit harder than she expected, but as far as she knew he never met the man before today.

"Jeremiah? Sorry if I was a bit harsh."

"No, it's fine, Julie. I'm just trying to figure something out."

He moved to where Timothy had been, then he then moved over to where Elliot was standing and shook his head. He then began acting out the events in a way that Julie was positive was not for her benefit. He seemed to be trying to piece together a puzzle. She kept quiet, curious where it would lead.

"Elliot distracts the creature until Timothy has a panic attack. Ignoring everyone else it lunges for Timothy, even going so far as to just push Hank out of the way. Elliot then tackles it before it can sting Timothy and is then stung himself. It was more an afterthought, as it immediately went back to Timothy and fed. Hank even destroyed its stinger and wounded it and neither fazed it. The creature finally flees after having its fill."

"I was there, Jeremiah. What's your point?"

He didn't respond immediately to Hank and instead rubbed his chin, looking deep in thought.

"When he gets like this, Hank, it's best to just let him run the course. He's trying to figure it out in his own way."

Hank shrugged. As much as Julie liked him, sometimes he was very stubborn and showed little understanding for others when they really needed it. She frowned slightly at him and turned her attention back to Jeremiah.

"I can't understand why it attacked Timothy above all else. Threatened, it should have gone for Elliot first."

He looked up at Julie, and there was an intensity in his eyes that she'd never seen before.

"I need to finish inspecting it. I have an idea what happened, but I need to see the lizarpion again to be absolutely sure."

"Lizarpion?" Both Hank and Julie raised an eyebrow at that, waiting for an explanation.

"It's a terrible name, but Elliot came up with it a bit before he died. Since I'm at a loss for a proper name, it will do for now. Can you take me back to the morgue?"

"Uh...sure. We can take my car. You going to be ok to drive, Hank?"

"I'll be fine. When you're done with Jeremiah, meet me at the station. This amateur hour bullshit ends now."

Hank had an intensity all his own as well in that moment, but his was more focused on vengeance than anything else. Jeremiah's was intellectual. She knew he was on to something, and when Jeremiah got an idea in his head he kept it to himself until he could prove or disprove it. She'd just have to go along for the ride.

"Alright. I'll finish my prelim inspection of Elliot and prep his body to be moved. Then I can take Jeremiah to the morgue and you and I can talk with the sheriff."

Jeremiah looked at the body and then at Julie.

"If you don't mind, I'll wait by the car."

"Sure, Jer."

Waiting until he was well out of earshot, she glanced over at Hank who was staring down at Elliot. His mouth was moving but he wasn't making a sound. Instead of saying anything, she waited patiently for him to finish. She could clearly make out the word 'amen' as he finished and turned to her.

"Think Jeremiah's gonna be alright? Need his head in the game."

"Since he's got a new theory about the lizarpion, or whatever you want to call them, he'll be obsessed until he can figure it out. If anything, his head is more in the game now that ever before. I've never seen him so intense."

"Good. If he can find out anything new to help us, it'll be worth it. Don't wait around for him, though. Drop him off and come meet me. I'm gonna need your help convincing Tusk to play it my way, now."

Tusk. He never referred to the sheriff like that unless he was really pissed off. Usually it was John, Sheriff Dragert, or Sheriff Tusk if he was joking around with her. The only other time she had heard him use just Tusk was when he told her the story of how he almost walked off the force because of how the sheriff blundered an investigation, years before she moved to Stonesworth.

Hank never went into specifics, but something about the chain of evidence being broken and the case being thrown out completely. According to Hank he felt the sheriff had, at best, done some shoddy police work. At worst? That Dragert had been bought off. But he had no proof. Without proof, he never outright accused him of anything, but he sure as hell alluded towards it. Their relationship had been strained since, with Hank pretty much dropping it in the years that followed.

"I've got your back. Elliot makes the sixth person, and I have a feeling that if we don't stop those things now, we're going to have a lot more. Frankly, I don't want the extra work."

Giving a bark of a laugh he shot her a smirk, which she reciprocated with one of her own. Things may be going to shit around town but at least they still had one another.

***

Sheriff Johnson P. Dragert. The sign on his office door was etched in golden letters on an oak-colored nameplate. Originally it had been designed to be replaced easily but since he'd held the office for the past twenty years, uncontested, there was no reason to move it. Dragert tried to slide it out and found it wedged tightly into the metal runners. Giving it a little more pressure with his thumb, it started to move slowly. Satisfied, he pushed it back into its original place. This was a little exercise he repeated every few months to remind himself that nothing was permanent.

About now, however, he truly wished some things were. Letting himself into his modest office, he headed right for the most opulent thing there: his desk. In the bottom left drawer, to which only he had the key, was the object of his visit this time. Just as he was about to unlock the drawer, Hank burst in unannounced. Dragert stiffened at first, but eased up a bit despite himself. He just didn't have it in him to fight tonight, and already knew what this would be about.

"Take a seat, Hank."

When the other man remained standing, Dragert took the initiative and began to speak to break the strained silence between them.

"Dorris told me about your call and what happened to one of the zoo personnel. It's a damn shame, that."

"A damn avoidable one, you son of a bitch."

Ok, I deserved that, at least once, he admitted to himself as he let Hank continue.

"If you would have let me use proper deputies instead of the fucking Mystery Gang, that man would still be alive and maybe we wouldn't have one of those creatures loose in town!"

Hank placed both his hands on the desk and leaned forward, getting right in Dragert's face.

"You're gonna tell me what the fuck has gotten into you and why you've been playing hardball since Wilk died, or I'm gonna shove my badge so far up your ass your teeth will be under arrest!"

There were two things Dragert didn't take kindly to. The first was liver. He hated the stuff more than anything. The second was threats that couldn't be backed up. He called them 'idle banter' and viewed anyone who made them as a blowhard. Hank though? He was the one man who would honest to god try and shove his badge right up someone's ass.

"Hank, just sit. Please."

Dragert knew that there was no use fighting against Hank any longer on this. He finally took the seat on the other side of the desk but sat awkwardly, as he leaned too far to one side.

"That man's death is on me. I accept that, and have already written a letter of resignation."

Hank's eyes went wide and he started to protest. "Now just a minute here, John; why would-"

Dragert held up a hand and waited for Hank to fall silent so he could continue.

"I've made some bad calls in all of this. I also blame myself for Ms. Ferguson's death. Had I taken her initial call more seriously, maybe she would still be alive. I've let my own personal fears and biases get in the way of being a good sheriff, but that's going to change. I'm letting you have full access to the department's resources. You just need to hear me out."

As he spoke, he reached down to unlock the drawer and pulled out his half-filled bottle of golden-hued treasure. "A bottle of Johnnie Walker Blue Label, circa 1991. This was a gift from the mayor at the time, on my very first appointment to sheriff. He told me to treat the job like this bottle: a rare gift."

Realizing he only had the one glass in the drawer with the bottle, he offered it to Hank, emptied his pen holder onto his desk, and wiped it clean with the edge of his cuff. Pouring about two fingers worth into each glass he didn't wait for Hank as he downed his. The liquid both burned and soothed him, and he savored the smoky flavor.

"Blended whiskey always tasted better to me."

Hank held his glass for a moment before taking a sip, probably debating whether to drink on the clock or not. Dragert smiled at that.

"I wasn't in a sipping mood. Guess you know how to enjoy a good scotch."

"This isn't about the whiskey, John. You just said you were finally going to be straight with me, so what's the deal?"

Sheriff Dragert poured himself a second glass and downed it just as quickly as the first. The second time always went down a bit easier. It also helped to loosen his tongue a bit. Since he was going to resign, he saw no use in keeping things to himself anymore.

"You were right, you know. I took a bribe, and I let that kid walk. Tampering with the evidence was easy and the pay was too good to pass up."

Dragert expected a big fat 'knew it!' or for Hank to come right around that desk and cuff him for obstructing justice. Instead, the man looked saddened, as if the last, faintest glimmer of hope that Dragert was innocent of the accusations had just been snuffed out. Despite their numerous disagreements over the years, and the strained friendship they now shared, it was a hard thing to take. He couldn't look Hank in the eye after that, but he continued.

"Guilt soon followed and I made a vow then and there to not let myself fall into the same trap of temptation ever again."

"Alright. You finally admit to doing what you were suspected of. You're a fucking saint. What the hell does that have to do with the lizarpions?"

"The what?"

Hank rolled his eyes and put his glass down. "It's what they're calling the damn things now, I guess. Just get to the goddamn point, John! I'm not here to be your priest. I won't absolve you of doing the one thing a cop never should."

That comment stung far more than it really should have, and Dragert felt his anger boiling to the surface. He poured himself another shot and downed it. Liquid courage it was.

"Fuck you, Hank. You want the point? This ain't the first time I've seen or heard of these goddamn things!"

It was as if the world stopped between the two men. Dragert could only hear his own breath going in and out and Hank looked like someone shot his dog and told him it was for the best. Finally he seemed to snap out of it and he stood up to leave.

"Wait, Hank! Don't you want to hear this?"

Hank didn't turn to speak. All Dragert could see was his hands clenching at his sides as he spoke in an unnervingly calm and even tone.

"You knew about these things. You knew there was something out there that was this dangerous and didn't deal with it properly. Six people are dead and all that blood is on your hands. Nothing you say right now matters, John."

"Just listen you stubborn fucker. It was six years before you started here, and only my third year as sheriff. A family had gotten lost in the same woods and I was part of a small search party investigating what might have happened to them. We ran into a group of these lizard things near a hot spring. I was the only one who made it back."

Hank turned slightly and listened, his hands still clenched into fists.

"It seemed almost like some kind of ambush. Myself and four other deputies had followed the path the family took to that hot spring and the things came out at us. Two deputies were killed instantly and the other two in the ensuing chaos. Even though I was the last man standing, I managed to kill every last one of those lizards. Never did find that family, but I'm sure you can guess what happened. It was too unbelievable, so I covered it up. Placed the blame on a pack of rabid wolves and that was the end of it."

"You goddamn coward."

"Hank, no one woulda believed me even if I went with the truth! When you told me what happened to Wilk, I knew it was those damn little shits all over again. I did my best to protect not only you but this town from another incident! You just had to keep poking that hornet's nest and now here we are. If we coulda just kept people out of those woods it would have blown over. Now everything is a mess!"

"The only thing you managed to protect was your own ass! You're a real piece of work, John."

Hank then walked over, reached across the desk, and ripped the sheriff's star right off Dragert's chest. It left a ragged tear in the cloth of the uniform. John didn't have time to react at first, but his blood boiled and he jumped up out of his seat and rushed toward Hank.

"The fuck you think you're doing?!"

"You said it yourself. You made some bad calls, and I feel you are now unfit for duty. Being the most senior officer in the station puts me as acting sheriff in the interim until a proper election can be called." Hank affixed the sheriff's star on his own chest.

"I may be resigning, but I'm not leaving a stubborn hothead like you in charge!"

Dragert pulled his arm back to take a swing at the other man but found his jaw aching as he was hit first. Landing with a thud on his ass, anger and shame brewed to the surface as his face went red. Hank had injured his pride and he simply could not let that slide.

"I made this office what it is, Hank! This town is safe because of me! Me!! You've done shit all but get in the way of that, and you are just as responsible for killing those people, you crazy fucker!! Especially Wilk!"

Dragert looked up at Hank, suddenly feeling very small as the other man towered over him. He simply stood there for a few silent moments, steely eyes bearing down on him. Hank broke the silence with that same even tone from before.

"I will carry Wilk's death with me until I die. Just as I hope to god his and all the others haunt you until the day you're cold in the ground. You're a drunk and a fucking pathetic disgrace. People are dead because you thought ignoring a serious problem would make it disappear."

He turned and left, pushing open the door so hard it left a dent in the wall with the handle. Over his shoulder he called back, "You tainted your career, John. At least leave it with a bit of dignity."

Dorris had been eavesdropping the entire time, Dragert guessed. Not only was the old hag staring right at him but the look on her face was about the same as Hank's had been a few moments ago. Grabbing onto the side of his desk and hoisting himself up, he walked to the door and quietly shut it as he watched Hank storm out of the office.

He then went back to the desk, poured another shot, and placed the bottle back into the drawer. Locking it, he removed the key from his keychain and placed it on the desk, right next to the keyboard. He then downed the final shot, hit a button on his phone, and waited for Dorris to answer.

"Y-yes, Sheriff?"

"Can you please get me the mayor? I have something I need to discuss with him."

"Right away, sir."

May as well make it official then. As much as his pride had been wounded, Hank was right. He had been a disgrace since he let those others die in vain two decades ago. He was a disgrace when he took his one and only bribe. Now, he was a disgrace for letting six more people die on his watch because he somehow thought sweeping it out of sight would make those things disappear again.

The phone started to ring and a familiar voice picked up on the other end.

"Sheriff Dragert! To what do I owe the pleasure this evening? I hope you have some good news concerning all the hullabaloo around those lizard things. Imagine, people believing they actually exist!"

He didn't respond but instead sat in silence for a few moments.

"Uh...John? Are you there?"

"Never mind It's nothing that can't wait until morning.."

Reaching forward, he hit the disconnect button and got up, grabbed his coat and hat, and left his office. Closing the door behind him he looked up and saw his name again. Nothing was permanent. Except the stains of the past.

"I'm going home for the evening, Dorris. Direct any emergency calls to Hank would you?"

"Everything alright?"

That's a loaded question now, isn't it? He thought as he replied "As well as they can be. Goodbye, Dorris."

He stepped out into the crisp late afternoon, got into his car, and drove towards home. Halfway there, he turned off the road and went down a dirt path. He'd gone down it dozens of times as a child; the road to Lake Summerset. It looked like a perfect painting of fall, capturing all the beautiful colors of the sunset and reflecting them back in a kaleidoscope of autumnal wonder. Just like he remembered it. He got out of his car and phoned his wife.

"Hello?"

"Hello, dear. What's for dinner tonight?"

"Oh, I hadn't bothered to start anything. I thought you weren't going to be home until late. Would you like me to make you something?"

"No, that's quite alright. I love you. Very much. And I'm sorry I wasn't the man I should have been all these years."

"Oh stop it, you big silly. I'll have a nice little meal waiting in the microwave for you when you get home. Love you, too."

"Good bye, Christa."

"Bye, Sweetie."

She hung up, and he held the phone in his hand for the longest time, contemplating what he was about to go do. His whole life and career felt like it had been built on lies. He was not a good man and he didn't even have much of a legacy to show for all his mistakes.

"Just a fucking drunk."

He pulled his gun from the holster, placed the barrel between his lips, and cocked the hammer back. Seconds seemed to last for ages as the bitter taste of metal filled his mouth and the scent of gun oil filled his nostrils.

Shaking, he pulled the gun quickly from his mouth and collapsed, there at the end of the pier. He buried his face in his hands and wept.

"A coward, too," he managed to say to himself between sobs.

XIII

Hank was sitting in a booth at Jay's Diner, a local haunt that had managed to stay in business despite all the other more popular chain restaurants opening up in the area. It had changed ownership several times, but managed to keep the same cook, Xavier, for the past ten years. Hank was certain it was *his* food that kept the place afloat. If he wasn't in the back slinging hash and frying burgers, the place was a ghost town. Hank was lucky that Xavier was working tonight, and ordered a steak, medium rare.

Despite how his day, and more importantly his week, was going, he was famished and needed a good hunk of barely cooked flesh. Just as his steak arrived Julie walked in, spotted him, and joined him in the booth. The waitress took her order, which was the same every time: cheeseburger, extra onion, hold the pickles, and swimming in ketchup. Hank never understood how anyone could like ketchup that much.

She sat across from him and looked like she was about to say something when her eyes went wide and focused on his chest. She'd noticed the sheriff's star right off the bat. His fault for wearing it.

"It's a long story."

"Good thing we've got all night."

As he sliced into his steak, Hank began to tell Julie everything that had happened with Dragert and how Hank now came to own the badge. Every time he took a moment to shovel another bite of meat into his mouth, she had a handful of different questions. He shook his head yes or no as necessary, and continued with his story.

"After I left I got a call from Dorris, telling me the Sheriff said I was to take all emergency calls. I phoned the mayor after, told him everything that happened, and told him what my plan was. He reluctantly agreed, after I reminded him how many were already dead."

"What plan?"

"I got a hold of the media. Told them there was an escapee from the state penitentiary up north, and they were to advise all citizens to remain inside and lock their houses up tight. A bit of a white lie, sure, but it got the job done. They're going to run the story on the evening and late night news. If the one is still in the area, or more are coming, this should keep people safe."

"Smart thinking. Maybe you won't make a terrible sheriff after all."

"Fuck that. I'm only keeping it warm for the next guy. I just couldn't stand the thought of Tusk keeping it any longer."

"I don't blame you. What's going to happen now?"

"I get a few well trained men and we go hunt down the one in town first and then the rest in the wild. We end this once and for all."

"I meant about you being sheriff, but I guess that counts."

Hank smirked at her and finished off the last of his steak just as her burger arrived. She licked her lips and dug right in. Hank ordered himself a slice of blueberry pie.

***

Things had taken a bit longer than expected and Jeremiah had been dropped off by Julie only a little while ago. He was eager to get back to the morgue to finish his analysis. The organ that surrounded the lungs confused him so much that it was all he could think about after Elliot.

He tried to get his mind off it. Having never seen someone die before, it really hit him hard, and he felt for the man, even though he barely knew him. Even the awful name Elliot came up with, lizarpion, was sounding less and less ridiculous the more he used it to refer to the creatures. Using the code Julie had assigned him, he let himself in and went right for the storage slab where they had placed the remains of the reptile.

Within minutes he had a bone saw out and was fully ready to dig into the cranium. He needed to extract the brain and investigate the nasal cavity to see how developed the vomeronasal was. He cut the skin and peeled it back, exposing the white dome underneath. Seeing that reminded him of something important, but he couldn't quite place what. Shrugging off that nagging feeling, he started up the saw and began to cut the skull.

After he finished with that task, he pulled the piece of skull off and had his first surprise of the evening. The brain was far more developed than any reptile he was familiar with. If he had simply been shown this brain blind, he would have guessed it came from a higher primate, such as a chimpanzee or a gorilla.

Although it was far cry from a human brain, it was developed enough for these creatures to be cunning problem solvers. Remembering the actions of the one today made Jeremiah shudder as he considered more of them working in tandem to achieve a goal. He would have to let Hank know about that as soon as he finished.

Continuing his examination of the skull, he cut into the nasal cavity and began to search for the vomeronasal organ, which was responsible for pheromone detection in most animals. Reptiles usually had theirs towards the front of the nasal passageway, so he was eager to see what this one had, and how developed it was. Probing about, he became increasingly frustrated as his search turned up nothing.

"This doesn't make sense," he said to no one in particular, and continued to dig away until he'd nearly destroyed the nasal cavity in the skull searching for something that obviously was not there. How on earth did this creature detect pheromones? It was far too unlikely that it did *not* have one. Perhaps he was looking in the...wrong....

His attention turned back to the organ wrapped around the lungs. No, that was impossible. Vomeronasal organs were smaller, almost minuscule in size, and only used to detect faint chemical signals. If that organ really *was* one, it was the largest he'd ever seen. Taking a quick biopsy, he looked around for Julie's microscope. Even though she lacked the equipment the University had, she still had the basic necessities. Preparing a slide he slid it under and gasped in amazement.

He was right. That was in fact the vomeronasal organ for the reptile; the cell structure was simply too similar for it not to be. Going over the behavior he witnessed earlier, when they were attacked, Jeremiah came to a horrifying realization.

Running back to grab his cellphone from his coat, he didn't notice the tear in the side of the bag they had brought back with them from the woods.

***

Julie was just licking her fingers clean when her phone started to buzz on the table. It went off once, then twice. The third time Hank looked at her and pointed at it.

"Gonna answer that?"

"It's just Jeremiah. He'll call back if it's important."

"Right now, everything he might say is important."

Invading her privacy for a moment Hank reached across the table and entered her pin to get into her phone.

"How the hell do you know that?!"

"It's my job to know," he grinned as he placed it to his ear. "Jeremiah?...Yeah, I answered her phone...She's right here, finishing dinner...Whoa!...Slow down, alright? Take a deep breath and just spit it out."

Julie's face started to transition from looking curious to frustrated at being privy to only this side of the conversation. Hank noticed.

"Jeremiah, hold on a sec. I'm gonna put you on speaker phone."

Hank handed the phone back to Julie and looked around. They were the only two patrons in this corner of the diner, and he gave her a hand signal to lower the volume to avoid anyone else getting suspicious.

"Ok, Hank and I can both hear you now. What's got you so excited?"

"It's about fear. They track by fear."

"What do you mean?"

"Today, when the creature attacked, it went for Timothy while ignoring Elliot, whom it had stung, right?"

"Yeah, I remember. Why did it do that?"

"The creature's vomeronasal organ is huge. Larger than any other animal's I've ever seen. It's so well developed that I honestly think it can not only sense fear, but it hunts by it. Think about it: if you fed on hormones usually secreted when your prey was afraid, wouldn't you go for the frightened victim first?"

"Holy shit. This explains why it went after Ms. Ferguson instead of Andrew. Her pheromones were stronger since she was aroused and angrier than he was. It may have even thought it found a mate. This is insane. These things must have an enormous range for detection then!"

Ignoring the fact that she was sounding a bit too excited, Hank tried to get her attention.

"Julie...the news. The warning. If people panic or start getting afraid..."

"The news?"

"Hank sent out a bogus report about escaped convicts to keep people inside. They should have run it on the evening news by now."

"Only...if what you say is true, Jeremiah, do you think the lizarpions have that kind of range? That pack was a good twenty clicks outside of town."

"It's entirely possibly. But there is something else you need to consider."

"Maybe we should try and get the word out anyway? Tell people to remain calm, not to get too agitated? Hell, maybe even hijack the Emergency Broadcast System." Hank interrupted.

"You know how to use that?" Jeremiah's voice sounded full of doubt.

"No, but how hard can it be?"

"Still, the thing you need to consi-"

There was the sound of something breaking on Jeremiah's end of the line and both Hank and Julie leaned in closer to listen better.

"Jeremiah?"

"Nnngnaah!!"

His scream cut through the air suddenly and caught them by surprise and even a few of the patrons on the other side of the diner looked up from their meals to glance in their direction. Hank and Julie exchanged a worried glance.

"Jeremiah! Jeremiah!!"

There was no answer, but there was a distinctive sound of a struggle. Hank tossed a fifty, far more than both their meals were worth, onto the table and was headed for the door as fast as he could. Julie scooped up her phone and was right on his heels, hoping they wouldn't end up being too late.

XIV

How could he be so stupid and careless? The creature snapped its jaws at Jeremiah as its tail waved dangerously close. While it was only about the size of a cat, he didn't want to take any chances with getting stung by it. Almost all venomous creatures were just as potent in their juvenile stages as their adulthood.

When he and Julie first got back to the morgue to perform the autopsy, he had completely forgotten about the egg and was paying for it now. It must have already been close to hatching and the bag turned out to be a perfect place for its remaining incubation period. If he had paid more careful attention to everything, instead of focusing on one singular task, he might not be in this situation.

Using a medical tray as a shield, he had managed to corner it near Julie's office. If it hadn't broken the beaker while he was on the phone with her and Hank, he would probably be a dead man by now. The little bastard had gotten within striking distance, and that sound was the only thing that saved him.

He shook his head to clear it, wishing he wasn't so pumped up right now. He must be going off like a dinner bell to the little thing. Pushing down his fear and anxiety he tried to think about the situation far more scientifically, and with an analytical mind.

The size of the egg was about half of a football initially. Assuming it hatched sometime that day, maybe an hour or two after he left, then the lizarpion had nearly doubled in size after only approximately 8 hours. If these creatures had a low gestation period, coupled with a fast initial growth rate, it could spell big trouble for the entire community.

His hand stung and he glanced down at where the creature had both bit and scratched at him. That occurred right after he dropped the phone and managed to avoid the stinger. The creature had lunged immediately and latched onto his hand, biting hard and scratching at the tender flesh. He was lucky the head and jaw were still so small, as well as its strength diminished. Had it been any more powerful, he'd be missing a finger or two.

When it bit, he cried out and managed to toss it across the morgue, where it hit an examining table. It began thrashing about and tossed stainless steel tools in every direction.

He kept trying to push it into the office so he could lock it inside. He'd figure out how to deal with it properly later. Displaying an uncanny level of intelligence, it looked over at the small room, the door, and finally back to Jeremiah, giving off an angry hiss. He could hardly believe it; the thing had the presence of mind to know when it was being trapped, even as a newborn.

Jeremiah made a mental note, promising himself to study that more as soon as he survived this encounter. Providing he did at all. Whenever it made a move towards him he swatted at it with the tray, managing to keep it at bay. However, his fingers were horribly exposed, which caused him to be a little more reserved in his swings. He give it far too wide an opening as he swung once more and it darted past him, giving him barely enough time to jump out of the way of the stinger as it ran off to the other side of the morgue.

Having lost sight of it, he cautiously moved forward, keeping a keen eye out for any movement, and trying to listen as intently as he could to any odd sounds. Only moving a few feet away from his starting position, he just about shit himself as the lizarpion jumped up onto the table of the dissected one and started to feast with abandon.

"Haven't eaten since you were born, and I'm proving to be too difficult to catch, huh?" he muttered to himself.

The creature had no adrenaline glands of its own and had yet to feed on anything since it hatched. Of course it would be starving, and turning cannibalistic was a better alternative than being killed by a larger creature.

It was kind of fascinating watching it feast. Instead of simply biting down onto the flesh and ripping away manageable chunks,, which it could then swallow whole, it instead would carefully cut away at the flesh with its claws and pull out strips. Those strips were then quickly consumed.

It was a unique and odd feeding pattern, but Jeremiah realized he was as mesmerized by it eating as it was by the food. An opportunity presented itself and he had to decide what to do. Try and subdue the creature alive, or just bash it over the head with the tray until it stopped moving.

Mere seconds felt like hours as his own sense of self preservation warred against the rational, scientific side of his mind. There was no way to tell how long it would feed for, and he only had once chance to take it by surprise.

"Forgive me," he whispered to himself and raised the tray high over his head. Leaping forward he brought it down as hard as he could, trying not to look as he destroyed the creature simply for existing.

Only, the tray kept moving past the place where it should have connected with the beast. It kept going until it rattled in his hands and the sound of metal on metal clanged and echoed in his ears. Eyes wide with panic, his gaze darted around, looking for where it could have gone. A blur caught his eye as the stinger came down into his hand.

Yanking back with all his might, blood shot from his hand just as a spurt of toxin exited the stinger. His breathing was quick and shallow as he held his wounded appendage close. Fear overtook him, and he was afraid to see if any of the toxin had actually gotten into the wound or if he had managed to pull away in time.

What was odd about these creatures was the fact their venom injection system was so delayed. He wondered if it was because the bulb the stinger protruded from, at the end of their tails, acted more like an eyedropper and pushed the venom out. Since it had actually contracted as it shot out the toxin out, could this mean they're able to shoot it without stinging a victim? Even under duress, his mind wouldn't turn off.

His movements were starting to become a bit sluggish and he could feel his heart racing. He chanced a moment to look down at his hand, but it was bleeding too much for him to tell if any of the toxin had managed to get into the wound initially. It was also impossible to tell if his own adrenaline and subsequent blood loss were causing his reactions.

Stumbling backwards, he bumped into the table the dead creature was on and caused something to fall to the floor with a crash. Both he and the creature were surprised and distracted by the sound, and he took the chance to try and get out of the morgue.

It was of little use, as the creature, perhaps believing its sting was true, now toyed with him and ran ahead to block his exit. He was well and truly trapped. Had he ever seen this much blood before? Just how badly was his hand hurt? It just seemed like there was far too much coming from the puncture wound as he turned his back on the creature and stumbled towards the way he'd come.

Suddenly there was a weight on his back as the lizarpion pounced on him, claws digging into his skin as it tried in vain to make him fall forward. Its tiny mouth bit into the meat of his shoulder as it tried to fillet his flesh like it had with its previous meal. The pain was white hot and caused his senses to return to him as a burst of energy flooded his system. Rushing backwards, he slammed into the wall, causing the creature to cry out in pain and let go of him.

Looking up, he saw his only chance at survival. Dashing across the morgue, he dived into Julie's office slamming, and locking the door. Just a few scant moments later the creature leapt up at the glass, smacked against it, and fell backwards. Jeremiah couldn't help but laugh at such an absurd sight. It tried a second and third time before giving up and resorting to its stinger.

Tack! Tack! Tack!! The sound of it hitting the glass was jarring, but it didn't seem the hatchling had enough strength yet to break through the glass to get at its prey. Jeremiah suddenly felt exhausted as both blood loss and an adrenaline crash hit him hard. Looking for a place to sit, he noticed the couch on one side of the office and fell into it. He welcomed the suddenly soft-as-a-cloud cushions. He chuckled himself to sleep in a delirious sort of way as his last thought was that he hoped he would wake up.

***

Julie rushed up to the door and entered her code. She was about to yank the door open and run inside when Hank put his hand on the knob and kept it shut.

"What are you doing? Jeremiah is in trouble and we have to get in there!"

"For all we know one of those things could be waiting to sting either one of us. We can't help anyone if we're *dead*, Julie. I'm going in first, so stay back."

It was hard to argue with his logic. She was being reckless and not thinking about the consequences of her actions. Hank talking to her like a child, however, didn't sit that well.

"You may be old enough, but you're not my father, Hank."

The stunned look on his face hurt her, probably as much as her words hurt him, and she immediately regretted it. They still had a friend to go and help though so she swallowed her frustration and hurt and pushed him forward.

"Let's go."

Hank removed his revolver from the holster and cocked back the hammer as he gripped the handle. She had to re-enter the code, and, once the door light went green, he opened carefully and waited a moment to see if anything tried to dart out of the morgue. When nothing moved, he slowly crept in, with Julie right behind him.

Her eyes scanned the room and the mess it was in. There were splashes of blood and small pools of it here and there. The creature on the table looked like a good part of it had been picked clean, and there were a number of items strewn about the floor. The sight of everything made her blood begin to boil.

Julie took great care to keep her area clean. It was a source of pride, and not just because it was her job. To see it practically ransacked like this just made her hate the lizarpions even more than she already did. Christ, even she was starting to call them by that godawful name.

Thankfully, the lights were still on and there were few places one of the creatures could hide. Noticing a smear of blood on the handle to the door of her office, she nudged Hank and pointed, afraid of making any more noise than necessary. His gaze followed hers and he gave a curt nod. *At least he understood what I meant*, Julie thought.

They both, slowly and carefully, made their way over to the door, wincing as bits of glass crunched beneath their feet. Hank took in a sharp breath as his foot hit a scalpel and sent it skidding across the floor. Remaining perfectly motionless after that, they both waited to see if anything responded to the sudden, loud noise. Nothing. Julie was starting to think the lizarpion had escaped somehow when a shadow caught her attention, just in the corner of her eye. Whipping around to see what it was, she barely had time to dodge as the creature lunged at her.

"Gah! No!"

She cried out and flailed at the thing, managing to keep it at bay. There were small lacerations all along its legs, and what looked like a large bruise on its side. *At least Jeremiah didn't go down without a fight,* she thought grimly. The creature's tail started to swing back as if it was about to strike, and Julie couldn't help but scream.

The sound of the gunshot was deafening. For the tiniest moment she had forgotten Hank was even there, she was so transfixed on her possible demise. A spray of warm fluid hit her face and she gagged when she realized it was the creature's blood. Wiping at her face with her shirt she yelled at Hank.

"Did you have to shoot it so close?!"

"No, but I've grown accustomed to having you alive."

"...Thanks."

He just gave a nod and flashed his winning smile as she finished cleaning the blood off her face. "Are there any others?"

"Don't see anything. My guess is that the egg he brought back hatched and this thing surprised him." Hank made his way to the office and looked through the window.

"Julie! Get over here, now!" He tried the handle and it just rattled in his grip. "Jer's in here and the door's locked!"

She ran over and fumbled with her keys, trying to find the right one to let them inside. Once she unlocked the door, both of them burst through and rushed to Jeremiah's side. Jeremiah was lying face down on the couch with a small a pool of blood on the ground underneath him. Julie could only bring her hand to her mouth and say a silent prayer of thanks when they turned him over to see his face wasn't contorted in fear. "Thank god."

Jeremiah looked dazed but very much alive. A string of drool fell from his mouth as he took a coughing gasp. It was then Julie could see what had caused the pool of blood. There was a nasty wound on the back of his hand, with several superficial ones on his back. Heading back out into the main area, she found some gauze and rubbing alcohol to clean and treat his hand and took it back to the two men.

By the time she came back into the room, Hank had Jeremiah sitting up, and was slapping his face, gingerly, to try and rouse him.

"Earth to Jeremiah...Earth to Jer...you in there, buddy?"

"Nnn...w...what..?"

Julie went to the mini-fridge by her desk and pulled out a bottle of water which she then tossed to Hank. He cracked it open and held it to Jeremiah's lips. Tipping the bottle a bit towards him, some spilled but most ended up in his mouth. "Shhh, it's alright. Just take a drink of this." Realizing what it was, Jeremiah then grabbed the bottle with his good hand and thirstily gulped. "Easy, easy! It'll still be there, Jer! What the hell happened in here?"

Taking another gulp Jeremiah pulled the bottle away, took in a deep breath of air, and closed his eyes. "Thank god you two showed up."

His words were a bit slurred and Julie figured he'd be in a mild state of shock after the encounter and blood loss. She sat next to him and gently took his hand into her lap. "This will sting like a bitch."

"What wi-"

She didn't give him time to finish his sentence; she just grabbed his wrist and then poured a liberal amount of rubbing alcohol over the wound.

"FUCK!"

Jeremiah tried to pull his hand away, but Julie kept her grip firm. He was too weak to really resist anyway, and she had to make sure to clean it as well as she could to prevent infection.

"Hold still, or I'm gonna have Hank hold you down!"

He gave a weak whimper as she continued to clean the wound, before patting it dry and wrapping gauze around it. The stinger hadn't gone clean through, which surprised her. It looked like it went about halfway into the back of the hand, and then tore the flesh a bit as Jeremiah obviously pulled away. Thankfully, it looked like it avoided doing any major damage. Hank broke the silence as she worked on the hand and then tended to his back.

"How the fuck did you get stung and not die?"

"Their toxin isn't injected immediately, like a scorpion's. I can't theorize as to why, but the bulb at the end of their tail, that holds the gland, squeezes to inject. I think they can actually spray the venom at their victims, if necessary. When it stung me I just pulled my hand away and got lucky."

"Good to know, I suppose."

Jeremiah just sat there breathing and taking reserved sips of the rest of the water as Julie finished dressing his wounds. "You're damn lucky. How could you forget about the egg?!"

He smirked weakly and looked at her. "You did, too."

Julie could feel her face grow hot as she began to turn red from embarrassment. He was right. Somehow they both managed to lose track of the stupid thing, and now here they were in a ruined morgue with Jeremiah's hand needing stitches.

"Let's head to the ER. They can get that hand properly cleaned and stitched up."

"Wait, there's something you need to know."

"If you're talking about the pheromone thing, we already know. You managed to tell us before you were attacked."

"No, no!" He sat up, his eyes wild with panic. Hank placed a hand on his shoulder trying to calm him down.

"Look, we'll get the word out. Everything will be alright Jer."

"That's not it! As I was trying to tell you on the phone earlier, their vomeronasal organ is so well developed they can probably detect pheromones from miles away. If a curious one came to town because of Andrew, then others will surely follow *its* scent."

"You don't mean..." Julie felt the words die in her throat as her own eyes grew wide in fright. Realization then dawned on Hank's face as well.

"More are coming. No matter what we do, more will come."

XV

Andrew woke with a start, feeling slightly disoriented. It took him a few moments to realize where he'd woken up; the surroundings were foreign to him. As his eyes adjusted with a few blinks it all came crashing back. The deaths of his uncle and brother, the fight with his mom, and his subsequent squatting at his uncle's place.

Not like he was gonna use it ever again anyway, Andrew mused. It was a pretty sweet little cabin, too. Right at the edge of the county, near a lake he never bothered to remember the name of. It was dark outside, but for all he knew it could be as early as four or five o'clock. He hated the autumn months. Give him sun and fun any day.

Scratching himself, he made his way from the guest bedroom, since he couldn't bring himself to sleep in his uncle's bed, to the bathroom. He emptied his bladder and reapplied some deodorant instead of bathing. It wasn't like he had to impress anyone today, anyway. Running his fingers through his greasy hair, he tried to lay down a nasty cowlick towards the back. After the fourth time it popped back up he just said fuck it.

In the kitchen he turned on the lights and glanced over at the clock. It was a little past seven which surprised him. During a binge of video games and his uncle's porn stash, he polished off the better part of a dozen beers and eventually blacked out. Now he had a bit of a hangover.

"And the best cure for that is more booze!"

It felt a little weird to be talking to himself, but he shrugged it off. He was on his own now. Hell, if he played his cards right he might be able to get away with living here in his uncle's cabin for quite some time before anyone got wise about it. Opening the refrigerator, he began to poke around.

His uncle hadn't been much of a shopper, usually eating frozen dinners or heading into town to eat at this shit hole diner he raved about. Andrew had eaten there once, and couldn't get the smell of a deep fryer off his skin for two days. He joked about the plates being fried along with the food, and got a smack across the back of his head for his troubles.

In the fridge was a half-empty jar of pickled eggs, an empty gin bottle, a few packets of soy sauce, a takeout container he didn't dare go near, various bottles of condiments, and the case of beer. Reaching in he felt his hand hit cardboard much to his dismay. He must have drunk the last of it. Being underage, he wouldn't be able to refill his stock until he got a friend to do the deed for him. For that, he'd need money. Money he usually got from working for Uncle Greg or taking it from Mom.

Fuck, he thought. Maybe he should go back, apologize to his mother, and try and get back in her good graces. While she hated beer, she kept an ample stock of boxed wine and it was easy for him to steal a few drinks from that without her noticing.

No. His mom was a royal bitch yesterday and the only way he'd go back is if she came crawling on her hands and knees for forgiveness. But he knew it would be a cold day in hell before she said sorry 'bout a damn thing she did in her life.

Getting more and more angry thinking about it, he kicked an empty can across the floor and smirked when it smacked into a rat trap and set it off, causing both to go flying. Wait, a rat trap? *Ew. What the fuck, Uncle Greg?*

Looking around, he only then realized what a dump the cabin actually was. Paint was peeling off the wall in some places, garbage littered the floor, and nothing looked like it had been cleaned in years. Andrew glanced over by the sink and saw a plate that looked clean. Reaching in to lift it up, he found it stuck. Giving a good tug to free it, he turned it over and just about puked. What looked like mold and some sort of dried red gunk had glued it to the counter. He dropped it immediately.

Ok, maybe he needed to find a better place to squat for a bit. He was sure one of his friends would have an extra room. Plus they'd have beer, or at least better access to it. Maybe tomorrow he'd head out...after packing up anything of worth here, like the video games and the guns.

A pounding at the door scared the shit out of him, and was instantly followed by the sound of someone yelling. This cabin was miles from town and as far as he knew the cabins on the lake weren't occupied year-round. Whoever was there pounded on the front door again, this time more frantic and insistent, and he could almost make out what they were saying.

"...me in...ammo...please!"

Andrew was never a brave man and the day his brother and uncle died he proved it by doing the one thing he could do well: running. Running got him away from those things and running got him out of his mother's house. Maybe now was another good time to run.

Turning and walking quietly to the back door, he was about to open it when a figure appeared in the glass.

"LET ME IN, PLEASE!!"

Andrew looked at the lock, and realized it wasn't set. The stranger must have noticed how his gaze went to the lock as well, because he pushed on the door, hard, sending Andrew flying back. He then threw the door shut, made sure it was locked this time, and ran into the living room.

"Do you have a phone?!"

Getting up, Andrew started to act defensively, looking for anything he could use as a weapon. Maybe that disgusting plate.

"What the fuck do you think you're doing in my house?!"

It was then the stranger turned around and Andrew got a really good look at him. Suddenly he felt like he was about to be in a heap of trouble. The man wore a police uniform and looked like one of the cops he had talked to down at the station. The only weird thing was, his shirt was torn right about where his badge should have been. The man's demeanor suddenly shifted as Andrew tried to play this off as his house.

"Ain't you a bit young to own something like this, you little shit?"

"Doesn't matter. You still need a warrant to come inside!"

"This isn't a goddamn search and seizure, this is life and death! Now, do you have a phone or not?!"

The sheriff stopped and glanced at Andrew and then his eyes widened as he got a good look at him. "Oh my god. You're the Ferguson kid."

"This is my uncle's place. Since you didn't arrest me, I decided to go out on my own. What of it?"

"I don't give two shits if you decided to become the king of Ireland. I just need your phone. Where is it?"

The way he was agitated and scraped up kind of had Andrew worried. There was a large gash across his forearm that he could see, as well as his gun missing from his holster. Oh god, was he attacked? Were they still after him?

"I...I dunno. I just use my cell."

Reaching into his pocket, he pulled it out and the sheriff snatched it from his grasp.

"What's the pin?"

"Fuck you. Give it back and I'll unlock it."

Sheriff Dragert shot Andrew a look that could freeze beer, but relinquished the device. Andrew typed in the code and handed it back.

"Zero Zero Zero Two? Seriously?"

"You fucking looked?!"

"You really are as dumb as your mother said you were."

While the sheriff tried to dial out, Andrew leaned back against the sofa and glanced over at the back door which he could still see from his position. There was a shape at the door that he only saw for a moment, but it made the blood drain from his face. It was distinctly reptilian.

"Oh my god...oh my god, you brought them here?!"

Andrew felt like his heart was seizing as panic began to overtake him. His breathing came in gasps and he tried to calm down. It was everything he could do not to wet himself right there in the living room.

"Keep your voice down!" the sheriff hissed. Andrew could hear the rings through the phone and the click as someone picked up.

"Stonesworth Sheriff's Department. Is this an emergency?"

"Thank god. Dorris, this is the sheriff."

"Hank?"

"No, Dorris, Sheriff Dragert! You need to send all available units to my location."

"I thought you gave Hank your job?"

"For once in your goddamn, worthless life, Dorris, shut the fuck up and do your fucking job!"

There was a silence on the other end for a few moments followed by a simple click.

"She hung up on you! Why did you yell at her?!"

"Don't you start with me, you punk! These fucking things tracked you to your house and now here!"

Andrew suddenly forgot about how panicked he felt and looked the sheriff dead in the eye.

"My...my house? What do you mean, my house?"

"...Shit. Look, I didn't mean for you to find out this way, but may as well get it out there. Your mother was killed by one of those things last night."

It was as if the world had been pulled out from under Andrew. He slowly walked around the sofa and sat down. He could vaguely hear the sheriff talking to him, but the words sounded so far away. A rush of memories, good ones, flooded his mind as tears began to form in his eyes. His mom was dead, and it was his fault.

As much as he may have hated her at times, he never wished for her to be dead. Even when he caught her making out with his P.E. teacher at a school dance once, he managed to forgive her. Hell, he was even going to forgive her after he cooled off from *this*. In just a few days time, everyone he ever loved or cared about was dead, and he was to blame. He was the center of it all, he had to be.

He could still hear words coming from the sheriff, but he didn't listen. He knew what he had to do. Getting up, he slowly made his way through the kitchen and to the back door. He placed one hand on the knob and the other on the lock. This was karma. If the world wanted him dead so badly, he'd just give it what it wanted. Maybe then people would stop dying.

"...fuck you think you're doing?!"

For some reason those words rang clear. Maybe it was a last ditch moment of clarity from his mind, trying to give him a reason to run again. No, not this time. He'd been a coward his whole life, but this time he'd face his destiny like a man.

"I'm saving you and everyone else! They just want me!"

Before he could go through with his heroic act, a stinger attached to a tail smashed through the window, sending pieces of glass flying. While the stinger managed to miss him, a large shard of glass hit him in the shoulder with enough force to embed itself. The sharp pain suddenly knocked him out of his heroic suicide moment and brought him crashing back to reality, just in time to be face to face with one of the lizards. It squawked threateningly at him.

"Ahhhhh!! AHHHHH!!!!!!!! I DON'T WANT TO DIE!!"

He screamed, and felt strong hands grab his arms and pull him back as a set of jaws filled with jagged little points snapped at the air he'd just been occupying.

"Move, goddammit!"

Andrew didn't resist as the sheriff pulled him into the living room. He just wanted the pain in his shoulder to stop and for his mom to be alive again. Wanted to play games with his friends and have sex with a hot girl. *Oh god, am I going to die before I even get my dick wet?*

He began to wail as the sheriff dragged him deeper into the house. The sound of crunching glass, and a pained cry from one of the creatures, told him they were in the house and he just wailed harder.

"Shut the hell up! Is there an attic?!"

Andrew's mind drew a blank for a moment before he blurted out, "Basement!"

"That's fuckin' peachy. Let's go!"

Andrew started to pull at the glass embedded in his shoulder when Dragert yelled at him. "Leave it in! You could bleed out, you stupid son of a bitch! Where is the door to the basement?"

Andrew could swear that he felt the hot breath of those things as they rushed through the living room towards the stairs. There was a door that led down to the basement, and he just pointed. The sheriff didn't waste anytime pulling it open, and then followed it up with a string of curses. It was a broom closet.

"No! The floor!"

Andrew pointed again, remembering that his uncle built the basement not for storage, but as a 'panic room' of sorts In case he was ever cornered by the police. Sure enough, on the floor was a rug that he pulled aside to expose the trap door. One of the creatures jumped onto the couch about fifteen feet from them and gave a cry. Another turned the corner and replied.

"Open it...open it!!"

"I'm trying! Give me a hand!!"

They both grabbed the rusted latch and gave a hard pull. Andrew felt pain blossom in his shoulder and the sheriff gave a strained grunt as the door gave way and flew open. Both men fell on their asses, but scrambled for their only hope at salvation. The sheriff dived in, head first, and Andrew was right behind him. He collided with the sheriff at the bottom of a ladder, knocking the wind out of the older man.

"Get...off...me!!" He said in between wheezing gasps. "Close...the...door!!"

Andrew tried, but the pain in his shoulder was too much. The glass had been pushed further in by the fall, and part of it had broken off inside the wound. It made climbing the ladder back up to the trap door nearly impossible.

He barely managed to reach the pull cord tied to bottom side of the trap door, and was thankful that his uncle was a paranoid bastard as he grabbed onto it. The last thing he saw was one of creature's bright blue eyes looking right at him, as he pulled with all his might sealed the two of them in the basement.

Then, darkness.

***

Julie filled out the paperwork for Jeremiah as they sat in the ER. Hank scratched his beard and wondered what their next move should be. He wanted to go back out and track the one that got away, but both Julie and Jeremiah told him that going after it at night would be suicide. They were natural nocturnal hunters and, as such, would have the upper hand. Even so, he hated sitting around on his ass with no plan of action.

There was also no telling if the one in town was attacking again, or how often it needed to feed. Since extracting hormones wasn't enough to sustain it, it would need nourishment sooner rather than later. The whole ordeal gave Hank the willies. He just wanted this all to be over with.

"How is he holding up?"

Instead of getting a reply from Julie, Jeremiah gave a weak thumbs up with his undamaged hand. "Alive. Might have to give up calligraphy now." His demeanor changed slowly after his little joke. Becoming quiet, he met Hank's gaze with a deadly seriousness. "You both need to go. I'll be alright for now, but you both need to warn the town."

Hank got in very close to the two of them and whispered so anyone else nearby wouldn't hear. "How can you be so sure they're coming? So far it's been just the one, and no other reported attacks. If we're lucky, the rest are still in the woods and we can hunt them down first thing tomorrow."

The doors to the ER burst open as a pair of EMTs came in pushing a man on a gurney who looked as if he was having a seizure. The nurse at the desk came running around to meet them.

"What happened?"

"Wife said he was attacked by some animal. Said she killed it by hitting it with a bat, but it had already squirted something at her husband. A few minutes later, he started seizing."

"He looks like he's going into cardiac arrest! Get him over to..."

The group of people had already gone down a hall and through a set of double doors. Hank watched them go and hoped the man would make it. One thing stood that out to him was the fact that no one mentioned the man being stung and the one he shot had a ruined stinger.

"He wasn't paralyzed. Maybe it wasn't the lizards."

"Actually, that may mean it was more than anything else."

"What do you mean, Jeremiah?"

"Snake venom isn't like a poison. It's not readily absorbed through the skin. It needs to be injected. However, the ramped up ACTH is probably easily absorbed. So you get the effects of that without the loss of movement."

Julie didn't like the fact that even touching the stuff could be lethal to the wrong person. The more she learned about these creatures the more she just wanted to crawl under her bed and never come back out.

"We need to see if that's the same one I shot today. Only way I'm gonna rest easy tonight."

Julie bit her lip as she looked up at Hank and then back to Jeremiah. "You're going to be alright?"

"Promise. Once I'm done here I'll give you a call."

"Alright."

She stood up and Hank pulled out his phone hitting the speed dial for the sheriff's department. After two rings Dorris picked up.

"Stonesworth Sheriff's Department. Is this an Emergency?

"Dorris, it's Hank."

"Oh, hi, Hank. You will never guess who called."

"Not now, Dorris, I need some information."

"Jesus, you're just about as rude as the sheriff was. Well, not you, the other one."

"Other one? What the hell are you talking about? Did John call?"

"Yes, and he sounded panicked. He was also rude as shit so I hung up on him, figuring he'd call right back in a bit of a better mood. But the line only rang once after that and I haven't heard anything else from him."

Hank's mind raced. Where the hell had Dragert gone after their altercation? And how long ago had it been? "When did he call, Dorris?"

"About twenty minutes ago."

"Dorris, this is very important. Can you pull up the 911 logs for tonight? I need any within the last half hour."

"Alright, give me a second to pull it up in the computer."

If Dragert *had* been attacked, he was likely dead by now if he hadn't managed to get away. Dorris was a prideful woman and acted like a mother hen more often than did her job properly. Once he got this all sorted he'd see about replacing her. Maybe just relegate her to daily duties.

"Ok, there were two. One was a disconnect that they couldn't place about thirty minutes ago, and twenty minutes ago there was a report of an animal attack near Crescentwood Drive and 50th Street."

Crescentwood Drive was on the other side of town from where Ms Ferguson and Elliot had died. It was possible that the creature had made the trek across town, but it seemed unlikely. The last he saw of the thing, it was headed away from town, not deeper into it.. A knot formed in his stomach as his gut told him more were already showing up, but he had to be sure.

"I need the exact address, Dorris."

He made a frantic motion to Julie that he needed a pen and paper, and she tore a bit off the entry form for the hospital and handed him the pen she'd been using. Jotting down the address quickly he said thanks and hung up. It was then he noticed three missed calls from a number he didn't recognize. He handed the address to Julie and looked to Jeremiah. "Take it easy and we'll come pick you up after we get this sorted."

He nodded and waved them off. "Go on, save the town. Or whatever it is you do for fun around here."

Hank smiled at him, gave a nod, and headed off, with Julie close behind.

"So what's with the address?"

"We need to head there to see if that's the creature I shot. If it is, I don't go into full on panic mode."

"If it's not?"

"Then we're in some real deep shit. I would say evacuate the town, but that might attract them even more. Wish we never heard of these fuckers."

Julie walked to the car and Hank motioned her to the driver's side while tossing her the keys.

"Me, drive? I'm not a cop, Hank."

"No, but I need to see who called me and make a few more calls myself. I don't have any hands free shit in this thing so you're driving. Why I gave you the address."

Getting into the vehicle she started it up and pulled out of the parking lot and onto the road heading south towards the house on Crescentwood Drive. Hank dialed the number on his phone and waited as it rang once, twice, and then a third and final time. He was then met with an automated message service.

"Yo, this is Andrew. If you're a hot chick, leave your name and number. If I owe you money, I'll get it to you later. Leave a message!"

Hank hung up the phone before the beep sounded and redialed. It went right to the voicemail message again. He did this three more times before finally giving up. Julie must have sensed his frustration, because she glanced over at him.

"Who was it?"

"It was Andrew. He called around the same time Dorris said they got a disconnected 911 call."

Thinking for a moment, Hank got an idea. Even if the call disconnected before they could get a proper bead on the location, it should have pinged off a nearby tower. The only problem was if it was in town, there was only one tower for the whole area, and he'd be back at square one. Praying Andrew was somewhere remote, he called back to Dorris.

"Stonesworth Sher-"

"It's Hank again, Dorris," he interrupted, "and I need you to check something else for me. Can you tell what tower that disconnected cell phone pinged from?"

"Ugh, Hank. I swear. Can't you just come in and get this done?"

"Dorris, please. It's a matter of life and death."

He could hear her audibly sigh; she made no effort to mask her frustration at being asked to actually do her job. He was definitely going to fire her when he got the chance. Another minute passed in silence, and he was afraid they got disconnected.

"Dorris?"

"Hold on I'm looking! Jesus, you guys are just rude as hell tonight."

Rolling his eyes, he took the time to audibly sigh right into the phone, which didn't seem to faze her one bit. "Looks like it only pinged at the one tower over by the lake, just outside of town."

"What's out there? Are there any houses or gas stations?"

"Well..." he could hear her clicking on her keyboard and typing a few things before she came back with an answer.

"There's a few cabins out there. It's impossible to tell which one the call came from however."

"Ok, thanks for your help, Dorris."

"Next time you call, someone better be dead!" she hung up on him and it left him with a frustrated, bitter taste in his mouth. The knot in his gut seemed to be growing bigger, and it told him that the place to be was out at the lake.

"Change of plans. We need to head to the lake."

"But...we're almost to Crescentwood. The lake is way on the north side of town. What the hell is out there?"

"I think Andrew is."

Hank began to wonder what the hell that stupid kid was getting into now. Why would he be out by the lake? As far as Hank knew, his mom only owned the house and they didn't have any friends that owned property out there. Then it hit him: his uncle must have had a cabin. Being a poacher, he probably wanted to be close to the woods, to be able to get in and out easily under the radar. The real question now, was which cabin would be his?

The car came to a slow stop, and Julie put it into park.

"Why are we stopping?"

"Like I said, we were almost there. Now we're actually there. Look."

She pointed through the windshield to the flashing lights across the street. Hank, wrapped up in his own thoughts, hadn't registered them. It looked like two deputies were talking to a woman on her front porch. At this distance he didn't recognize them, but he knew there were only about six possible cops on the clock right now.

He got out of the car, but when Julie hopped out as well he held up a hand.

"Wait here. I just want to see if the creature is the one I shot."

"But, Hank-"

"No buts. We can't stay long, because we need to see if Andrew is alright. Might be a wild goose chase, but if those things are at the lake then there's no telling when they might spill into town."

"Fine. I'll keep the car warm. Just hurry."

He nodded to her then jogged across the street and up to the house where the two deputies were still talking with the woman. Up close, he finally recognized them as Jefferson and Gains. Jefferson he knew well enough, but Gains was a rookie whom Hank had never said more than three words to. He seemed to surprise the two men because their eyes went a little wide at the sight of him.

"Deputy Murphy? What are you doing here?"

"Sheriff now. I actually need to see the creature that attacked the woman and her husband."

"We've called animal control, sir. Damnedest looking thing, too."

The woman butted in before either deputy could say anything.

"It's around back, near the shed. Is my husband alright?"

"I'm sure he'll be alright, ma'am," Hank lied through his teeth. The man's only real hope was that getting sprayed actually made a difference, rather than being injected. The fact that he survived the ambulance ride boded well for that theory, at least.

Not wanting to deal with the two deputies continued questions about his presence there, or new position, he made his way around to the back yard and towards the shed. A brilliant white light glared in his face as he stepped closer. Motion detector. Unfortunately it was blinding him and killing his night vision. Holding up a hand against the light, he made his way over to the side of the shed. Waiting a moment for the floodlights to click back off, and another moment for his vision to return, he pulled out his mini flashlight and clicked it on.

He found it behind the shed. The baseball bat had been discarded into the grass with a large amount of blood along the wood. He smirked, glad that at least the woman had managed to defend herself against being its next victim.

"Atta girl."

Immediately, he lowered the light to the tail, hoping he'd find exactly what he wanted.

"Fuck me."

The tail was intact. He looked at the leg and saw it, too, had no sign of a wound. Part of him tried to rationalize it. Lizards regrow limbs all the time, so why not a tail? The rational side of his brain won out, though, reminding him that lizards took far longer to regrow limbs than a few hours. And as far as Hank knew, these animals didn't possess miraculous healing powers.

It wasn't the same lizarpion. Rushing back to the car, he ignored the calls of the two deputies trying to get his attention. Hopping back into the cruiser, his expression must have given away that it wasn't the one, because Julie's demeanor changed as well.

"Was it dead at least?"

"Head was bashed in, with a crater the size of my fist. One less to worry about. Hop out, I'm gonna drive. I know a shortcut."

Swapping positions, Julie spoke up once he put the car into drive.

"Ok, so we're headed to the lake. Any idea where to start looking?"

"Maybe we'll know when we see it."

XVI

When the call got dropped for a third time Dragert tossed the phone to the ground in frustration.

"Hey! That's my phone, you asshole!"

This Andrew kid was getting on his last nerve. He thought he was annoying back at the station, when they first met, but this only cemented the opinion. Sure, Andrew had a nasty piece of glass embedded in his shoulder, but the way he whined about everything and refused to just shut up was starting to wear thin. If the things upstairs didn't kill him, Dragert might.

"It's worthless down here. Being underground must fuck up the reception or something. Every time I get through, the call is disconnected. I tried the station again, 911, and even Hank a few times. Nothing."

"So...they're not gonna come save us from those things?"

"Not any time soon at least."

After Andrew had closed the hatch to keep the things out, the two of them were stuck in the dark. Instead of floundering around like fools, Dragert told Andrew to stay put. But, now he regretted tossing the phone before using it as a flash light.

"This place have any working lights?"

"Oh, yeah, I think so. I've only been down here once. Uncle Greg showed it to me in case I was over and we had to make a break for it."

"Make a...you mean to tell me there's another entrance to this place?"

"Yeah."

"Another entrance they can get in through, you idiot!"

Getting down on his hands and knees, Dragert started to feel around for the phone. He hadn't tossed it hard, and hoped it survived the landing. Some of these phones were about as resilient as tissue paper in a strong breeze. His hand brushed against something and he grabbed it. It wasn't the phone, but a flashlight. Fumbling for the switch, he turned it on and a beam of light shone right into Andrew's face.

"Hey!"

Other than a nasty stain of blood on his shoulder, the kid looked alright. A few other minor scrapes, but as long as they left the glass in place he should be ok until they could get to a hospital. If those things had followed him to the cabin then his car shouldn't be surrounded anymore. They had a chance, providing they could slip away undetected.

"If getting blinded is the worst thing that happens to you tonight, consider yourself lucky kid. We barely got out of there alive. What the fuck did you think you were doing at the back door?"

Turning the light away from Andrew, Dragert started to search the basement, which really looked more like a root cellar. Multiple beams held the bracers in place and provided structural support, but there wasn't much else except some crates and a workbench against a wall. Probably filled with all manner of things which were illegal to some degree. Andrew answered his question as he continued to search.

"I...thought they were just after me. Figured since everyone else I love is dead, I may as well join them. End all this. At the last second I chickened out...I don't wanna die, sheriff. I don't wanna end up like my brother and uncle and mom."

Dragert could hear the kid's voice crack, and rolled his eyes. Christ on a pogo stick, that kid whined a lot. He cut him a little slack, on account of losing those closest to him in such a short time, but he really needed to man up. It was fight or flight time, and Dragert expected to fly all the way back to town and set up a real hunting party to eradicate these things. What had Hank called them?

"Fuckin' lizarpions..."

Failing to notice Dragert was actually talking quietly to himself, Andrew stopped lamenting long enough to question him on what he'd just said.

"Liz...arpions? They have a name?"

"Sure, kid. Whatever." He replied absently, far more intent on finding the exit that Andrew spoke of. He kept looking at the same four walls, over and over again. There was the ladder leading up, no windows, four walls and a dirt floor. Claustrophobia had never been an issue for him before now, but then he'd never been trapped in what looked like a grave, by a bunch of creatures he thought he had killed twenty years ago.

"So where's the exit, kid? I'm just seeing a whole lot of nothing."

Andrew didn't immediately reply, so Dragert turned the light back to him. Instead of looking for the light switch, if it even existed, the kid was curled up on the floor, with his hands around his knees, rocking back and forth. For a moment, John almost felt bad for him.

"Fuck if I know. He just said it was a place to lay low."

"This is a fucking dead end?!"

"I dunno! He said he was almost done with it, so after a while I just figured he finally was."

It was true. He looked carefully at all four walls, and, other than a few boxes here and there, the only way in or out was the ladder and door above their heads. They were trapped.

"Well. Isn't this just fucking dandy. If those things don't manage to get down here we're going to starve to death. Or die of dehydration. I forget which one kills you first."

"Water. Three, maybe four days without water. Food, you can go a few weeks before you croak."

This was what the kid knew? Of all the things he could have known about, this was the one item, in all his life, he actually paid attention to? It was slightly useful, but Dragert was at the end of his rope with this kid. All patience was out the window, and, now that he'd pretty much signed their death warrant, he could give a shit about him.

"Thank you, Mister Wizard. Just wish I still had my gun. We might have a chance to pick them off one by one, using the trap door as a bottleneck. It'd be better than dying in the dirt."

"Oh, guns?"

Andrew got up with a groan and moved over to the workbench in the corner. He moved a little sluggishly and it seemed like his energy was fading. If they didn't get him to a hospital soon there was no telling how much longer his strength would actually keep him going. The shock of the situation could only mask the pain for so long.

Once at the bench, he reached around for something and grinned as he found it. Dragert heard a click, and suddenly the place was bathed in a cool fluorescent light. There were lights installed right into the support beams that Dragert had missed.

"If you knew about that the whole time, why didn't you say anything?" There was annoyance in his voice and a touch of anger bubbling to the surface. Wounded and in shock or not, this kid was certifiable.

"Dunno. Just thought about it when you said guns. This is where Uncle Greg kept his special collection and ammo. I think."

"By 'special' I'm guessing you mean illegal?"

Andrew looked a little sheepish at the question, and fidgeted a bit before answering. "Yeah."

"If it's got stopping power I could care less if it was the gun that shot Lincoln. What's he got?"

They both began to look around the workbench for anything usable, and then moved on to the crates scattered haphazardly around the small basement. Dragert was actually quite thankful there was no windows. Windows could have been an easy escape, but could just as easily be an entrance for the creatures.

After about fifteen minutes of searching through the items in the basement, they assembled their haul on the workbench. Between the two of them they had found another flashlight, a case of MREs, two boxes of .22 ammunition, a half-empty box of shotgun shells, twenty five .38 caliber rounds, which would have been perfect for his revolver had he not lost it, two .338 caliber rifles with no ammo, and three grenades.

"This is a bunch of jack and shit, son. Thought you said he kept the 'special' stuff down here?"

"That's what he said, sir. Coulda just been blowing smoke, though. I've only ever been down here once, and there was a lot more stuff."

"With no ammo for these rifles, and no guns to use the ammo we *do* have, we're right back at square one."

"What about the grenades?" Andrew picked one up and tossed it to the sheriff.

"JESUS FUCK!"

Dragert felt his heart pound in his chest as he scrambled to grab the flying projectile, dropping the flashlight in the process. He barely managed to catch it in time and glared at Andrew with venom in his eyes.

"You are, by far, the stupidest piece of shit I've ever encountered. Who the fuck told you tossing a live grenade was *ever* a smart thing to do?!"

Andrew just looked at him like a deer in the headlights, moments before it was struck by the oncoming car. Just this dumb and lost gaze that had no real brain power behind it.

"Just...don't ever do that again. Coulda killed us."

A scratching came from the trap door and Dragert felt his grip tighten on the grenade. He wondered if they might actually be useful if he could toss one up and out. He didn't know anything about explosives other than what he'd seen in the movies, and he knew that was woefully inaccurate at the best of times. Blowing up the cabin around them or blowing his arm off were very real possibilities if something went wrong.

Being trapped led him to consider some very dangerous ideas, though.

"Is there any duct tape around here?"

"Probably? Why?"

"We're gonna make these grenades into shrapnel bombs. Take the shotgun shells and tape them around the damn things and then toss them through that door."

"No way! That's gonna fucking kill us too!"

"Either way, we're dead men. We gotta try something, and this looks to be the best way of clearing those things out.

Even if we only kill one or two, the others might get spooked enough to hightail it outta here!"

As much as he told himself he was trying to convince Andrew to go along with the idea, he knew he needed just as much convincing. In theory, it seemed like a sound idea. Grenades were a concussive force, he knew that much at least, and expanded as they blew out. While the bullets wouldn't go off in a traditional sense, the metal would add shredding power. At least, he thought it might.

"Trust me kid, this is sure to work. Grab the tape and let's get to work."

Under the bench they managed to find a sorry-looking roll of duct tape, with only enough tape to assemble two of their bombs. Just as well, Dragert figured, because there weren't enough shotgun shells, either.

"Why don't we use the other bullets?"

"These are filled with buckshot, and should add more pieces of metal to fly into those bastards. We use regular bullets, then we only get one or two extra little bits."

"Won't it fire like a gun when the grenade explodes into a fireball?"

"...Andrew, I don't have the time, patience, or desire to tell you why this will work better. Just do as I tell you and roll the tape under the lever on the side, or they'll never go off at all."

The kid nodded, and Dragert could hear the sound of him pulling the tape off the grenade, and then reapplying it. Good thing he mentioned it, he thought. Most people, he wouldn't need to look after them to such a crazy degree, but he seriously thought Andrew had some sort of mental deficiency. No way was he just naturally this stupid.

Placing both grenades on the workbench, he admired their work. They'd managed to tape four shotgun shells to the sides of two of the grenades. Crude didn't even begin to describe the two bombs, but if he was right they should have some serious destructive power. The hard part would be opening the trapdoor wide enough to toss them out without letting those things in.

"Alright, now we just need a plan to use these puppies. One of us needs to open the door and then drop out of the way so the other one can toss the grenades up there. Then we both need to take cover as they go off, to avoid any shrapnel ourselves."

Looking right at Andrew's shoulder he added, "Looks like I'm throwing."

"I'm gonna get killed! What if they sting me like they did my Uncle Greg?"

"Then it's gonna hurt! Get the hell up there and get ready for my signal kid."

"What's the signal?" Andrew asked as he moved over to the ladder.

"Me yelling at you to open it! Now get up there."

Watching Andrew struggle to get up the ladder with his injury made Dragert feel a little bad. He probably could have done it himself, without getting Andrew involved, but at least this way there was a better chance of it going off without a mistake. Last thing they needed was one of those bombs falling back on them.

Once Andrew was in position, with his good hand against the trap door, he unlocked it carefully so as to not make a sound. He then gripped the tug cord in his other hand.

"Let go of the cord, you idiot!"

"But don't we need to close it after I drop?"

"I can't throw past you until you're out of the way. And if the door shuts we're as good as dead."

Andrew sighed, and his shoulders slumped a bit as he let go of the cord. His body tensed and he winced; the slumping probably aggravated his injury.

"This will work. We're getting out of here, ok?"

"Alright. Ready when you are. At least I won't die starving."

Whatever, kid, Dragert thought. Saving Andrew was the last thing on his mind right now. If he got extra lucky, any surviving lizarpions would descend on the kid while he made his way out. It was an awful thought, true, but it wasn't as if he actually wanted it to happen. That made it ok, right?

Dragert waited a few moments, listening to make sure none of the creatures were right on top of the trap door. Then, he took a deep breath, tensed his arm, and prepared to pull the pin and throw.

"Open it!!"

Andrew did was he was told, shoving on the door with all his might and tossing it open. He then dropped to the floor. stumbling a bit, as Dragert pulled the pin and let the grenade fly. Thankfully his aim was true and the homemade bomb sailed through the opening and out into the living room of the cabin. The last thing he saw before he grabbed Andrew and pulled him back behind a beam was one of the creatures glancing into the hole in the ground.

The explosion that followed was a lot louder than he expected.

***

They arrived at the lake faster than Julie had thought they would. Hank said he knew a shortcut, but every time anyone had ever said that to her before it usually ended up costing more time than it saved. She always wondered if they ever actually *took* their own shortcuts, or if they just guessed and then hoped it would work out.

He had taken them down a dirt road and slowed the car to a stop as they arrived at the lake. There, in the headlights, was another cruiser. It had to be the sheriff's. Former sheriff, Julie corrected herself.

"That's his car."

"Alright, let's go see if we can find him."

She had her hand on the door and was just about to open it when Hank grabbed her arm and gripped it firmly. Not hard enough to hurt, but the pressure was starting to build.

"Hank what are...you..."

It was then that she saw it. Or at least she guessed they both were looking at the same thing. The cruiser had several large scratches along the side and the driver's side window wasn't just rolled down, it was actually smashed out. Tiny pieces of glass still stuck in the door frame glinted in the headlights.

"Are we going out there?"

Hank took a moment to look around. Julie wasn't sure if he was looking for Dragert or the creatures, but suddenly she felt very vulnerable in the car and reached to lock her door. It was already locked, but the act gave her some measure of comfort.

"No. We're going to drive around the lake and see if anything pops out at us. Keep your eyes peeled."

He put the car into reverse and backed out enough so that he could turn the car around to follow the dirt road along the perimeter of the lake. It was difficult to see *anything* in the darkness, let alone the creatures. There was a new moon coming and that, coupled with the heavy amount of trees, caused the night to seem pitch black.

Whenever they passed a cabin, Hank would slow the car to try and give them both a better chance to see if there was anyone inside. After three houses Julie wondered if they were going to find anything.

"Maybe the lizarpions left?"

"I got a gut feeling Dragert is still kicking, if only to spite the damn things. There aren't that many houses around the lake, thankfully. We should end up back at his car in about ten minutes."

Passing the fourth house, she wondered if she should bring up something to talk about beside the lizards. There was something she had always wanted to ask Hank about but never had the courage. Seeing as they could die any minute now it seemed as good a time as any.

"Hank."

"See something?"

"No, not yet. There is something I'd like to talk about though, if you don't mind."

"Shoot. Just keep an eye out while you do."

She nodded, not sure if he took his eyes off the road to notice. Now or never.

"Why is it we never...ya know?"

Hank glanced over at her from the corner of his eye, quirking an eyebrow as he did.

"Never...uh...what?"

"Dated, Hank. There's something there. You know it. I know it. Half the town knows it."

The only sound in the car in response was Hank, clearing his throat nervously. Julie rolled her eyes and kept talking.

"Seriously, Hank. We've had playful banter since we met but it never went anywhere more significant. Not saying I'm without blame on this one," she turned to look at him, "but you never made a move either."

"Keep your eyes on your side."

Oh, so he didn't want to talk about the elephant in the room? She folded her arms indignantly and went back to looking out her side for any movement or for Dragert himself. Stewing in her own juices for a few moments was enough to make her boil over. She was about to give Hank a piece of her mind for dismissing her so quickly when he spoke again, this time his tone a little softer.

"There were two reasons I never acted on anything. The first of which is our age. Calling it a summer and winter romance is being generous. I'm at least twice your age, and even if I'm not, I am certainly old enough to be your father."

She swallowed down her anger and let him continue, this time turning in her seat to regard him as he spoke.

"Hank, age...it isn't that big a deal."

"Keep looking, or I stop opening up."

"Fair enough," she said, agreeing to the compromise and turning back to look out her window again.

"Age may not be a big deal to you, or even to me, but it would be to the town. Word spreads like wildfire, and I can just hear the gossip now. Cradle robbing deviant. Daddy issues. I'm sure we could suffer the words and rumors for a time, but for how long?"

"Ok, I still think that's a horseshit excuse for a reason. Since when have either of us cared one ounce for what the people of the town think of us? Your second reason better be a good one."

"Alright. Number two is my wife."

Hank could have said anything else and it wouldn't have fazed her one bit. This she was not expecting or prepared for.

"Oh..."

"You know what happened to her, and how bad it got at the end. I have reservations about moving on. No matter how much time passes, it still feels off to me."

How on earth could she compete with a dead woman? He obviously still loved her and kept that feeling close to his heart. It shouldn't have surprised her so much, but in the few years they had been friends, and gotten closer, he never opened up about her.

"There's still a bit of pain there, I guess."

Silence filled the car as they both went back to looking for Dragert. Julie felt the silence was a bit awkward but was unsure of what to say.

"Doesn't stop me from getting horny as fuck though."

"Hank, you perv!"

He flashed her that winning smile of his as she slapped his arm, hard enough to elicit an ouch and causing the car to swerve a bit. That was when Julie caught the movement on Hank's side of the woods.

"Stop!"

Slamming on the brakes, they both lurched forward a bit as the car slid to a halt on the dirt road, causing a cloud of dust to stir up. They both tried to peer through the fog they'd created, waiting for it to settle, when one of the lizarpions leaped onto the hood through the haze, gave a loud squawk, and then attacked the windshield with its tail. The stinger pushed all the way through, and got lodged there.

While the creature tried to free its tail, a strange sound filled Julie's ears, and it took her a second to realize it was her own voice, screaming in terror. Something slammed into her side of the car, and a second creature peered through the window with its bright blue eye.

"DRIVE!"

Before she even finished the word, Hank had already slammed his foot on the gas. The one on the hood lost its balance and fell off, towards the front of the car. It's tail was still stuck in the windshield and as it fell over it was dragged under the car. The tail ripped free as a sickening crunch filled the air.

Glancing behind her, she could see far more than she expected in the tail lights. They had originally counted about eight at the nest. She lost count, but she guessed there had to be at least twenty now.

"There is way more than we thought, Hank!"

"Looks like a goddamn herd. Hold on!"

Julie had never seen Hank so focused. His knuckles were white on the wheel but he was in an almost zen-like state as he shifted into a lower gear. They crested a hill and suddenly went into a steep decline.

"Fucking backwoods roads."

At the bottom of the decline was a sharp turn. Instead of riding the brakes, Hank yanked on the emergency brake and sent the back end sliding, just enough to match the turn, and then hammered the gas as he shifted back up again.

"Where the hell did you learn to drive like that?!"

She could see the corner of a smirk on his face as he focused on the road, picking up speed. "If we survive this I'll tell you over dinner."

"Deal."

Both of them saw the cabin coming up; the lights were on.

"Fuck. Should have turned right instead of left from his car. Would have seen the lights right off the bat."

Hank slammed on the brakes right outside and was about to lay on the horn to let whoever was inside know he was out there when the side of the house exploded outward. There was no time to react.

Debris pelted the side of the car, and Julie's window shattered inward, showering her with the tiny shards of tempered glass. The next instant she felt a white hot pain as something struck her right above the ear. She and Hank both were jostled in their seats, and the car rocked, tilting onto two wheels before settling back down again with a bang.

Only able to blink, she slowly looked around at her surroundings. Reaching up to where she had felt the pain she was relieved there wasn't a hole or a hunk of something sticking out of her skull. Looking at her hand though, it was covered in blood. Head wounds always looked worse than they actually were, she tried to reassure herself.

Hank! She turned to look at him and he was yelling something. At least his lips were moving like he was trying to tell her something. The explosion had clearly made her a bit deaf. Slowly her hearing began to return, and Hank's voice started to get louder and louder with every word.

"...ulie! Julie! Are you ok?!"

Managing a nod, she licked her lips and looked Hank over. He had a few scratches but since she was closer to the blast she had the misfortune of taking the brunt of it. *I must look like shit right now,* she thought.

"Stay here!"

Words wanted to come out, but she still couldn't manage to talk. She shook her head violently instead, but that was a mistake. The movement caused her to see stars and she had to close her eyes tightly to keep from puking and passing out. There was a pretty good chance she had a concussion.

Opening her door to follow Hank, she watched in horror as two of the creatures ran from the ruined cabin. One looked badly injured, limping as it ran, and the other just took off like a bat out of hell. Neither paid any attention to her or Hank.

"How's it feel to be terrified for once you bastards!" Hank called after them. Moving carefully, but quickly, he stepped over the exposed hole and called out. "Andrew! John!!"

A painful moment of silence passed and Julie wondered if the two were still alive in there when a familiar voice came from deeper in the house.

"Over by the stairs!"

Hank bounded over to the area in question with far more energy than a man his age should have. Julie followed after and they both looked down into a hole in the floor. Dragert and Andrew both looked up at them.

"Hank? Julie?!"

"Stop gawkin' and get the hell out of there! There's a whole fucking herd on our tail and we need to *go*!"

Dragert's eyes went wide as he pushed Andrew up the ladder before him and the boy only muttered a weak groan as he climbed. As soon as both were out everyone headed out of the house. When they passed what was left of the television, Andrew picked up a demolished game controller and sighed.

"Move it!!"

As they started to climb out of the wreckage, they found that the herd had caught up to them. Julie instantly started to panic. There was no way they could get to the car in time. They were trapped. They were going to die out in the middle of nowhere in a cabin that looked more like a warzone than a house.

"Take cover!"

Dragert came up behind her, pulled a pin out of something that looked like it was covered in duct tape, and threw it at the approaching herd. A few of the creatures glanced at the item now in their midst. Julie was slightly confused too, but Hank grabbed her and they ran back inside the house.

The second explosion was just as deafening as the first, but they weren't so close this time. A small tingle of glee ran up her spine as she saw lizarpions, and parts of them, fly through the air. The rest immediately scattered and the explosion had bought them enough time to get to the car and hop in.

One of the scattering creatures ran right towards her. It was in such a panic that it either didn't know or didn't care that she was in the way, it just wanted to get as far away from the explosion as possible. Bracing herself for the inevitable impact, she heard a shot as the thing fell in a heap and skidded to a stop just in front of her. Hank had his revolver out and a thin wisp of smoke trailed up from the barrel.

Hank had left the engine running and he threw the car into reverse as the remaining herd regrouped itself. Many squawked and screeched at the car as it disappeared from sight. The view of so many in the headlights was surreal. It wasn't just a herd; it seemed like a whole damn colony of the things.

Looking out behind them, Andrew and Dragert tried to lay low in the seat so Hank could focus on reversing. Without looking, he grabbed the emergency brake again, yanked it, and caused the car to go into a tailspin. Letting off the gas at the right moment and slamming on the brakes, he turned the car a full 180. Letting go of the emergency brake handle, he put the car into drive and hit the gas.

Satisfied the creatures were a memory again, he looked in the rear view mirror at Dragert.

"I got your call. Sort of. By the way, Dorris-"

"Is fired."

Both men paused and then burst into hearty laughter. Julie didn't know what was so hilarious. Dorris was annoying, but was firing her really that entertaining? Maybe they were both in a bit of shock. Lord knew she was. Gingerly touching her head wound again, she was pleased to find the blood flow slowing. Turning back to Andrew, she noticed the large blood stain on his shirt and the tear in the shoulder.

"Did they sting him?!"

"Just about," Dragert replied. "This damn fool was about to go kamikaze on them when one busted the back window of the cabin. A shard of glass got shoved into his shoulder. We need to get him to a hospital, quick."

"Just what the hell happened here, John? And why are you at the lake?"

Dragert got very quiet all of a sudden and looked out the window. It seemed like he was debating something, Julie thought, and when he spoke again and told them everything, including why he'd come to the lake, she understood why.

"Hell of a story, John."

"Hell of a night. If you two hadn't showed up when you did..."

Julie was happy they'd taken the chance of coming to find Dragert and that they'd managed to get him and Andrew out of the situation alive. But there was still something nagging at the back of her mind.

"We know why you were out here but why the hell was Andrew?"

"It's my uncle's cabin, actually. Was." Andrew frowned as he looked out the window. "After the fight with my mom last night, I came out here to crash. Sheriff Dragert here showed up a few hours ago and then you two rescued us.

Julie felt sick wondering how to tell Andrew what happened to his mother. Her face must have betrayed her thoughts because, Andrew just shrugged and went back to looking out the window.

"It's alright. He already told me what happened to my mom. It was my fault, wasn't it?"

"No, actually. These things hunt based on pheromones. Your mom was...angrier than you were that night, and that's what attracted it."

He turned to look right at her, his gaze far more tortured than his words let on. "I led it to the house though, didn't I?"

"We...don't know exactly why one came to town. It may have followed you, but you are *not* responsible for her death, Andrew. Understand?"

He just shrugged again and went back to looking out the window. Julie felt for the kid, she really did. His entire family, that they knew of at least, had been killed in a matter of days and he was left to live with it.

"Either of you have a phone with you? Dropped the kid's back at the cabin and I need to get the mayor on the horn. We're gonna need the fucking army out here."

Julie handed him her phone as Hank asked, "Think they're gonna believe you?" There wasn't doubt in his voice, Julie noticed, but an odd degree of hopefulness. If nobody believed them about the sheer number of the creatures, the town could be overrun.

"They better."

He punched some numbers in and hit send, waiting a few moments before he started speaking loudly into the phone. Julie turned around and looked back out the front window. In a few minutes they would be in town and then she could go back to her apartment, lock the door, and hide under her bed until all this blew over. There was something strange about the horizon, though.

"Hank...is the town..."

"Glowing?" Andrew finished her sentence as he leaned forward to get a better look. There was no separator cage between the front and back. There hadn't been a violent offender in town in years, so the cruisers didn't have them. It cut costs.

Hank's jaw tightened as he started to speed up the car. Not only was the town glowing, but the closer they got the more they could make out the storm clouds. It took Julie only a few seconds to realize those weren't storm clouds but smoke. Something in town had caught fire.

"Downtown's WHAT?!" Dragert yelled into the phone and joined the other three in looking at the horizon. Stonesworth was burning, and they were driving right into the heart of it.

XVII

Things looked a lot worse when they were farther from town. When they arrived at the downtown core, they found it had been just one large building that housed three businesses. Jay's Diner, a dry cleaners, and an antique store.

Even though it was late, a small crowd had gathered to watch the fire and it looked like the owners of the property were talking with one of the firefighters about the damages. Hank kept the car at a regular speed, doing his best to avoid attracting any excess attention.

"We'll be at the hospital in about five minutes. How you holding up back there, Andrew?"

"Just...peachy."

"At least you're still breathing. Count your blessings, kid. We all could've died back at your uncle's place." Hank then looked at John through the rear view mirror "Dragert, what did the mayor say about getting the military involved?"

"...He didn't believe that there were that many, and told me to sleep it off. Damned fool thinks I'm drunk."

Hank sighed and shook his head. If they weren't going to get any sort of backup then the town could be overrun, and that was something Hank did not want to see or deal with.

"Keep trying. Maybe he'll get so sick of your calls that he'll send them just to shut you up."

"Sure. Not like I have a career or anything anymore."

"I still haven't forgiven you for the shit you pulled, Dragert. Could've avoided this whole mess."

"Noted, Hank."

Hank did his best to ignore the dismissive tone as he pulled into the ER lane at the hospital. They had more pressing concerns than his wounded pride.

"Ok, Julie, take Andrew inside and get the two of you checked out. See if you can find Jeremiah. If Dragert can't convince the mayor on the phone to send help then maybe I can do it with the bodies of the creatures from the morgue."

Julie got out with Andrew, leaned back in through the driver's window, and kissed Hank on the cheek. He could feel his face go flush from the peck.

"Stay safe. John, you've still got my phone."

"Oh, sorry about that." Dragert reached over and handed her the phone and Hank dug his out of his pocket and tossed it to the other man.

"I still owe you a dinner."

"Better come back. I hate eating alone."

"Start calling the media. We need to evacuate the town. With the escaped convict story we already had them run they're probably going to believe it if we tell them it's escalated."

"They won't evacuate for just a couple prisoners, Hank. What the hell do I say?"

"Anything. Just get them to believe it. Those things are coming, and that fire was probably just like ringing the dinner bell."

Hank watched as she went inside with Andrew and then turned to Dragert. He had yet to turn on the phone he'd given him.

"What the hell are you waiting for? Get up here, get the mayor on the horn, and try and convince him to help!"

"The convict story...I axed it." Dragert said as he climbed into the front seat of the car.

Hank just turned to glare at the man sitting next to him. Just when he thought that John had sunk low enough, with all the shit he'd been pulling, he drops this nugget of truth onto Hank's lap.

"You *what*?!"

"I got a call a little after you gave the phony story. They wanted confirmation and the prison refused to comment. So, I told them the truth. Did you really think they wouldn't double check your story?!"

"So, you're telling me..."

"No one's prepared for anything, Hank. They're all a bunch of sitting ducks."

***

Across town, Mrs. Hernandez was sound asleep in her room when her dog's barking suddenly woke her up. Cursing at it in Spanish, she got quietly out of bed, so as to not disturb her husband, and went downstairs, fully ready to kick the stupid mutt in the head if it didn't shut up.

As she reached the bottom of the stairs, the barking stopped for a moment and she thought that maybe little Kahlua had tired herself out and gone back to sleep. But after another moment of silence the dog started up again, only this time it was a high-pitched whine.

"...Kahlua...?"

Rounding the corner she saw that the doggie door on the back door had been ripped from the frame and something was leaning over her dog. Screaming, she moved to find a broom or something to knock it away. The first thing she grabbed happened to be the mop leaning against the wall and she swung at the creature; unfortunately she missed. The lizar-pion stripped a chunk out of the dog's hide and chewed, practically ignoring the woman.

Mrs. Hernandez swung again and this time she hit it. It merely winced and leaned in to take another bite of the dog at its feet, while its tail darted out like a striking cobra. The attack was strong enough to knock her off of her feet, striking her just above her right breast. It had instantly punctured her lung and was filling it with the white toxin. Gargling noises emitted from her throat as pink-hued fluid gathered around her lips.

The wound began to bubble as the last air from her lungs tried to escape. Her heart began to race as the creature loomed over her, giving two short squawks, before turning her over and grabbing onto her back. The pain was excruciating and she felt a sucking sensation, but all she could do was gurgle as she tried with all her might to take a breath.

The thing on top of her began to make a series of noises, almost like barks, and the last thing she heard before slipping away into oblivion was her husband yelling at the top of the stairs for her to shut up the goddamn dog.

***

David finished laying out rose petals in a path leading from the front door to the bedroom and paused to admire his handiwork. It had been three weeks since his wife had kicked him out for cheating on her and he was still determined to get her back. It was a one-time fling with a client, and he'd promised her it would never happen again. Unfortunately, she wasn't taking anything he said to heart, so he was doing his best to romance her.

He had managed to convince her sister his intentions were genuine and she gave him an extra copy of the house key. He snuck in that night, knowing she would be home late from work. Every detail was planned perfectly. The trail of rose petals led to their bedroom where he'd be laying on the bed, waiting for her in just a robe. Chilled pink champagne, her favorite, would also be waiting for her as well as an assortment of her favorite chocolates.

Even if she rebuffed him tonight, he still had a few more ideas of what to try to get her forgiveness. He was wearing her down. Any day now, if not tonight, she would come running back and then their lives could finally get back to normal. Grinning like a fool he jumped onto the bed and leaned back, making sure to carefully open the robe, just enough to give the faintest peek at his growing excitement.

It was 11:55PM, and he'd been waiting for her for over thirty minutes. He was just about ready to call it a night and head home when he heard the front door swing open. He didn't hear it unlock...had he left it open? It really didn't matter, because this was it! She would notice the petals any moment now and be so overtaken with desire and longing for her husband that she would just have to take him back. *There was nothing a little bit of good sex couldn't fix,* he thought.

The fifth stair creaked. He had promised her two years ago that he would fix it but he never got around to it. If she took him back tonight, he promised himself, he'd make sure to fix it right away. It was the least he could do, after all. Seeing a shadow in the dim light of the hallway, he called out.

"Don't be scared, Sheila. Your sister gave me a key, and I just want you to hear me out. I've got two of your favorite things in here waiting for you." He glanced down at his manhood and smirked devilishly. "Well, three."

A huge lizard head poked inside the room and looked around, its nostrils flaring, smelling the air. David took a moment to process what he was seeing, to try and understand why he didn't see his estranged wife walking into the bedroom, but something from a bad horror movie.

"Sh...Sheila?"

As soon as it heard his voice it turned to look right at him, cocking its head to the side, as if noticing him for the first time. It entered the room slowly and he could see it would be as large as a Great Dane if it were on all fours, but it walked on its two hind legs. There was a nasty gash across its leg and its tail looked like it had been through a meat grinder. Some sort of white fluid oozed out of the mess at the end of the tail, and David gagged a little at the sight. All thoughts of reconciliation with his wife slipped from his mind.

"What the fuck are you?!"

Scrambling back as it crept closer, he pulled at the impossibly small robe, trying to cover himself, and looked around for a weapon. Grabbing the lamp off the nightstand, he ripped it from the wall and tossed it at the thing approaching him.

The make-shift projectile missed, but it shattered as it smashed into the opposite wall and succeeding in distracting the creature. Taking advantage of the opportunity, David tried to run past it but cried out in pain as it turned and jumped onto his back. Clawed hands dug into his shoulders as powerful legs kicked at his lower back, shredding his flesh with deadly efficiency.

He dropped immediately, from both the weight and the pain, and tried weakly to shake the thing from his back. Suddenly the thing got off him, and he thanked god for the respite. He hadn't crawled more than two or three feet away before he began to scream, shriller and louder than he ever had in his entire life.

He actually felt the skin and muscle being peeled from his back, and he could hear the creature's jaws rhythmically opening and closing as pieces were removed. The realization it was actually eating him is what caused his bladder to empty all over the floor.

"KILL ME!...KILL ME!!" he babbled over and over as it continued to pull pieces of meat from his back and greedily consume them. Bawling and carrying on like a baby, tears streamed down his face and snot flowed from his nose.

The next thing he felt was the strangest sensation in the world. Scaly hands groped around inside his back. He felt them grab onto something near the surface, tugging. His whole body lifted off the ground for a moment, then fell back to the floor with a sick, wet plop as whatever the creature had tore free from inside him. He vomited immediately, but without comprehending. The creature continued digging, extracting another piece from his torso.

As the sounds of more chewing filled David's ears, one of the things the creature pulled from his body fell onto the carpet right next to his face. Had be been capable of rational thought at that moment, he would've recognized it as a partially eaten human kidney. His kidney. Seconds later he was dead.

The creature had what was left of the right kidney in its hand, having eaten off the adrenal gland with its first bite. Tossing the ruined organ aside, it continued to peel pieces of meat from David's back, exposing his ribs by the end of its meal. It then dragged the dead husk over to the bed and pulled it up onto the mattress. It bounced slightly and began to assemble the pieces into a crude nest of meat and bone .

***

"This is gonna turn into a massacre."

"Maybe, or maybe the herd we saw will just stay near the lake. People aren't anxious or agitated, and most animals have the instinct to run away from fire. There's one or two in town that we need to find and kill, and we can contain the rest until help arrives."

"You have any idea how stupid that sounds, John? They were deep in the woods before, not a fifteen minute drive from the center of town. Keep trying the mayor."

Hank could tell Dragert was rolling his eyes as he redialed the number and got the same result as he had the past three times. Straight to voicemail. Either the mayor had turned his phone off for the night, or he was blocking the calls. Either way, they were up shit creek without a paddle.

"If we don't get people out of here, or at least try, their blood is on your hands, Tusk."

"Fuck you. This isn't all my fault, you know. How the fuck was anyone supposed to know there were so goddamn many of them?! That was a good twenty or thirty back there, and you told me there were only around eight."

Anger boiled deep inside Hank and he was at a loss about how to convince the man of the real danger the town faced. He resigned himself to keeping his mouth shut, and decided to do whatever *he* felt was necessary to protect this town. He was about to say something to Dragert when he noticed a man running out into the street, his eyes wide with fright and panic. Hank slammed on the brakes.

"Look!"

There was a creature chasing him, and even before Hank could jump out to help the man, the thing was on him. Its stinger stabbed down quickly multiple times. It then began to feed.

"What....what the fuck is it doing to him?!" Dragert turned a sickly shade of green as they watched, both transfixed by the ghastly sight. It grabbed onto the man's back, and arched it head to the sky and cried out in a series of barking grunts.

"It's sucking out his adrenal hormones. Needs them more than we do, apparently."

Hank grit his teeth. Saying a tiny prayer for the man, who was clearly beyond help, and another one for forgiveness, he gunned the engine and put his foot down hard on the gas. The creature looked up a fraction of a second too late, just as Hank slammed into it with the car. The force of the impact sent it flying about twenty feet before it rolled to a stop. It did not get up.

"You killed that man!"

"You know as well as I do that he was dead as soon as it stung him. They're in the town, John! How the fuck is that possible? We had a good twenty minute head start by car!"

"Few stragglers arrived early?"

"Christ. There's no telling how many made it this far before our encounter at the lake. We need to do something. Where's the PEP station for the Emergency Broadcast System?"

"Uh...about that..." Dragert fell silent after that and his delayed answer only made Hank even angrier.

"Well?! Where is it??"

"We don't have one."

Fuming was the mildest word to describe how Hank felt as he started to drive a little faster through the streets.

"Are you fucking kidding me?!"

"That one wasn't my fault. The mayor was looking to make budget cuts and that was the first thing to go. With the news and the media and computers and shit, it just seemed less and less relevant."

"This whole county is run by ignorant as fuck sons-of-bitches."

Lizarpions were in town. There was no way to warn people of the impending threat and Hank had no plan of attack. This was turning into even more of a cluster fuck than he'd initially thought it was. Inspiration hit him as he passed by the one he'd hit with the car and he pulled to a stop.

Getting out of the car he quickly scanned the area for any other signs of the things. Porch lights began to turn on in the area. The commotion was drawing attention and a few people were starting to leave their homes to investigate.

"Everyone! I'm with the sheriff's department and I need you all to go back into your homes and lock all your doors and windows! Do not leave your homes until you are told it's safe to do so!"

"Fuck you! This is America! I can do whatev-AHH!!!"

The lone dissenter was attacked by one of the lizarpions as another came out of the bushes to Hank's left and squawked at him. Pulling out his revolver, he got off a shot, dropping the creature before it attacked. Someone else screamed and Hank swung around in time to see a pair of feet being dragged inside the open door of a house on his right.

"Everyone inside. NOW!"

A chorus of slamming doors greeted him as he reached down to pick up the dead lizarpion at his feet. Carrying it to the squad car, he tossed it into the backseat.

"Why the fuck are we bringing that thing??"

"Because people believe what they can see!"

XVIII

Unsurprisingly, every news outlet and radio station she tried to call about what was going on treated her like a prank caller. One classic rock station thought she was going along with their promotion to win tickets. She won, but they still ended up hanging up on her, saying she was 'taking the joke too far'. It was impossible.

Andrew had been admitted and she left him with the doctors and nurses as she tried to call Jeremiah. He had to have been released by now and she hoped he had gotten back to her apartment alright. She couldn't help but feel very exposed, even standing in the middle of the ER. There was no place to really secure herself, besides her office downstairs.

In fact, that didn't sound like a bad idea. She could turn off all the lights, lock her door, and crawl under her desk. The mini fridge was stocked so she could last at least a few days. *Damn smart thinking Julie*, she thought, and she patted herself on the back just as Jeremiah's voice came in through the phone.

"Julie? Are you alright?"

"You were right. There was a whole herd of them out at the lake. At least twenty, and I think they were all headed back here."

"Shit. I had hoped I was wrong, but I think they have a rapid spawning and growth cycle."

"Meaning?"

"That twenty may only be a small percentage of the whole."

"You really know how to find the silver lining to the dark clouds, Jeremiah. Are you back at my place at least?"

"No. I had no ride and no wallet and you called me just as I was about to call you. Can you come pick me up?"

"I'm here already. I had to bring that kid Andrew in. What floor are you on?"

"Still on the main, down a corridor near the ER. Found a vending machine and spent what little change I had on what I believe is an expired candy bar."

"I know exactly where that is. Stay put and...I'll..."

The phone slipped out of her hand as her heart began to race. She was standing towards the back of the main ER where patients with various injuries were waiting to speak with a triage nurse. From her position she could just barely see around the corner to the entrance. Three of the lizarpions waltzed in like they owned the place, nostrils flaring.

A man with his hand wrapped in a blood-soaked towel was the first to fall. He bumped right into one as it turned the corner into the ER waiting area. A stinger stabbed right into his neck and he dropped like a sack of flour. A woman screamed, and the other two descended on her next.

In an instant fear and panic exploded among the rest of the people there and they fought to escape. Those who could move quickly managed to get past the lizarpions but those who were more injured, and slower, became the next victims. One man with a steak knife sticking out of his forearm somehow got the knife ripped out and began to bleed profusely. This caused a woman with a limp to slip and fall in the blood, cracking her head open on a coffee table edge.

Time seemed to slow down as Julie watched another two creatures enter the hospital and add to the chaos. Those who were running for the exit tried to turn around, but stingers shot out and stabbed at those who tried to flee. Any who were not stung seemed like they were being funneled towards the other three creatures. Were they being...herded?

Another woman had three creatures descend on her at once, with one of them feeding on her with its hands. Uttering an almost gleeful bay as the others ripped hunks of flesh from her struggling body.

Gore and blood were everywhere. All but one of the nurses had run deeper into the hospital. The one who stayed tried to help a man in a wheelchair escape but was stabbed repeatedly in the back for her troubles. She slumped over the chair and looked oddly as if she were humping it, the way her body convulsed. The man in the chair just screamed, until one of the lizarpions ripped out his throat and began to feed on his stomach.

The rest of the creatures were feeding, both traditionally as well as draining hormones from their victims. In some gruesome cases they were doing both. Julie had her back against the wall and had so far avoided detection. Slowly she slid along the wall towards a door leading to the vending machine where Jeremiah was.

Just a few feet from the door one of the creatures looked up at her, a long piece of skin hanging from its mouth. It squawked once, waited a moment, and then honked twice, quickly. Two of the others looked up from their feast as well.

They were coming for her. Giving up being slow and cautious she bolted the remaining few feet to the door as one jumped at where she had just been standing, crashing into the wall and leaving a sizable hole. Julie swung the door open, slammed it shut, and took off in a run down the hall.

Jeremiah was standing at the end of the corridor and was tossing a half eaten candy bar into the trash when she grabbed his arm.

"The call got cut off. What happened?"

"We have to go. They're here!"

"In the town? Already?!"

"In the hospital!!"

One of the animals had managed to push the door open and they could hear the sound of claws tapping against the linoleum floor as it rushed towards them. An unfortunate orderly exited one of the rooms in between it and the two of them and the creature ran right into him, knocking both to the ground. The creature injected him and immediately began to feed. Jeremiah's eyes went wide and he took off without even waiting for Julie. She was right on his heels, cursing under her breath.

"Shit. We need to get to the morgue, now!"

"Why there?"

"We can hide out in my office until help arrives."

"We'll be trapped!"

"We already are!"

***

By the time Hank and Dragert arrived back at the scene of the fires the crowd had dispersed and the buildings were just smoldering. Hank's heart sank as he didn't see what he was looking for.

"Shit. Shit!!"

"What? What the hell are you up to?!"

Hank pulled the car around one of the firetrucks and finally saw what he wanted: one news van was still there. The crew looked like they were packing up and the woman, who was obviously the reporter based on her outfit, was enjoying a smoke.

He pulled the car right up to the news crew, jumped out, and swung open the door to the back seat. Grabbing the dead creature, he tossed it onto the road right in front of the reporter. She cried out in surprise and horror at what lay at her feet.

"You need to get this on the news. Now!"

"Who the hell are you and what the *fuck* is that thing??"

"I'm the acting sheriff, Hank Murphy, and that is a lizarpion. It's a dangerous reptile and there's a whole herd of them headed into town. We need to get the word out that no one is to leave their homes!"

"Fucking shit, this looks real. Jim! Come take a look at this!"

One of the men who was packing away equipment came around the side of the van to see what all the commotion was about and leaned down to look at the creature's dead body.

"Shit, this does look almost real. How the hell did you get the polyurethane to look like real skin?"

"It's...what?! No! This thing *is* fucking real and we need to warn people! They hunt by detecting pheromones and everyone in town is in danger!"

"Wow, it even looks like it's breathing."

"...breathing?" The color drained from Hank's face.

A bright blue eye shot open and looked around wildly as the thing scrambled to its feet. Its claws lashed out at Jim, and cutting deeply across his chest.

"Oh my god! What the...what the fuck?!"

The stinger was flailing around wildly, spraying white toxin everywhere. A large glob of it landed on the reporter's leg as she stood there dumbstruck watching the thing come back to life.

He'd only managed to daze the stupid thing, and he immediately kicked himself for not making sure it was dead. Now the reporter was yelling at the other man in the back.

"Get the camera! Get the camera, now!!"

He came out, camera hoisted onto his shoulder, and focused it on the creature which seemed just as surprised as they were. One of its eyes was ruptured, and it kept squawking at them, trying to keep them at bay instead of attacking them. Not waiting for it to change its mind, Hank took a shot and ended it.

"Like I said, they're real and there are more of them in town. We need to warn people. Tell them to stay indoors and remain calm."

"Jim, are you alright?"

"Looks...worse than it is, Sheila." His words sounded a bit strained as he gingerly poked at the gash on his chest. It wasn't bleeding much, but Hank had no idea if that was a good thing or not.

"Sheila, we need to get this on the air. Can you do that?"

"We were live the second Rich turned on the Camera. Where did these creatures come from? What is the town doing to keep people safe?"

She shoved her microphone right into Hank's face and he wondered for a moment where the hell she'd been hiding it, as well as thinking that she was insane to try and do an interview right here in the road where one of those damn things could jump out at any moment.

"We're trying to warn people! They won't enter your home if you remain calm. They track things like fear and arousal."

Beads of sweat were starting to form on Sheila's forehead, and she was swaying a bit as she stood there, her breathing becoming more ragged.

"And...and what ...do...."

Her eyes rolled back and she fell against the van, sliding down the side, and dropping the microphone. Her body convulsed and she appeared to be having a seizure.

"Was she stung?!"

The other two men shook their heads and Hank tried to prop her up. Her body wasn't reacting as badly as a sting, and that was when he noticed the glob of stuff on her calf, already absorbing into her skin. *Her body must be reacting to the chemical in the venom without the paralysis,* he thought.. He really wished he could remember what Jeremiah had called it.

"You two need to get her to a hospital!"

Both men stood there without moving, their gaze fixed on the reporter.

"NOW!" Dragert boomed, surprising not only the two men, but Hank also. Dragert leaned in to help get her up, carried her to the back of the news van, and set her down. The other two men scrambled to the front doors, hopped in, and sped off without being told twice. Dragert turned to Hank.

"What are we gonna do? These things are overrunning the town and we've got no way to warn people."

"We need a goddamn miracle, John."

Instead of a miracle three of the creatures rounded the corner between their car and the two men, blocking their path. A low hiss emanated from the throat of one as they advanced. Hank pulled his revolver out, aimed, and pulled the trigger. A hollow click came from the gun and his heart sank like a stone.

"I'm empty. Get ready to run, Dragert."

"Shit. I am not in the shape or the mood for this."

Both men turned and bolted in opposite directions with one creature going after Dragert and two going after Hank. He found it grimly amusing that they'd go for the leaner man as opposed to the fatter one. As he turned a corner he saw an open dumpster and hoisted himself inside it before they could follow. If he was lucky, and kept quiet, they may run past. Maybe the smell of garbage would interfere with his scent.

He heard the clicking of their claws on the asphalt as they entered the alley and they both ran past the dumpster just as Hank had hoped. *Yes! I'm in the clear.* Then the clicks slowed, stopped, and started to advance slowly towards his hiding spot.

Doing his best to remain silent and calm, he hoped they were just going back to help the other one track down Dragert. As much as he disliked the man, he did hope he had gotten away. But the clicks stopped right in front of the dumpster and he heard a snort as one jumped onto the side of the dumpster and looked right at him.

"Fuck!!"

This is it he thought. This was how he was going to die. Defenseless and sitting in a pile of trash. The tail raised high and was about to dart down when a long piercing cry cut through the night. Immediately the lizarpion looked up, head turning in the direction the sound came from. The tail hovered in the air as though unsure if it should still strike or not.

"What are you waiting for?!"

Hank hated waiting. If it was going to kill him he wished it would just do it. But the thing looked down at him, snorted again, and then leapt off the dumpster. It took off with the other one, running in the direction of the cry, which sounded again. A few seconds later the third one ran past the entrance to the alleyway as well. What the hell were they all up to?

Dragert followed a moment later, his face flush as he gasped for breath.

"What the hell just happened?"

The other man held up a finger, signifying he needed a moment to catch his breath, before answering Hank. "Some sort of rally cry or some shit. I was sure I was a goner. It tackled me and was about to strike with that damned tail when it heard that cry. It just stopped and went running. Looks like you had a similar experience."

"Yeah. This can't be good. We need to find out what the fuck is going on, right now. Could be the key to ending all this."

"Alright. You smell like shit, by the way."

"And you look like it. Give me my phone."

Taking the device from Dragert, he dialed Julie's number and waited. When it went to voicemail, he frowned and tried again. On the third ring she picked up but she was barely audible.

"Julie? Are you there? Is everything alright?"

"Lizarpions are in the hospital, Hank. Jeremiah and I barely made it to my office. We're hiding under my desk right now."

Shit. He just sent that news crew off to their deaths. No time to feel guilty, though. He had to get to Julie out of there. "We'll be right there!!"

"No, don't. There are too many of them. Two of them were following us but they just left and we don't know why."

"I might."

Hank quickly relayed his story to Julie, making sure to emphasize the fact that the creatures left before attacking, even though they had the upper hand. There was no way he would have survived if they had ignored the call.

"Whatever it is, it's bad. We're going to try and follow them to find out what."

"Hold on, Jeremiah has a hypothesis."

There was a small shuffling sound on the phone as she handed it over. They must both be crammed under her desk, which was a small space to begin with. With the way these things track, it was probably more for comfort than hiding.

"Did you see the one making the call?"

"No, just heard it."

"I've been thinking a lot about the sex of these creatures."

"Hell of a thing to think about in a time of crisis, Jeremiah."

"No, no! Not *having* sex, their gender! It didn't occur to me before, but so far they've all looked almost identical. Dark coloring, similar shape and size...at first I thought they were a species that was more difficult to determine gender. But, when you brought up the cry, just now, it made me wonder if the ones we've been seeing are actually all males."

"….You don't mean that was some sort of goddamn mating call do you??"

Dragert's eyebrows shot up at Hank's question and he gave a low whistle.

"It very well could be. If there is only one breeding female in the group it could be that they are matriarchal in nature and answer to her. Remember the one you shot in the forest? It was both larger and a lighter color than the rest. It also only attacked for hormones."

"Now every horny one of those goddamn things is running for her."

Hank's mind raced. There had to be a way to exploit this, to try and defeat these things once and for all.

"You two hang tight. I'll call you in a few. Right now, I've got to come up with a plan." He hung up the phone and headed back to the car calling to Dragert over his shoulder. "You may be able to atone for your past sins, John. Just tell me you've got the key to the armory."

"Never leave home without it. Why?"

"We're gonna go bag us a queen."

XIX

Even as Hank spoke his plan aloud it sounded like something out of an action movie. They would see if they could find where those things were congregating at, capture the queen, and drive her back to one of the old warehouses down in the industrial district. They would trap her and the rest inside, torch the place, and be done with it once and for all.

"Two things, Hank. First off: how the hell do we find out where she is?"

"Every so often you see one of the fuckers running toward something. We just need to follow one. He'll lead us to her."

"Alright, logical enough. Second problem is, how do we get close enough to capture her, alive I might add, without all her boy toys ripping us to shreds?!"

"It needs work, I admit."

Dragert scoffed loudly and shook his head. "I'm in. God help me I'm in."

"Didn't give you a choice."

Turning sharply he drove into the station's parking lot. Tires squealed as he slammed on the brakes and hopped out. Both men jogged up to the door, ripped it open, and were actually glad to find it a ghost town.

"Glad to see these fools are actually out doing their jobs."

"We hope. Come on, we need to go shopping."

The armory was a bit of a misnomer for what they had locked in the small supply room towards the back of the station. It held a number of munitions, but really nothing that could wage war against the creatures. At best they could keep them at bay for a little while.

Hank looked over the selection. There were several shotguns and rifles, a dozen or so handguns, a few revolvers, and plenty of ammunition for all of it. What caught his eye though, and helped him form a more concrete plan, was the box for a multiple grenade launcher tucked almost out of sight.

"When the hell did we get this?!"

He leaned down and pulled the case out to the middle of the floor. Popping open the crate, he regarded the weapon with an almost child-like reverence.

"This is military issue, John. How did we end up with one?"

"I called in a few favors. Remember when we had those hippies protesting the logging up north, and we had about two hundred of them camping out?"

"Yeah. We managed to get them to disperse legally and without incident when the company agreed to several of their demands for better logging practices."

"Well, at one point that seemed a pipe dream. So I got this baby shipped to us with several flashbangs and some tear gas. We never used it and, honestly, I forgot about it. It's useless right now, though. Nothing lethal. All crowd-control ordinance."

"You saw how those things scattered at just the sound of those grenades you tossed up their asses. This might work very, very well. Plus, Jeremiah said they're nocturnal. If their eyes are sensitive enough we might be able to blind them with the flashbangs and give ourselves time to grab the bitch."

Dragert got quiet and he seemed to be mulling everything over. Maybe even convincing himself it was their only shot. At least that was what Hank hoped, as he grabbed the case and placed it on the counter.

"What's on your mind, John? Think it has a shot?"

"Maybe. With this stuff we have a shot to confuse and disorient them long enough to get in there and grab her. If we find them. If she's even there. If we can get close enough. If. If. If. A lot of variables in this, and a lot of room for it to go tits up and takes us down with it."

Hank nodded, reaching over and grabbing a shotgun. He started to load it with buckshot rounds. As much as he trusted his revolver, they'd need all the stopping power they could get.

"It's crazy, and we'll probably be killed, but it's either this or the town becomes their new feeding and fucking grounds."

Dragert got a funny grin on his face as he grabbed a shotgun of his own and loaded it. Not saying a word, he grabbed a second shotgun and did the same, as well as a bandolier, which he filled with more rounds. Looping the straps of the shotguns around his arms and over his shoulders, he positioned them like swords on his back.

Hank smirked and stifled a laugh. "You look ridiculous."

"Feel pretty damn good though."

"Can you even fucking move in that getup?"

Dragert twisted his torso, and Hank could only laugh. It was obvious that the two guns and bandolier around his chest were restricting his movements a good deal. Hank Helped the other man remove one of the shotguns. Then Dragert grabbed a small snub nose pistol.

"That isn't police issue, John. What the hell is it doing in the armory?"

"It was confiscated from a case as evidence, and then turned over to the department after the fact. I always felt they were neat little guns."

"That ain't gonna do shit against them, John. Put it back."

Shrugging, Dragert slipped it into his boot. "Never know when you might need it." They then grabbed the rest of their equipment and headed back to the car.

"Got your cuffs?"

"Yeah, why?"

"We don't have a cage for this thing, so I figure we can cuff its hands and feet, and maybe even cuff it's tail to a leg or something."

"Good luck with that. You think I'm going anywhere near one of those tails after tonight, you're crazy."

"We'll figure it out when we need to."

Hank popped the trunk of the car and was about to load the weapons in, when he looked across the parking lot and saw a truck.

"John, whose truck is that?"

"Dunno. Been parked here since...shit, you don't think it's Wilk's do you?"

"Hard to say. I can't remember what car he drove. His wife never said anything?"

"She was too upset about how he died."

"Fair enough. Come on. Let's see if we get lucky with the keys."

Moving quickly, Hank ran over to the driver's side of the vehicle and tried the door. It was locked. A second later he heard the sound of glass shattering as Dragert busted in the passenger side window.

"The hell do you think you're doing?!"

"I can see the keys. I'm getting us in! Since someone locked the keys inside it's no wonder it's been sitting out here. Their fuck up is our gain."

He unlocked the door, brushed the pebbles of glass off the seat as best he could, and reached over to grab the keys from the ignition. By the time he hopped in, Hank had loaded the grenade launcher onto the truck bed along with the extra items they had grabbed. Getting into the truck Hank started the engine and was pleased to see the tank was half full. More than enough to get the job done.

"If this doesn't work I want you to know something, John."

"Been an honor working with you, too, Hank."

"No...I just want you to know you were a lousy sheriff."

Hank smirked as Dragert laid into him with a string of curses, then he put the engine into drive and pulled out onto the road.

***

Things weren't looking good. It had been at least fifteen minutes since they last saw any of the lizarpions and their window of opportunity was closing quickly. If they didn't find a way to locate the female, their plan would be a bust and the town would be over and done. As they drove through the residential area they noticed some of the populace trying their best to escape.

Some drove in cars that zoomed past their truck and others ran on foot through the roads to get to safety. Hank and Dragert both decided that going in the direction everyone was feeling from was probably their best chance of finding where the males were all headed.

Just when it seemed like they had screwed up by taking too much time to arm themselves, Hank noticed one creature moving parallel to the truck. Slowing down and killing the lights, he watched as it went down the street, turned left, and disappeared.

"Got you now, you horny little fuckers."

Following after it, Hank and Dragert were unprepared for what lay before them. About halfway down the road, thirty or forty of the creatures milled around in front of a house. It wasn't their numbers that was strange, though; it was what they were doing.

Several had grouped off and were attacking one another. When one fell, another went in to challenge the victor. Some just idly stood about, snapping at one another. Dragert vocalized what was going through Hank's mind. "Jesus. They really wanna fuck, don't they?"

"Don't we all?"

"Yeah, but I'm not about to behead a guy just to lay some pipe. This is insane. How are we even gonna get close to that place?"

They hadn't been noticed yet, so Hank quickly pulled into a driveway, next to a minivan, and killed the engine. They waited a few moments before exiting the truck and took care not to slam their doors. Both men spoke in a strained whisper.

"Stay calm. They might wanna fuck but there's nothing saying that they won't come looking for a late night snack."

"You never answered me, Hank. How the fuck are we gonna get past that mob?"

"Flashbangs."

"Won't that spook her, too?"

"If she's making a roost, my guess is that she's not about to give it up without a fight. We'll start with the flashbangs, and follow up with the tear gas."

"You're guessing she's inside?"

Hank peeked out from their hiding spot behind the minivan and scanned the group of lizarpions. As far as he could tell under the porch lights and street lamps they were all smaller and darker. Male.

"If she's not outside she has to be inside. No reason for them all to gather here like this if she's not in there and in heat."

"This is suicide."

"Only if we die. You good, John?"

"Yeah. If I die, promise me you'll let my wife know I'm sorry."

Hank glanced over at Dragert and shook his head. "Just tell her yourself."

"Shut up you old fart and promise me. You've got speed, I've got weight. If it comes down to a run, you need to use my death as a distraction. Got it?"

Hank turned to look at him, and for once saw a degree of conviction he hadn't seen on Dragert's face since they first started working together. He gave a swift nod. "Alright. Better not fuck anything up then."

Dragert nodded in return, and Hank gripped the stock of the grenade launcher. The directions for its use had seemed fairly self-explanatory. He'd never actually fired one, but he hoped it was as easy as it looked. Clicking the safety off, he took a quick breath and ran out into the middle of the street. Taking aim at the largest cluster of bickering males, he let loose one round and then quickly aimed at a closer group, fired again and then looked away to avoid the flash.

Flashbangs were quite aptly named. Hank had never used one of those either, but the explosion caused the whole street to light up like it was midday. Even though he was some distance from the initial blast, the sound it produced was enough to make his ears ring.

It had the desired effect. Lizarpions scattered immediately, suddenly forgetting about the whole reason they had come here in the first place. Hank thought they might even get away without having to use the tear gas.

"Come on!" he yelled back to where Dragert was providing cover, and both men moved in closer to the house. A couple stragglers noticed the two, hissed, and leaped toward the men. That's when Dragert took advantage with his shotgun.

The first blast tore an arm clean off one creature. It spun from the force of the blow and fell, struggling to get up as it bled out on the ground. The second caught one in the face, which all but destroyed its snout. Before it could utter a sound, another shot ripped its throat apart.

Dragert is one hell of a shot, Hank thought, as he aimed right at the front of the house. Letting loose his third grenade, it smashed through the front window and, a few seconds later, gave off the same loud noise and blinding light. Several creatures ran out the front door and, thankfully, none of them looked to be their quarry.

"We need to get in there! Cover me!"

Hank rushed inside the house and dropped to one knee, ready to shoot a flashbang into the face of anything still in the house. The foyer and living room were empty, but he didn't have time go through every room looking for the female. Thinking quickly, he tried to deduce where she might be.

When they first encountered her in the woods she dropped down on them from a tree. The feeling in his gut told him she liked being up high. Upstairs. Fifty-fifty chance he was right and he always did favor the high road. Taking the steps two at a time he raised an eyebrow at the rose petals everywhere.

Dragert was right on his six, covering the way they'd just come. If any came back too soon he hoped they had enough ammo to keep them at bay. They could've tried to kill them all in the street but there was still the chance of most escaping back to where they came from. They had to kill as many as possible at once, and be sure about it.

At the top of the stairs his gut told him to follow the petals. If it had attacked whoever laid them down then dimes to dollars they were in the bedroom. Moving quickly but cautiously he held up the grenade launcher and kicked the door open fully. He gagged.

On the bed was the female, presenting. It wasn't the most attractive thing in the world, but what caused him to gag, and then Dragert to blanch, was what she was presenting on. A mass of human bodies, some picked clean and others still fairly meaty, had been cobbled together to make a crude nest.

Not being mounted immediately, she must have sensed that something was off, and she turned. Seeing Hank and Dragert there she let loose a shrill cry, one they'd not heard from any of the creatures so far. It was immediately answered by a few more that sounded similar.

"We're gonna have company!" Dragert yelled as Hank aimed the launcher near the creature. Firing, he yelled, "Get back!" just before ducking out into the hallway and slamming the door behind him as the grenade went off. Even with the door between them and the explosion, both men were stricken deaf, and the female freaked out immediately, her ruined tail thrashing wildly and spurting out toxin as it did.

Opening the door, Hank wondered how they were going to get her out of here with her thrashing like that. It was far too risky to get close to her, but they had no choice. Any moment the males would come back to protect her, judging from their cries, and they only had one shot to get this to work.

It turned out he didn't need to get close to subdue her. In her panic and fright she jumped off the bed and right out the window. Shards of glass cut into her skin as she sailed through the air. A moment later there was a thud and a crunch and Hank looked down, fearing the worst.

Thankfully, the female was not dead. She had managed to land on another one of the creatures. It broke her fall, but was killed on impact. That solved how to get her out of the room.

Bounding out of the house and heading towards her, Hank saw a few of the males approaching and commanded Dragert, "Keep them off me while I cuff her!"

Unsure at first if the other man heard him, Hank's fears were allayed when Dragert's response was to fire at one that got too close. The buckshot was tearing through the bodies of the creatures like they were made of nothing more than paper. Whenever one fell, the others backed off a bit. Seemed they were beginning to learn that humans with guns were dangerous.

The female cried out in pain again which made the males hiss their displeasure. They began to advance again, despite their reservations.

"Hurry it up, Hank!!"

Hank's hands were shaking a bit as he approached the female. Thankfully her tail wasn't a spike anymore but it was still just as deadly. Her legs were kicking wildly and she still hadn't managed to right herself. Getting a good look, Hank guessed that one leg was broken. Readying the cuffs, he grabbed onto one leg, slapped them down, and then did the same to the other while they were still close to one another.

This caused her to kick her legs even more and Hank couldn't get close to her hands or her tail. Gritting his teeth he hoped this wouldn't kill her as he hit her with the butt of the grenade launcher. The force knocked her out cold but also caused the gun to go off, firing a flashbang into the night.

It went off before he could try to warn Dragert, blinding both men as well as the creatures in the immediate area. They were both still somewhat deaf from being so close to the last explosion so they only felt the sound from this blast. The light was another matter.

Even with the grenade being twenty or thirty feet up in the air, it was like looking directly into the sun. Hank shut his eyes tightly to block out the sudden brightness and blinked repeatedly to try and restore his sight.

Panic began to set in when his vision remained hazy and he couldn't make anything out clearly. Was that Dragert, or a creature advancing towards him? Where did the female go? He was dumb, deaf and blind, stumbling in the street like a drunk. Part of him wished he'd died in the dumpster if this was how he was going to bite it. At least then he knew it was coming; knew what to expect.

Taking a chance, he closed his eyes and counted to ten, praying the creatures were far more affected than he was. They had night vision, and worked on primal instinct. He didn't have superior vision but he had reason and logic on his side. Opening his eyes again, he breathed a sigh of relief. His vision was better. It wasn't perfect yet, but he could make things out. He had one hell of a headache, too.

The female was still on the ground, thrashing about and carrying on. He could barely hear her screeches as he moved towards Dragert, who was bent over and vomiting. Poor bastard had gotten the worst of it. Hank put a hand on his shoulder and Dragert spun around and fired his shotgun.

If Hank had been standing on the man's left side, he would have been shot at point blank range and died right there, within seconds. Knocking the gun out of Dragert's hand and grabbing the man by the shoulders, Hank tried to get him to listen.

"DRAGERT! JOHN! IT'S HANK!!"

The other man blinked furiously, yelling back in a voice barely audible to Hank, "HANK?! THE FUCK HAPPENED??"

"GRENADE WENT OFF. WE NEED TO LEAVE. NOW!!"

Almost all the creatures nearby had been affected by the grenade. Hank hadn't realized how powerful they were in close quarters and suddenly he had doubts about his master plan. He'd intended to toss the queen in the truck bed, drive through town leading the males to a warehouse, and lock them inside to pick off easily.

How the hell was that going to work, now that he had blinded and deafened nearly all of them? This is what he got for not thinking things through fully. Should've just gone in, guns blazing. Could have probably taken out the mob in one shot, then and there.

Dragert was stumbling like Hank had been and he tried to stand only to fall back on his ass. Hank grabbed him by the arm and hoisted him up. As time passed his vision started to get back to normal and his hearing was getting better. Dragert had blood seeping from his ears and they both probably had permanent hearing loss now. *Smooth move, Hank.*

Pushing Dragert in the direction of the truck, Hank went back to the female. She'd stopped thrashing and now looked like she might die from the blood loss. He was easily able to finish cuffing her extremities, and he began to drag her towards the truck. Moving her must have caused a great amount of pain though, because she started up again with the squawking and honking. Before he could get her into the back of the truck four males appeared at the end of the street.

Unfortunately, these ones didn't appear blind or deaf. Dragert was leaning against the side of the truck, his eyes shut tightly, and Hank grabbed him.

"Help me get her in here!"

Dragert slowly opened his eyes, looked at Hank, then to the creature, and wearily nodded his head. Dropping the tailgate, both men hoisted her up, being careful to not get the toxin on their skin or get cut by her claws when she began to thrash again. Slamming the tailgate shut, Hank hopped into the driver's seat and Dragert joined him as he brought the truck to life and gunned the engine.

Glancing over to see why the four males hadn't attacked he saw a small group of people that had come out of their homes to see what the explosions were. Two were already dead and another was running screaming back into the house. There was nothing he could do for them, aside from seeing the plan through.

Throwing it into reverse, he slammed into a trashcan at the end of the driveway, as well as a fifth male they hadn't noticed before. The tires made short work of it. They felt the bump of reversing over its body, and then again as they accelerated forward out of the cul de sac they'd found themselves in.

"Good god, we made it."

"What?!"

"I SAID, WE MADE IT!!"

"SHE MATED? WE CAN'T LET HER LAY THOSE EGGS!!"

Whatever, thought Hank. The important thing now was to try and round up the males. If he was right, then they had really fucked things up with those flashbangs

***

Julie had no idea how much time had passed since they last talked to Hank. He had said something about a plan, that he would call back, and then hung up. However long it may have actually been it felt like hours, cramped up next to Jeremiah, under her desk.

She wasn't entirely sure why neither of them had moved from their hiding spot. They both knew the creatures could detect pheromones and had superior night vision. If they were still truly being hunted one would have found them by now. She guessed there was just something reassuring about hiding. Comforting even.

As comforting as it was though, she'd had enough. Whispering quietly, she spoke to Jeremiah and she began to move, her joints aching from being stuck at an odd angle for such a long time."We need to get out of here. Those things are gone."

"We don't know that!" His reply came out as a panicked hiss

"Fine, stay here. I need to move."

Halfway out from under the desk she felt and heard a vibration and nearly had a heart attack. She was so intent on listening for any sign of the lizarpions that she'd forgotten her phone was still in her hand. The glare of the screen was bright, causing her to wince as she looked to see who was calling. She answered it quickly

"Hank!"

"You two still sitting tight?"

"Yeah, we were about to move, though. How did the plan go?"

"Good. And not so good."

Julie bit her lip as Hank explained to her first his idea, and then how everything went. She had put the phone on speaker so Jeremiah could listen as well. He was shaking his head by the end of it.

"You ruined any chance you had at luring them. You might get five or ten but the whole group? They've scattered and are licking their wounds so to speak. It could be hours before they recover enough to go find her."

Hank's voice boomed through the phone, causing Julie to lower the volume. It was highly unlikely one was still around, but she didn't want to take a chance.

"We don't have hours! She's going to be dead soon and we need to lure the males so we can kill them all!"

Jeremiah looked deep in thought for a moment, and then his eyes went wide. "She's in heat and is producing a large amount of pheromones. Those, coupled with her mating calls, are what got every male in the area to come to her. If we can concentrate that scent, we might be able to lure them in despite themselves."

"Make them so horny that god himself couldn't stop them?" Julie chimed in, a smirk on her face as she got what Jeremiah was getting it.

"Exactly. Problem is we don't have the equipment here. Everything is back at the University, and that's a good forty minutes out of town, even if you were speeding. We would also need time to isolate exactly what the chemical makeup of her sex scent was so we could duplicate and enhance it."

"Like I said, we don't have time. She fell out of a second story window and is fading, fast. There has to be something we can do right now!"

Jeremiah furrowed his brow, and Julie couldn't help but bite her lower lip. She was glad Hank was ok, but his plan could have been thought through a little better. If he had told the two of them, they might've been able to offer some insight. In any case, it wasn't like she and Jeremiah were doing anything to help the situation by hiding out in her dark office.

A light bulb went off in her head and she couldn't help but giggle a little at the notion. It was a gross idea but might be their only option. "Um, Jeremiah."

"Yes?"

"What if she were stimulated?"

"What do you mean?"

"What if she were stimulated...sexually? Would that cause her to produce the scent the males would follow? Even if they were deaf and mostly blind?"

The look Jeremiah gave her was a cross between utter disgust and downright confusion. She had never had anyone look at her like that before and she couldn't help but stifle a giggle fit. It was life and death out there, and here she was thinking about helping a lizard masturbate.

"Tell me you aren't fucking serious." Dragert's voice sounded very much like Jeremiah's face looked.

"Would it work?"

"Maybe? They have a huge vomeronasal organ, so they would be able to pick up the scent easily enough if you drive around town with her. If she were stimulated enough it could possibly lure the males, even the wounded ones."

"Julie, we're not going to...*stimulate* the queen!!"

"You're the ones who blinded all the males! You wanted ideas and I gave you one."

"...we'll call you back."

The line went dead and Julie finished pulling herself out from under the desk. Letting her eyes adjust to the darkness for a moment, she moved over to the light switch on the wall. Glancing out the window of her office she saw a thin sliver of light coming from the door between the morgue and the hallway. It did little to light up the room outside the office.

"Do you really think it will work, or did I just goad them into doing unmentionable acts with the queen?"

She could hear shuffling as Jeremiah also pulled himself out from under the desk. A second later she heard him bump into something and curse.

"Shit!.....uh, yes actually. If they got her worked up enough, it could send the males into a frenzy. Even wounded, they'd be compelled to follow. But it's still a *huge* long shot. We may miss a few, but without a female to breed with at least we'd stop the population from increasing."

Julie couldn't help but laugh to herself again as the image of Hank and Dragert and the lizarpion popped into her head. Man, that'd be a story. *We saved the town by helping a lizard get off!*

Shaking her head and satisfied they were finally alone, she clicked on the lights causing both her and Jeremiah to blink reflexively at the sudden change in brightness. Turning to open the door of her office and finally get out of there, her breath caught in her throat. Across the way, under one of her examining tables, were the two creatures they thought had left earlier, sleeping.

XX

"I thought they left!" Jeremiah hissed as she quickly turned off the lights again and ducked down behind the door. Thankfully, they didn't appear to be waking up.

"So did I! They must have given up searching for us and took a nap. I don't know! All I know is that we need to get through them to get out of here!"

"Let's just wait for Hank. They're sleeping and we're safe in here."

"Until they wake up and start to look again! They're nocturnal, or have you forgotten? No telling how long they'll be asleep and when they do wake up, they're gonna be hungry. The window on this office kept out a baby, but it's gonna do shit-fuck-all for two grown ones!"

She couldn't see the look on Jeremiah's face but she had a feeling that he knew she was right. If they waited for help to arrive there was a good chance the things would wake up anyway. If they got even a whiff of their scent they could easily break into the office. Suddenly her comforting hiding spot felt more like a coffin.

"We need to either find a way past them or kill them before they have a chance to react. The hall door is still open so we could make a break for it and slam it behind us, trapping them."

Jeremiah moved slowly towards the door and peeked over. Very little of the light from the main door filtered through, but Julie's eyes had adjusted enough she could see his head move in a nod.

"We don't have any weapons, but if we move quickly we can get out the door before they get up. I think."

She could hear him start to twist the knob and reached out to grab his arm, fumbling around for a moment before latching on and squeezing hard. Leaning in she spat out, "Are you crazy?! I'm not ready!"

He held his position and slowly let the knob return to its default position, then stood and helped her up. Looking out into the morgue she wished she could see the lizards under the table, but it was completely black.

"Maybe we should turn on the lights in here. That way we're not totally blind. They can see at night anyway, right?"

"It could wake them!"

"Knocking something onto the floor because we're going for the door like a couple of blind people will too!"

"...Fine. Do it. But we need to be quick. Just make a beeline for the door."

Flipping the switch, the fluorescent lights flickered for a few moments before humming back to life. Julie looked out the window and saw the two lizards still curled up and sleeping. Giving Jeremiah a nod, he began to open the door again. Once he had turned the knob all the way around, he held it for a moment before slowly pulling the door open.

The creak was loud and he immediately froze. One of the creatures stirred and Julie knew they'd only have seconds to react. Grabbing onto the partially open door, she swung it wide and made a break for it. If she lived through this she was going to empty an entire can of lubricant on those hinges.

The door didn't stop creaking until it was open fully, and now both lizarpion heads bolted up, searching for the source. Locking their gaze onto Julie and Jeremiah, the right one gave a short, two-squawk call and sprang up.

"RUN!" Julie screamed as she darted between the tables to the door, hoping Jeremiah wasn't far behind.

Five feet from the door one darted in front of her with its jaws snapping. Skidding to a stop, she actually fell over and landed in a heap on the floor next to it, barely missing the strike from its tail. Had she still been standing, she would be dead.

Jeremiah, who was right behind her, stumbled over her as she fell, and slammed right into the creature. It kicked at him with its hind legs, but the sudden force and weight were too much for it and she heard a satisfying crunch as Jeremiah landed. Both its legs were broken.

"Shit! SHIT!" Jeremiah cried out as he rolled away from it. It was thrashing about, squealing in pain, as its ruined legs wobbled to and fro. In defense, the tail lashed out, trying to attack anything and everything in reach. Its partner managed to get too close and got stung by accident which immediately caused it to turn on the wounded one.

While the two fought, Julie grabbed Jeremiah's arm and pulled him up. She bolted the last few feet to the door, slamming all of her weight into it and causing it to fly open. Eyes wildly scanning the hallway, she was glad to find it empty, and turned to make sure Jeremiah got out too.

He was seconds behind her and about to exit the morgue into the freedom and safety of the hallway when a third creature tackled him. How could they have missed one?!

"NO!" She screamed and ran back into the room, turning in the direction that the two had tumbled. Jeremiah had managed to grab the tail in one hand, aiming it to the side as white toxin spurted from the tip.

"Get it off, GET IT OFF!!"

The hind legs were kicking him, and were shredding his pants. Julie acted purely on instinct and kicked it as hard as she could. She felt something pop against her foot. The creature howled in pain as it flew off Jeremiah and landed motionless in a heap.

"Can you run?!"

"Yes! GO!"

They were both on their feet again and now had just one more of the things to deal with. It had either won the fight with the wounded one or gotten bored as it turned to them with its jaws dripping crimson.

This was the only thing standing between their death and freedom and Julie would be damned if she was going to let this creature stop her. Grabbing for something, anything, on the table next to her, she came back with a bone saw. Not exactly what she was hoping for but it would do.

The creature hesitated, at seeing her armed, and cocked its head. It looked at her, then Jeremiah, then her weapon, and then back to her. It gave a shrill noise before leaping towards her, and she swung with all her might.

The saw landed true, managing to tear through the skin of its belly despite the blunted edge, and she pulled as hard as she could. Blood and offal poured from the increasing wound and the thing shrieked once before falling silent. As it convulsed in its death throes she felt a stabbing pain in her shoulder. Looking to see if she'd been cut, was when she noticed the stinger, deeply embedded, and the bulbous growth at the base pulsing.

***

"You're not seriously going to finger-bang that fucking thing are you?!"

Dragert couldn't even believe it when it was first suggested. It didn't matter if it would work, it was beyond disgusting. There had to be another way. He breathed a sigh of relief as Hank agreed with him.

"Fuck, no! Do I look like some sort of deviant? We just need to hope her current state is enough."

He nodded in agreement, glad his hearing finally had returned.

"These things could hear her call all over town. Our hearing is pretty much back to normal, so I'm guessing theirs can't be far behind."

"What are you getting at, John?"

"She's in distress. She's already in heat and she's bleeding like a stuck pig. Combine that with her constant calls, she'd probably bring them in even faster."

"You think?"

"The only piece of ass in miles is dying and you don't think they're gonna come running? It's gotta work! It's all we got left!"

"Except she hasn't said a word in a while. She dead?"

Dragert hoped not as he looked out the window to the truck bed. She wasn't dead, as he could see her chest rise and fall, but she wasn't going to be alive much longer.

"Stop the car."

Hank pulled the truck to a stop, glancing around for any more of those things. People had been coming out of their homes earlier but either they'd already been killed or they'd gotten wise and were staying indoors now. Dragert opened the door and got out, heading to the back.

"John! What the hell are you doing?"

"Plan B. I'm gonna stimulate her, but not how you think."

Hank shot him a worried glance, but turned around and started the truck up again. Dragert lost his balance a little as the truck shifted, and wobbled his way to the female's head. Her eyes were half-closed and her breathing was shallow. Part of him felt bad about what he was going to do, but it was their only shot.

Grabbing one of her arms, still in the cuffs, he held it up and aimed with the shotgun. Hesitating for a second, he looked down at the creature again and closed his eyes. He thought of everyone who had lost their lives because he had been a coward and didn't deal with this properly from the start. *How many more people are going to die because of my mistake?*

Without hesitating another moment, he pulled the trigger. It severed the arm at the elbow, causing her to kick back to life immediately, her eyes going wide in pain. She opened her mouth and let loose the most hideous noise as she coughed and gasped for breath..

Torture wasn't really his thing, and he was hoping he hadn't just thrown the thing into agony for nothing, when the first reply came. Then more. Then a lot more. So many more that it actually frightened him, because every reply sounded like it was pissed that their queen was in danger.

All the males calling out in chorus sounded kind of like music and he could have almost enjoyed it, if not for the undertones of pure malice in the sounds. He made the mistake of taking his eyes off her as he looked out in the direction of the replies and she lunged forward with her neck and bit down into his calf.

"Fucking hell!!" He cried out and instinctively tried to pull back his leg, causing the razor sharp teeth to dig further into his flesh. Reaching back, he hit her twice on the snout, causing her to let go and cry out again.

He moved back out of her reach, being careful not to get near her tail, and inspected his wound. It felt like hell and looked even worse. Pulling off his belt he tied it hard around his leg, just below the knee, to try and help stop the bleeding. God, did it sting.

"Step on it, Hank....fucking step on it." He said to himself with a pained expression as the truck gained speed, heading towards the industrial part of town. They'd only get one shot at this, and if they fucked this one up, there wouldn't be any Plan C's.

***

"Oh god, oh god, oh god..." The words just came out, over and over again, as she looked at the tail pumping toxin into her system. There was no cure and there was no hope. In moments she would be paralyzed, and soon after that her heart would give out from stress.

Julie grabbed at the tail, ready to pull it out, when Jeremiah shouted at her.

"NO! Leave it in! Don't move!!"

"Wha...?"

She started to turn towards him, but he quickly stepped in front of her and grabbed her hands with his, gently removing them from the tail.

"It went all the way through. If you pull it out now the toxin coming out of the end will get into your bloodstream. We need to find a way to get it out without getting the wound contaminated."

Tears of joy and fear welled up in her eyes as both the good news and the bad news hit her. The stinger wasn't injecting toxin into her but there was no way to get it out without a huge risk of still being affected anyway.

"What the hell are we gonna do?"

"I have an idea, but you're not going to like it."

"It can't be any worse than having this thing jutting through my shoulder!"

Jeremiah looked at her and shrugged, shaking his head.

"Alright, that's a very valid point. We need to push it through."

"You're right, I don't fucking like it. Can't we just cut off the end and pull it out?!"

"Not without risking the toxin getting into your blood. If we cut right at the base of the venom sacs in the bulb, without puncturing them, I should be able to squeeze it down to a manageable size. The tail itself is only about an inch or two thick at this point, and the bulb is large but soft."

Without hesitation, Jeremiah took the bone saw from her and cut the tail free. Removing the excess weight that was pulling on her wound felt great, all things considered, but she had no idea how they were going to get the whole thing through a hole only about half an inch thick.

"There is literally no way that thing is going to fit Jeremiah! This isn't a goddamn arrow!"

"I know, believe me I know. I'm going to have to cut around where it punctured, on the other side, to make room."

"No. No fucking way! We can pull it out if you're careful. We are not pushing three to four inches of muscle and organs and bone through my shoulder. You need to pull it out as straight as you can, and then I won't be affected by the residual toxin at the tip."

Shaking his head violently, Jeremiah disagreed just as vehemently.

"Absolutely not! There's no way I can do that with an injured hand. The second I have a slight tremor and the tip touches you on the inside of that wound, you're dead."

"Guess I'm living with it then."

The joke was grim and neither laughed. This was not how she wanted to spend her night, this was not how she wanted to spend her week, and this was not how she wanted to die. The fact whether she lived or died was based on how carefully the stinger was removed infuriated her. Such a random, stupid thing.

"Fuck it." Grabbing onto the bulb, she gave a hard squeeze and felt fluid move under her fingers as it jettisoned out the end. "Clean off the excess as best you can."

Within seconds he had surgical gloves on and had a wad of gauze which he used to seep up as much of the toxin as he could. He then went over the area with an antiseptic wipe, hoping to pick up whatever he missed. Satisfied, he took the gauze, gloves and wipes and threw them into a hazardous materials bucket.

"Ok, so we're going to try and push it then?"

"Nope."

Bracing herself she grabbed the closest thing she could reach, a permanent marker, and put it between her teeth. Taking a moment to brace herself, she looked Jeremiah straight in the eyes, hoping he understood that if this didn't work it wasn't on him.

Thoughts turning to Hank, she hoped he was having an easier time of it as she bit down, tightening her grip on the tail piece. A final prayer, and she started to pull.

The pain as it was being pulled out was excruciating. Every instinct and nerve ending screamed at her to just yank with all her might. If she gave in to that wonderful idea, she risked twisting it as she pulled. Which in turn could cause the tip to rub against the walls of the wound. No. It had to be precise, and it had to be slow.

Seconds felt like hours as she continued the methodical extraction. The marker cracked and a few drops of ink leaked into her mouth, filling it with a sour taste. The damned thing was a poor substitute for a piece of wood. Were there barbs on this damn stinger? It looked smooth, but it felt like she was pulling sandpaper through the hole.

Please, she thought, *please let me live through this. Don't let me go through so much pain to fuck up at the end.*

Sweat formed on her brow and followed the channels of her skin down into her eyes. Blinking rapidly wasn't helping to clear them so she simply shut her eyes tight and kept pulling. As it started to become easier she had to concentrate even more to keep it straight and perpendicular to the wound. A moment later she felt nothing. Oh thank god...but was it out?

Her hand kept extending and extending for fear that if she let her guard down now it would be her end.

"You're done!"

Risking the chance of opening her eyes, she looked and saw the tip of the stinger was a good three inches from the wound. Letting go, it fell to the ground and a few final bits of fluid seeped out.

Bursting into tears, she grabbed onto Jeremiah and held him hard, sobbing into his shoulder, overcome with a torrent of emotion.

"It's alright. You did it."

After holding the embrace for a few long moments she finally pulled back, took in a deep breath, and let it out slowly. It felt wonderful that she was alive, despite the horrible pain in her shoulder. Gingerly pulling off her shirt she turned toward Jeremiah with a weary smile.

"Ok, let's get this cleaned up and go see if everyone else is alright."

"What about Hank and Dragert?"

"We've got a lot more people right here who need our help. Those two will be fine."

XXI

They had been driving around in residential areas for nearly twenty minutes as the female lay dieing in the back of the truck, trying to get as many of the males rounded up as they could. Hank knew Dragert had shot it again, but he wished she didn't have to be so goddamn vocal about it.

Keeping an even pace to not outdistance the males following them was easy enough. Right now a mob nearly as big, if not bigger than, the one from the house was about fifty feet behind them. Glancing in the rear view mirror, he saw several stumble. Fuckers were still blind, or close to it, it seemed.

Looking over to the edge of the mirror, he noticed that Dragert seemed to be doing about as well as the queen was. Reaching behind himself to unlatch the window, he slid it open a few inches and called out to him.

"You look like shit! You gonna be alright?"

"We need to get to the warehouse, Hank. Her cries are getting quieter and we're gonna lose the males."

Hank nodded his agreement. They'd just have to pray they got them all and that any they missed were easy to flush out. Pulling a hard right, he headed back into the center of town glad when a few more emerged from the woodwork to join the herd at their heels.

"That's right, you fuckers, come try and save her."

Stonesworth wasn't a huge town, but it wasn't a tiny one either. They had to cut through the downtown core to get to the industrial district. Turning to take a shortcut, he slammed on the breaks just before ramming into a firetruck.

"Why are we stopped, Hank? WHY ARE WE STOPPED?!"

"Shit, shit shit..." repeating himself over and over he shifted into reverse and backed up to maneuver around the fire truck. Counting the sidewalk, there was just enough room for the truck to squeeze by, but their lead on the herd was becoming razor thin.

"Get us out of here, goddammit!"

Giving it gas he jumped the truck up onto the curb and moved past the engine. He overestimated how much space he'd need on one side, and the crunch of metal filled his ears as sparks began to fly.

Once past that little annoyance of a roadblock, he continued on his path hopeful there wouldn't be any more delays. Another one like that would cost them their lives. Noticing a movement in the rear view mirror, he saw Dragert shifting his way towards the window.

"She's just about dead. Could shoot her again, but I doubt she'd even feel it, let alone cry out again like she did before. How much further?"

"Fuck...a good ten minutes or so."

"Better hope the leaders of the pack have excellent senses. Gonna need them to lead the rest into the trap."

Silence fell between them, the only sounds being the engine of the truck and the dying calls from the female. Dragert was the one to break the silence.

"Hank. How exactly are we going to trap them?"

"Remember that one cracker factory that shut down about seven years ago?"

"Yeah. About a third of the town lost their jobs."

"I've been in there since but they gutted the place of all the equipment. We should be able to drive right in and close the doors behind us.

"Sounds dumb as fuck, but we've made it this far. May as well see it through to the end."

"That's the spirit. Now hold on, I'm gonna try and speed up a bit to get there in time."

***

Blood and gore were everywhere when Jeremiah and Julie emerged from the hall, back into the main area of the hospital. It appeared no one had survived the initial attack and she rushed over to the doors to see if any more creatures were on their way.

Sirens blared in the distance and it actually filled her with hope; others had indeed survived, or at the very least she and Jeremiah weren't the only ones left in town. Moving quickly back to the main area, she tiptoed through the pools of blood and bodies and went right for the phone, picking it up and dialing 911.

The line was busy.

"Shit, of course it is."

"What is?"

"911 is busy, and I can't get through."

Walking around the side of the desk, she began to search for a phone book but thanked her luck when she saw an emergency contacts sheet near where the phone had been on the desk. One of the numbers was for a local branch of the state troopers. Dialing it into the phone, she waited anxiously, wondering how she was going to explain all this without sounding crazy.

"Thank you for calling the Wisconsin State Police. If this is an emergency, please hang up and dial 911. Otherwise, please stay on the line, our options have changed."

Rubbing the bridge of her nose between two fingers, she shut her eyes tight and sighed deeply.

"A fucking machine. Perfect."

***

"Finally, we're here!" Looking behind him, Hank was glad the herd of males had remained on their tail and even added more to their ranks. Hazarding a guess, he figured there were fifty or sixty of the damn things all thundering towards them. Jumping out of the truck, he rushed over to the sliding bay door and gave it a yank.

It didn't budge.

"The hell?"

Trying again, he gave it a good hard yank and it still didn't lift more than an inch. Limping over to see what was the hold up, Dragert came around the side of the truck. This was the first time Hank noticed that his lower leg was covered in blood and that the man looked rather pale.

"You've seen better days."

"We both have, you sorry son of a bitch. Why aren't we inside yet?!"

Even weakened, he still had some bite to his bark. Hank turned to look at the door and noticed a brand new padlock where there hadn't been one a year ago.

"Of all the times for them to finally lock this place up." Glancing behind the truck his gut sank and he thought he might piss himself. The males were closing in quickly and they had maybe half a minute before becoming a late night snack.

Not saying a word, Dragert spit on the ground, emptied the chamber of his shotgun, and reached into his pocket to reload it with slug rounds. Waddling over he placed the end of the barrel right against the lock and pulled the trigger.

The lock broke into two pieces but still held together. Another blast from the shotgun and the fragmented metal bits went flying and he reached to rip the rest off, cursing as he burned his fingers.

Wasting no time, Hank whipped the door open and ran back to the truck. "Get in here!!"

Dragert barely made it to the truck. One of the males jumped into the truck bed and sniffed the female. Pushing at her limp body with its snout, it tried to rouse her but to no avail. Not even waiting for the door to shut Hank hit the gas, causing the male to fall out of the bed of the truck.

Quickly righting itself, it gave a mournful cry and darted after them. Good, Hank thought looking in the mirror behind them. Vengeance can be just as powerful of a motivator as sex.

Heading onto the main factory floor Hank started to run over boxes and tents and for a few brief moments panicked that he was running over squatters. After a few seconds without screams, it seemed the homeless shanty town was empty.

"Explains the padlock."

Coughing in fits, Dragert seemed like he had lost too much blood.

"We need to get you to a hospital."

"Fuck that. We need to see this through. What's the next stage?"

"Stage?"

"Yeah, how are we gonna kill them once we double back around to lock them in."

"I...don't know."

"...of fucking course not. You got shit for brains, Hank!"

Slamming his fist against the dash, the glove compartment popped open and a bottle of vodka rolled out and into Dragert's lap. He got a wide grin on his face as he popped the top.

"You're in rough shape. Should you be drinking that?"

"If I'm gonna die, it's gonna be drunk. Fuck it."

Now was not the time to demonize him, or preach at him for his alcoholism. But, seeing the liquor caused him to develop an idea.

"Molotov! We need to make that bottle into a Molotov cocktail. Look at this place! It's a fire waiting to happen. We can set one off then hightail it out of here and shut the door behind us, making sure none of these bastards follow us out. Have an old fashioned barbecue."

Taking another swig of the bottle, Dragert belched and nodded. "Might actually work. We could-LOOK OUT!."

Focusing on the path ahead of them again, Hank barely missed a larger 'house' constructed right in their path that almost blended in with the surroundings. Splinters of wood flew everywhere and he heard the sound of a tire blowing out. The truck went into a spin, and then skidded to a stop right against a set of stairs at the far end of the warehouse.

"After this is over with I'm revoking your license."

"You can revoke whatever the fuck you want, just get out! We gotta move!"

Pushing against his door he saw that the creatures were almost on top of them. Dragert's door was stuck, so, without thinking, Hank grabbed him and pulled him out through his side and ran up the stairs, practically dragging him along. There was a factory supervisor's office at the top of the steps. Pushing Dragert inside, Hank slammed the door shut behind them just as one of the lizarpions jumped after them, hitting the door with a thud.

Looking around in a panic, Hank realized they were trapped.

***

Things at the hospital were starting to improve. Instead of directing incoming patients through the destroyed ER, they sent them to the main entrance and set up a triage with the surviving doctors and nurses. What was really making her feel secure though, was the police presence.

Convincing the officer on the other end of the line, after spending god knows how long navigating the archaic phone system, wasn't easy. She knew she was incredibly fortunate he didn't just hang up, mostly because another officer came to grab him after seeing some footage on the news of one of the reporters being attacked. They sent a patrol to check it out, and seeing the bloodbath in the hospital was all the proof they needed.

There weren't many people coming in, and that worried Julie. Trying to put the thought of how many were dead to the back of her mind, she convinced herself there weren't that many because they were all still safe at home.

Yep, that was it. Not dead or dying, but still asleep in bed tonight. It was a weak excuse, but there had to be at least a kernel of truth to it. Jeremiah was sitting with his head between his knees. Since Julie was a doctor she'd done all she could to help those who came in before more could take over and tell her to rest due to her injuries. Thankful for the respite, she made her way over to the man, and plopped down beside him.

He barely looked up to acknowledge her. "Is it over? Like, *really* over?"

"I dunno. Haven't heard from Hank, and every time I try to call him it goes right to voice mail. I've got a bad feeling, but at least *we* are out of the woods."

A weak nod and smile was his reply. Julie's worry must have shown, despite her best attempts at hiding it, because Jeremiah's expression softened to one of concern.

"He'll be fine, Julie. I may not know him that well, but he's resourceful and can think on his feet. He also is a lot stronger than I think even he realizes. Try not to fret. Besides, he owes you dinner. It'd be rude to cancel that on account of death."

Despite how she was feeling at the moment, that got a small smile and a soft chuckle out of her. "Would be a shame if I didn't get a free mediocre meal out of all this."

Turning away and looking forward, Jeremiah nodded and smiled. Julie had a good feeling about everything now, and was glad that at least the town was safe. Not normally a religious woman, she bowed her head, closed her eyes, and said a little prayer for Hank. After she finished, she looked up and an odd thought suddenly entered her head.

"Is Andrew alright?"

*****

Walking slowly away from the door, Hank hoped it would hold. Built solid and out of what he thought was steel, there were no windows, except a small two way mirror on the wall next to it. Thankfully, that seemed to confuse the creatures into thinking it was more of the mob instead of another means of entry.

Risking taking his eyes from the door, he turned to Dragert. Fading fast was an understatement; his skin was a pallid color and his breathing was short and shallow. Too much blood loss, and if they didn't get him to the hospital soon there was no way he'd survive.

"Be honest...how bad is it?"

"You look fine to me. Just a flesh wound, really."

"You lying sack of shit."

A smile crossed his lips as he began to cough violently. Hank wondered if there was some sort of venom or bacteria in the bite. There was some sort of lizard he'd read about whose mouth was so dirty the bite was practically toxic. Blood loss alone wouldn't account for how rapidly Dragert's health had deteriorated.

"We need to find a way out of here. The door's still open and the only thing keeping them inside is the fact that we killed the queen and they know exactly where we are."

Scanning the room for an alternate entrance, or, hopefully, a fire exit, he frowned as he saw nothing. It was just a glorified box at the top of a set of steel stairs used to look out over the factory workers as they toiled away.

"I already took a glance around. Judging from the look on your face, you've come to the same conclusion. We are truly and royally fucked."

Arguing the fact was pointless. Managing to lure the creatures out of the populated residential area wouldn't mean shit if they couldn't keep them here. Any minute now they would lose interest and start to head back into town to continue the slaughter. Kicking a desk shoved against a wall caused a loud bang to reverberate through the room, throwing the lizarpions just outside the door into a frenzy. Knocks and scratches came frantically as they tried even harder to breach the door.

The bang had another effect as a previously unseen hatch swung open, nearly hitting Hank in the face. Ducking out of the way just in time, he looked up through the secret opening and gave a whoop of a laugh. He could see the stars of the night sky and never thought he'd be so happy to see something that had always been so mundane to him before.

'It leads to the roof! Come on, we're getting out of here."

"Hank...you can't carry me up there."

The smile faded quickly from his face and was replaced with a frown as he realized that Dragert was right.

"Goddammit, John, there's gotta be some way of getting you up there."

"Not before the things get in here, end up escaping, or I just die. I got chills and feel hot all at the same time. That fucking thing bit me and infected me with something." Conviction crossed his face as he looked up at Hank with the bottle still in his hands. "We need a distraction to keep them here and they know I killed her. They can smell it on me."

There was no way they knew he was the one who had killed her, but he had a point. A distraction was needed. While Hank had no love for the man because of everything that had happened, he also didn't wish this fate on him. A brutal and violent end, but he could see no other way.

"You sure about this?"

"Yep. Just need your lighter. I left mine in the car."

A smoker he was not. Prepared, though, he always was. Hank made sure to have at least a cheap lighter on his person at all times. Reaching into his pocket, he pulled one out and walked over to John, who was busy ripping shreds of cloth from his shirt and soaking them in the vodka, before wringing them out and sliding them into the bottle.

"There's still time. I can get out there, lock them in, and find a way to get you out."

"We're not having this talk. Tell my wife I loved her and that my last thoughts were of her and not that hussy Fiona Hennessy from high school."

"Uh...really? That's gonna be your last words to your wife?"

"She'll understand. God damn. Few hours ago I wanted to kill myself but couldn't and now here I am going through with it and I want to live more than anything. Fuck you, Hank, for getting me into this mess."

Patting him on the shoulder Hank replied, "Anytime."

Both shared a bit of a chuckle before Dragert motioned towards the open hatch with a nod of his head as he struggled to stand. Using an office chair nearby as a sort of walker, he moved slowly towards the door.

"Get the hell out of here. I'll give you a ten second head start before I start the party. Find the fire escape and close that door."

Nodding, Hank headed to the hatch and climbed on top of the desk to pull himself out.

"Hank."

Ducking under the hatch so he could see Dragert, the other man took off his shotgun and tossed it to him. He barely caught it.

"Just in case."

"Crazy son of a bitch..." With a leap he was up and out of the room and on the roof, his footsteps echoing against the sheet metal.

***

Ten.

A lot of things were on Dragert's mind as he began to count down from ten. His wife, the fact that they never had children, his legacy as sheriff, what Hank would say about him when he was gone, the fact that Fiona took his virginity...All things he regretted to some degree and he wished he had the time to make up for them.

Nine.

He would have killed to eat that last meal his wife had cooked for him, waiting in the microwave for a husband that was never going to come home. His eyes got a bit teary as he thought about her, the same thing that had prevented him from killing himself at the lake earlier.

Eight.

She'd understand, no doubt. His wife knew the risks she was going to have in that kind of life and she always knew that every night she went to sleep she could wake up a widow. That he was going to do that to her, and that he consciously knew he was going to, made it all the harder.

Seven.

Not going through with it wasn't an option at this point. Even if he could shimmy out that hole there, was no way they'd get back to town in time to save his life. Either way he was a dead man. At least this way he was able to make up for all the stupid shit he'd done.

Six.

Licking his lips he reached for the lighter and gave it a few clicks until it flickered to life, the heat from the flame was almost too hot for the tip of his thumb as he held it there. Feeling a bit woozy he focused on that heat, the slight pain, to maintain his conviction.

Five.

There were two choices now, and neither seemed optimal. Opening the door would mean he was immediately swarmed by the things. He may be able to throw the bottle but there was a good chance he'd just drop it, setting the office ablaze and little else.

Four.

Throwing it out the two-way mirror might have a better chance, but only if it broke the glass. If it bounced back he would be burned alive and those things would end up fine. Fuck.

Three.

The gun! It was still in his boot. Letting go of the lighter for a moment he reached down and pulled it out, groaning as he did. Covered in blood it at least looked like it would still fire. Putting it down on the office chair, he grabbed the lighter again.

Two.

Lighting the Molotov, he picked up the gun, took aim, and prepped his arm to toss the bottle out the window. Only one shot to get this right and he prayed he had the strength to get it out into the factory floor to hit something flammable.

One.

This was it. *Christa, I'm sorry.* Pulling the trigger of the .22 snub-nose reminded him of the sound cap guns made when he was a kid. Weak as shit gun, but the window shattered, and any lizarpions caught in the shower of glass cried out in pain and surprise. Several bright blue eyes looked right at him in surprise as he threw the bottle with all his might.

Sailing through the air like a magnificent missile it soared above the group on the landing in front of the office and smashed against a series of boxes on the floor below. As the bottle exploded it spread flames across everything it touched. Growing quickly, the fire caused panic among those closest to it.

Smirking as he saw the billows of black smoke rise, Dragert knew he'd done his job just as several stingers pierced his torso. Barely registering the pain, he sunk to the floor of the office and thought how badly he wanted a drink.

***

Halfway down the fire escape Hank heard the shot and the sound of glass breaking. No time to drop the ladder; he shimmied down as far as he was able and let go, hoping he didn't break anything as he landed. Roll! Gotta roll as I land!

Trying to roll was a lot more difficult than he thought it would be, mostly because he wasn't moving in any direction other than straight down. Feeling something crack in his foot, he knew there was going to be a broken bone or two, or even a snapped ankle. Limping towards the door he gazed in wonder at the devastation they had wrought.

Already spreading to every corner of the shanty town, the fire was devouring everything in its path. Some of the steel beams even seemed to be on fire with how intense the blaze was becoming. What really scared him though was the sheer number of lizarpions running back in his direction.

Reaching up and grabbing the handle of the bay door, he pulled down with all his might and panicked when it stuck about three quarters of the way down. He gave a few more tugs, but it didn't budge, just rattled in place. Glancing under the door showed they were almost there, and he also saw the issue: a piece of the chain for the door had snagged on a piece of metal on the side.

Reaching under, he grabbed it, freed the chain, and pulled it the rest of the way down. The first of the creatures slammed against it, hard, just as it hit the ground. Fearing the door might give way under the force and weight he limped back and readied the shotgun.

More and more of the things slammed against the door and their cries grew more and more frantic. Thick black smoke billowed out of every vent, hole, and broken window in the factory, causing Hank to feel a sense of satisfaction.

Despite every shortcoming that night, he and Dragert had managed to lure, contain, and eradicate the threat. Dragert...he said a small word of thanks to the man for his sacrifice, and promised himself that his ultimate involvement would die with him. No sense in dragging his name through the mud needlessly.

The screeching and clawing at the door slowed until it finally stopped. Smoke inhalation or the heat of the flames must have finally gotten the best of them. It really was a death trap in there.

"We're done here."

Turning to leave, he was knocked off his feet by a powerful blow which slammed him against the door and knocked the wind out of him. Gasping for breath, he looked around to see what had happened and just about shit himself.

It was a lizarpion, but nothing like any of the others. Only the queen could have rivaled this one in size, which made Hank figure that this was the king. Standing about eight feet tall, the thing had skin so dark and so smooth that light hit it like an oil patch. Its eyes were a bright green, instead of blue, and it had a bifurcated tail. Luckily it didn't have stingers on the ends, but they did end in some sort of bony, club-like protrusion

The hands were covered in suckers, so it fed like the others in that regard. Being so large and powerful, it must not need the toxin to subdue its prey. Not that it would need any help inducing fear. As dark and black as the skin of this new version was, Hank could see that its maw, claws, and legs were covered in blood. It had been busy that night and just now was getting around to his lady friend.

Breathing was painful, and Hank guessed he had at least a rib or two broken. He stood and tried not to piss himself as he held up the shotgun. "Your wife sends her regards."

Pulling the trigger his eyes went wide as the gun simply responded with a click. Then another. Dragert had never bothered to reload it after emptying it.

"Fuck me!"

Roaring in defiance, the creature advanced on Hank who tried to run, only to be swept off his feet by a swing of the creature's tail. Landing with a thud, he noticed there were a few shells in the dirt. Guessing they fell out of Dragert's bandolier as they shot the lock off he praised the man for his poor choices and grabbed them, wincing at the pain in his chest as he began to reload the shotgun.

The king grabbed him with both hands and lifted him up. Roaring in his face, it was impossible for Hank to keep control of his bladder and he felt the warm liquid run down his legs. The thing snorted once and then gripped him tight enough to make Hank cry out in pain.

"No...no!"

Struggling made the pain worse as he felt the suckers dig into his skin. Just as he felt the sensation of being drained he managed to wriggle the shotgun free. He tried to aim it at the creature, but pulled the trigger too soon. The slug slammed into its ankle causing it to cry out and drop him. Landing on his bad foot, he cried out again and this time took better aim as he righted himself.

"Suck on this!"

Praying that wouldn't be the last thing he said, he squeezed the trigger. The slug blew a hole in its gut and the third and final shot blew off half its face. Teetering to and fro it gave a final, gurgling cry and toppled over. The king was dead.

Aiming his empty gun at the thing, as if that would ensure it stayed dead, he waited for a minute, and then two, for any signs of life. Satisfied that it wasn't going to spring back up he fell back against the dirt. Stinking of blood, sweat, and urine, Hank began to listen to the sound of his own breathing over the roar of the fire consuming the warehouse. Part of the roof collapsed and he closed his eyes, hoping that when he woke up this would all be a dream.

Maybe he'd take Julie to Red Lobster.

EPILOGUE

It had been a little over a month since the last encounter with the lizarpions. Hank and Julie were getting calls every day from all manner of people, ranging from scientists, who were trying to study the creatures, to movie and television producers, all eager to get them to tell their side of things. Early on they both agreed to push all the fame and fortune off onto Jeremiah who eagerly ate it up.

Hanging up the phone after another such call, Hank reached over and hit the intercom button. There had been several improvements to the sheriff's department that he was proud to admit had been his idea.

"Jennifer, could you please direct any more calls for me regarding the lizards to Doctor Jeremiah Besson at the university? You'll find his information in the Rolodex on your desk."

Firing Dorris and hiring Jennifer had been one of the best improvements he made in his new position, once things started to get back to normal. For one thing, calls weren't getting missed or disconnected with the same frequency as they had under Dorris.

"Sure thing, Hank. Have you started working on your campaign?"

"Not sure yet. Might only run if I'm unopposed; I hate politics."

"You're kind of a local legend. Anyone would be stupid to run against the town hero."

"Just forward the calls, Jennifer. I've got a lunch date I'm late for."

"Yes, sir."

Legend? Hero? He hated when people called him that. He was just a stupid old man who happened to get incredibly lucky. Feeling partially responsible for the ways things turned out, it was hard to accept that the survivors of that night regarded him and Dragert as heroes. There was even talk of a statue in the town square. Bah.

Getting up from behind his desk, he winced and rubbed his chest gingerly. His ribs were coming along nicely but it would still be a few weeks before they completely healed. The rest of his body, however, still felt bruised, and he walked with a limp and a special boot because of the bones he broke in his foot.

Still, if that was the worst to happen after all the shit, he was alright with it. The forest itself had been cordoned off by the military, just in case there were more of those things waiting to come out.

Building a fence just as the snow started to fall seemed foolish at the time, but Hank convinced the powers that be that it was necessary. It didn't block off the whole forest, but it did protect the side facing town. Military outposts had been set up at the edges, just in case.

No matter what they did or said, however, people were going in to search for the things. May as well keep everything nice and contained in case they got agitated again. So far, only government officials had been allowed past the perimeter. That suited Hank just fine. *They* could deal with it if there was a next time.

It only took him about ten minutes to arrive at the diner. It was still a burned out husk, but Julie had insisted they meet there first for some reason. Parking his squad car, he got out and headed towards the front of the building where she was already waiting for him.

"It's damn cold out here. You better have a good reason for dragging me away from my very busy schedule."

Hank smiled at her, flashing all the charm he could muster as he got closer. After everything they had decided to try their hand at a relationship, age difference be damned.

"Well, Mister Sheriff, I wanted you to be the first to know. I quit today."

"You what?!"

Julie nodded, the grin on her mouth widening as she spoke.

"I've seen far too much death in my short time on this earth and I figured I could use a break. I want to do something a little more...fun."

Unsure if he liked where she was going with this, he cocked an eyebrow. "Uh...such as? This isn't a Dear John letter in person, is it?"

Julie laughed long and hard at the accusation, so much so she doubled over.

"Dear John? Ha! As if I'd waste my good stationary on you."

Smirking, she pulled him in close, and leaned up for a kiss, which he happily obliged.

"Alright, you quit. What now, then?"

"I bought the diner."

Gaping at her, his eyebrows shot up. He glanced at the charred husk and then back to her.

"You *what*?!"

"More accurately," she broke from the embrace and pulled a paper from her jacket pocket, "I bought the land. Since the state paid everyone in town a nice settlement for what happened, I decided to invest my money into a place you and I both enjoyed. The owners were happy to sell it for a song, and I've got enough left over to rebuild it."

"Shit, this is a big decision. Are you sure about it?"

"I better be. I signed the papers this morning."

Shaking his head, he couldn't help but grin at her. Even after everything, she still had a spunk to her that he found both inspiring and intoxicating.

"Yer full of surprises, aren't you?"

"A few. I'm gonna need a business partner, you know."

'Ha! I knew there was a reason you tried to seduce me!"

"Seduce *you*?! You old dog…it was the other way around and you know it!"

"A rich, available woman is quite the catch this days."

He wrapped his arm around her, trying not to wince at the pain as he did so. Both of them looked at the ruined building, visions of the future going through their heads.

"Maybe I won't run for sheriff, after all. I mean, running a diner is sure to take up a lot of my time."

"I was certain you'd see it my way."

***

Winter had not been kind to Andrew but then, life hadn't really done him any favors in general. Since his family was killed by the lizarpions, he tried to cash in on the victim angle, doing the talk show circuit, and signing movie deals. Problem was, he didn't get a proper agent and got shut out of most of the profits.

Since his mother and uncle had no wills naming him as an heir, the bank seized the properties, which left him homeless. Drifting from couch to couch, he lost a good deal of friends as they got more and more fed up with his mooching attitude.

Ending up without a roof over his head at the start of spring, he started to stand outside of restaurants, begging for loose change or left overs. The chill of winter stuck to the area and even though 'spring had sprung', snow still covered almost everything. Most times he was chased off, but one time he was offered a helping hand.

A local dairy farmer saw him and recognized him from the news. Offered him honest work with honest pay, room and board, and three squares a day. Not one for manual labor, he almost refused the offer, but the prospect of getting off the street won out over pride and he agreed.

It was not easy work, and it took him some time to get used to not lazing around, but soon he was fit, healthy, and learning to enjoy the life he was living. The Carlson's had taken him in when he was at his lowest, and he appreciated their hospitality and generosity. By mid spring the whole business of the fall seemed like a faded, distant memory.

One day, about a week after the snow finally melted away and warmth returned, he was cleaning out one of the milking rooms when the Carlson's son ran up to him holding something in his hand.

"Andy! Andy!"

Turning around, he smiled at the boy. Kid was annoying as hell sometimes, but he liked how he'd taken to calling him Andy, like his brother used to. Something about the way he looked up to Andrew, like Josh had, also created a bond between the two.

"What's up, Timmy?"

"Look what I found!"

Holding up his prize as proudly as he could, Andrew took it from his hands and inspected it. It looked like some sort of shell, broken into several pieces.

"Huh. Looks like an egg shell. Where did you find it?"

"Over near the fence, by the woods. What do you think laid it?"

Shrugging, he handed the boy back the shell pieces.

"No idea. Maybe a goose or a hawk or something. Probably fell outta a tree." Andrew handed the egg shells back to Timmy, and turned back to finish his chores. "Now run along, I gotta get this done before dinner."

"Don't you wanna see where I found it? Aw, come on, Andy. Pretty please?"

He tossed the shovelful he had in with the rest and his shoulders slumped. When Timmy begged, it was hard to tell him no.

"Alright. Just a quick look, but then you gotta come back and help me finish up, got it?"

"Promise!"

Andrew couldn't help but smile at the kid. When he got excited it was downright infectious. Besides, what could it hurt? It wouldn't take them more than five or ten minutes to go scope out his 'find' and then he'd get help finishing. Pretty much win win.

Timmy led the way as fast as he could back to where he'd found the nest. When he ducked under the fence at the property line, Andrew spoke up.

"Timmy, you know your dad doesn't want you heading out into the woods. Hell, I don't like heading there either."

While they were in a different county and no where near where the creatures had been seen originally, Andrew still felt a sense of dread whenever he got close to a wooded area. Some things were harder to get over than others.

"It's ok, Andy, it's just here by the fence." When Andrew didn't move, Timmy came back and grabbed him by the hand. "Please? The nest is so cool!"

"Alright, alright. Just don't let your dad know. He'd probably fire me for letting you go past the fence like this."

They both headed towards a fallen tree about twenty feet into the forest. Seeing how happy Timmy was eased Andrew's nerves a bit, but that was short-lived. As they came around the tree to the nest, Andrew's blood froze.

The nest was around two or three feet in diameter, and filled with so many shells it was impossible to tell how many animals may have hatched. The nest itself was made of pieces of bone and animal hides, but what caused Andrew to freeze there in the woods was what Timmy was pointing at.

On the ground, about a foot across, was a track in the dirt. Three long toes in the front, and two shorter ones in the back. There was no doubt in his mind what it was, and he hardly registered Timmy's voice.

"Cool, huh?"

ABOUT THE AUTHOR

C.M.W. Hawkins is an American-born writer who has been living in Canada ever since his wife imported him. They both live happily with their preteen son in Alberta.

While the author has been writing for and working on various projects over the years, this is his first published novel.

When not writing, about toxic lizard creatures or otherwise, he enjoys reading other horror novels, various comic books, playing video games and spending time with friends and family.